THE HALFWAY TO HELL CLUB

A Sean O'Farrell Mystery

MARK J. McCRACKEN

KITSAP PUBLISHING

The Highway To Hell Club
Second edition, published 2018

By Mark J. McCracken

Copyright © 2018, Mark J. McCracken

Cover design by Sherri Shaftic

Paperback ISBN: 978-1-942661-89-4
Audio Book ISBN: 978-1-942661-95-5
eBook ISBN: 978-1-535069-99-1

This is a work of fiction. Names, characters, businesses, places, events and incidents are either the products of the author's imagination or used in a fictitious manner. Any resemblance to actual persons, living or dead, or actual events is purely coincidental.

All rights reserved. No part of this book may be reproduced or transmitted in any form or by any means, electronic or mechanical, including photocopying, recording or by any information storage and retrieval system, without written permission from the author, except for the inclusion of brief quotations in a review.

Published by Kitsap Publishing
P.O. Box 572
Poulsbo, WA 98370
www.KitsapPublishing.com

Printed in the United States of America

TD 2018

50-10 9 8 7 6 5 4 3 2 1

Acknowledgments

It is now common practice for first time authors to name drop the names of big time authors, giving them thanks when in reality they may not even know them. Why should I be any different? A couple of years ago I attended the Mystery Writers of America's University in Seattle, Washington. The one day training galvanized my resolve to finish this novel. It was wonderful to hear bestselling authors speak about their problems they have when they write. I found myself nodding my head a great deal, and I am sure my mouth was open equally as often.

Thanks to Reed Farrel Coleman, Hank Philippi Ryan, and our local NW MWA President Brian Thornton for helping me realize this dream. Likewise many thanks to Robert Dugoni who is not only been encouraging, but very generous with his time.

Many kudos to my editor Jim Thomson who worked his magic and helped shape The Halfway to Hell Club.

Many thanks to Robert B. Parker, Ace Atkins, Michael Connelly, Raymond Chandler, Nicholas Meyer, David Baldacci, Brad Meltzer, Sir Arthur Conan Doyle, Dashiell Hammett, and the many other authors who continue to influence me and my future writing.

To my brother in law John Gierlak for proofing the novel and making excellent suggestions.

Thanks to my sister Mary and my younger brothers John and James.

To Sherri Shaftic, graphic designer and book cover artist extraordinaire. The cover is fantastic; you can hear the cable car rumbling along the tracks.

To our wonderful all grown up children Michael (and his wife Stephanie), Sarah, and Jacob. Thanks for your love and support.

To my wife Kathy who allows me to hide and write, at all hours of the day and night. She listens to my cockamamie ideas, descriptions of shoot outs, allowing me to try out on her a long lists of quips from my various characters, allowing me to turn our cruise vacation into a plot for my next novel. She does not lose patience for all these things and many more. All my love.

Mark J. McCracken
Bremerton, Washington
November 2017

CHAPTER ONE

I was sitting back in my chair reading the morning Chronicle on what was a typical foggy spring morning in San Francisco, with the sun trying to pop through and failing as usual. It was a Friday and the week had been a good one. I had just finished a case for a nosy housewife who thought her husband was cheating on her. I tailed the gee for three nights and discovered he was a closet actor; he was auditioning for a part in a community theatre production. She was embarrassed, and I kind of felt sorry for her, a little. That all changed when I gave her a bill for $150.00 plus expenses. Her attitude changed, and so did mine. She paid.

Another case came from the law office down the hall. They needed a background check on a witness for an embezzlement case, and were glad to find out the witness in question was being paid for his testimony by the other law firm involved. I worked this case by day and followed the Shakespeare by night. For two weeks' work I collected $250 plus expenses from the law offices of Dunhill, Myerson, and Kindle. They were more than glad to pay; they were just handed a favorable verdict for their client.

As I read, I drank freshly percolated coffee with my feet up. The middle left drawer is halfway open, just in case.

I was reading a story about the new Golden Gate Bridge, which apparently came in under budget. Seems odd to me because nothing comes in on budget in this town, what with all the graft that needs paying. I had moved on to the next article about reduced ferry service to Sausalito—apparently everyone is driving the new bridge—when my office door opened.

Standing in the doorway—let me restate that: taking up the entire doorway and then some—were two mountain-sized Chinese guys in black suits and ties with white shirts. I took my feet off the desk and opened the left-hand middle drawer all the way slowly so my two guests would not notice. I straightened up in my chair and folded my hands on the blotter in the middle of my desk.

"What can I do for you two boys?" I said.

The mountain twins didn't move. These guys were so big that their arms didn't hang at their sides naturally; they bulged away from their bodies. But these two weren't fat; they were all muscle. The one on the left opened up the debate.

"You come with us," he said.

"Where to?"

"You come now."

"Sorry, boys, I was just getting to the funny papers. Maybe you can make an appointment for next week." I put my feet back up on the desk and re-crossed my legs at the ankles.

"You come now." The man knew how to turn a phase, all right.

"Shove off, sailor, I'm busy." I lifted the paper back up.

The one on the right smiled and took out what looked like a small baseball bat. It was about a foot long and hit my desk lamp as hard as he could. The lamp went off the desk and crashed into wall. I liked that lamp a lot too.

The other one allowed himself a small smile.

"You come with us now?"

"You know, I just put a brand new light bulb in that lamp twenty minutes ago. Why don't you two boys buzz off? I'm starting to lose my cool." I brought my feet to the floor.

The two mountains exchanged looks and smiles. One started to move east and the other west; they were ready to make me come with them. I had the .45 out of the drawer and in a spot to fire twice before they could move another step. The smiles were gone now. They didn't quite know what to do. What we had here was a Mexican standoff with two Chinese guys.

Lefty finally started yapping.

"You didn't rock a round in the pipe, bud." His English skills suddenly got pretty good. "That thing won't do you much good."

"I always keep my rod loaded and ready to fire," I said. I slipped my thumb over the safety and released it with a loud click.

"All I have to do is ease off the safety."

The two looked at each other, then the .45.

"Besides," I said, "there all kinds of vicious lawyers down the hall, and you never know who might stop by for tea and crumpets."

I couldn't see who it was, but someone was behind them, yammering in Chinese. Whoever it was, he wasn't happy. One went to one corner and one went to the other, and they stood against the walls. They looked like a couple of kids sent by the teacher to stand in the corner.

The man doing the talking, I could see now, was Jimmy Chan. Jimmy and I went to college together. I was glad to see him.

"Sean O'Farrell, is that coffee or are you drinking somebody else's tiger milk?" Jimmy said.

"It's nine thirty in the morning, Jimmy."

I released the magazine from the .45 and pulled back the receiver. The bullet flew out and up, and I caught it in the air. Righty gave Lefty a long hard look that said, Look, genius, the gun was loaded. I gave Jimmy a hug, and pointed to the clients' chair, then at Lefty and Righty. "These two world-class body builders work for you, Jimmy?"

"No, Sean. They work for Mr. Chin Wang." Jimmy didn't smile. Neither did I.

If you live in San Francisco, you damn well better know who Chin Wang is. He owns, operates, controls, and does damn near anything he wants in Chinatown. If there is such a thing as a list of people not to cross in this city, Mr. Wang is right at the top.

I gave Righty and Lefty each a look, followed with a nod and a simple "Sorry." Both men returned the nod. Okay, I said to myself, now everyone in the room knows the score.

Jimmy Chan was a sharp kid in school, a buddy who helped me get through algebra while I helped him with English. I played first base and Jimmy was the greatest shortstop I had ever seen. He was smooth, fluid, and catlike in gobbling up grounders. He was a terrible hitter, though. He was an easy out on the deuce. But Jimmy is a good egg.

When Chin Wang came to San Francisco in the Barbary Coast days, Chinatown was wide open. If it was for sale, it was available in Chinatown. Prostitutes, little girls, dope, booze, contract killing, arson, extortion, blackmail, loan sharking, as well as legitimate banking services. Mr. Wang slowly edged everyone else out in Chinatown. If they wouldn't deal, he had them killed. It was a simple matter of business, Chinatown style. After a while the mayor and cops left him alone too. After all, he was cleaning up a mess they couldn't take care of.

By 1910, Chin Wang owned everything, and anything he didn't own it wasn't worth having. He convinced locals to start putting money in his banks. All the nasty street crime went away. He brought in doctors and quality health care; he took care of people. The muscle was still there and feared, but it was rarely needed or used in broad daylight. The Chinese were able to live in Chinatown without being shaken down, and Chin Wang became even more powerful.

Jimmy brushed something off his sport coat sleeve.

"Mr. Chin Wang would like you to come and see him at his office. It is a personal matter. I told Mr. Wang I would come and assist in bringing you to him." His smile was broad and revealed pearl-white teeth. "There will be no difficulties, Sean."

I got up and reloaded the .45. I took out my double-rig shoulder holster from the bottom drawer and put it on. I adjusted both .45s and put on my coat. Righty and Lefty looked at me while I slipped on my coat and grabbed my hat.

"You expecting to run into an elephant on the way, boss?" Lefty said. "Why the double rig?"

I shrugged. "I'm not a very good shot. It may take both roscoes to scare away any street muggers in Chinatown," I said. "Let's go see Mr. Wang."

Lefty put his mitt against the door.

"Leave the roscoes, boss."

"If I take the rod out again, it will be to use it."

From the hall, Jimmy yelled something in Chinese and Lefty dropped his arm. We took an elevator to the lobby, and outside the front door was a Duesenberg waiting to take us to Chinatown.

I loved this car: a 1935 Duesenberg SJ LaGrande Dual-Cowl Phaeton, red with tan leather interior and a matching top. This was a car to end all cars. Lefty opened the door, and Jimmy and I slid into the back seat. Righty drove and Lefty took shotgun. They fired up the big turbo-charged V-8, dropped her into gear, and stormed up Hyde Street on a mission.

"Jimmy," I said, "I'd rather take the cable car, but I suppose this old beater will do."

CHAPTER TWO

The Duesenberg moved up the hill with ease; if this were my Ford coupe, I would be scared to death. We took a left onto California Street, and there the hill really got steep. We got behind a California line-cable car. I was worried we were going to have trouble with all the weight in the car. Righty and Lefty looked like they weighed three hundred apiece. But the Dusey did just fine.

We drove by the telephone exchange building, which looked like a red Chinese temple. After another block we stopped at the San Francisco Chinese Social Club. A couple of swells in tuxedos with white gloves opened the doors to the car, then to the front door to the club.

I had never been in there, but it was sure a swell joint. Everybody was dressed to the nines. We walked through a casino and a restaurant, past little old ladies playing Mahjong.

We went into an outer office. A couple of Chinese ladies stood and bowed. One young girl took my hat. Jimmy knocked and opened the door to Mr. Wang's office.

Before I walked in, Righty held out his hands. His eyes were saying, Please, no trouble. "Sorry, boss, there are no guns allowed in Mr. Wang's office."

I pulled both .45s out of the holster and handed them over. He nodded a thank-you and placed the two guns in a drawer of an end table outside the office door. Righty and Lefty looked greatly relieved. I was starting to get along with these two. They might be muscle, but there was a sense of grace and class to their work.

Mr. Wang stood as soon as I entered the room and came around from behind his huge desk. He was five-feet-five, with a round face that was not fat. He had on the glad rags: A smart-looking double-breasted gray pinstripe suit with a handsome burgundy silk tie and a white carnation on the lapel. He gave me a firm, professional handshake.

"Thank you so much for coming on short notice, Mr. O'Farrell. Please have a seat."

I took a red leather chair and Jimmy sat in the other. Righty and Lefty went to the corners behind Mr. Wang's desk. They folded their hands in the front. It was a subtle reminder to me that they were there. They were always there.

Before Mr. Wang could commence business, a side door opened and an incredibly elegant Chinese woman entered the room. Everyone, including me, went to his feet.

"Mr. O'Farrell," Wang said, "may I present my wife, Mrs. Anna Wang."

She bowed. She was a goddess, and Wang was a lucky man. She wore a white silk kimono and walked with a ballerina's grace. Her feet moved, but her body seemed to float like a cloud or a ghost. She shook my hand and gave me a smile that would melt any man.

"Please forgive me, gentlemen, for intruding," she said. "I came to remind my husband that we are leaving in one hour for the mayor's college scholarship charity lunch."

Mr. Wang gave a look of alarm. "I will be ready to go in a few minutes, my dear."

"It was very nice to meet you, Mr. O'Farrell." She gave her husband a nod of acknowledgement and gracefully left the room.

Mr. Wang turned to me.

"Mr. O'Farrell, I sincerely hope that my assistants did not inconvenience you a great deal. I have cautioned them in the past for being too bold."

Righty and Lefty both looked like two Siamese cats with a mouth full of bird. They both opened their eyes wide and prepared for their demise.

"No, Mr. Wang, they were most gracious," I said.

Lefty and Righty both took a breath and color returned to their faces. Mr. Wang spoke to them in Chinese. They came around to the side of the desk and bowed, then gave me nods on the way out.

As the door closed, Mr. Wang leaned back in his chair and crossed his legs. "Mr. O'Farrell, Jimmy here tells me you are a very good investigator and a man who keeps his word."

I nodded.

"You are, however, if I may be so bold, a terrible liar. My two assistants are not subtle or gracious." Mr. Wang gave me a small smile.

He nodded to Jimmy.

"That is why I sent Jimmy along. It occurred to me that these two men may not be very polite in their request. I sent Jimmy to save you from them, but I suspect I may have saved them from you." Again, he offered a small smile.

"First, I must ask you for complete confidence and discretion," he said.

"That goes without even saying, Mr. Wang," I said.

Mr. Wang stood and walked over to the window. He seemed to be looking at nothing.

"I know, Mr. O'Farrell that you know who I am and what I am. I make no apologies for that, or how I conduct my business affairs, or how I gain results." Wang adjusted his glasses and continued to stare out the window.

"When I arrived here, Chinatown was tearing itself apart with Tongs and daily killings. I am no angel, Mr. O'Farrell. I have performed many sins, and ordered many sins, but again, I am unabashed."

There was a knock at the door and the small Chinese girl that took my hat brought a tray with tea. She served Mr. Wang first, and then he offered us some. It was world-class stuff.

"Mr. Wang, I am no expert, but I believe this is Dragon Well Green

Tea, is it not?" I asked.

"Well done, Mr. O'Farrell. How did you know?" He said.

I smiled. "Jimmy here was always bringing a different tea with him to school. He made it a point to expand my horizons. I really enjoy an excellent cup of Chinese tea."

Mr. Wang took a sip and placed his cup into its saucer.

"Mr. O'Farrell, I have always been a frank man. I believe you should address all your problems head-on. In this case I am at a loss. I am a powerful man, but I am powerless as to what to do and I believe I need your assistance."

I put down my teacup. "Of course, sir."

Mr. Wang cleared his throat.

"My wife and I are blessed with five children. My first four children are girls. They are all very well educated, two doctors, a lawyer, and a dentist. My youngest is a boy. He is a double major at the University of San Francisco. He is an engineering and architecture student. He will graduate in six months with a double master's degree." Mr. Wang allowed himself a small smile of paternal pride.

"All of my children know what I am and what I do. All of my daughters have married powerful men and started their own families. Some of these young men are integral parts of my business ventures, some are not."

He took a moment and cleaned his glasses.

"My son Kuai will have nothing to do with my business. He intends to do public works, designing buildings, hospitals, and public housing. He rejects all of my business dealings. This is perfectly all right with me; my business life is not a life I would hope for my children. He has made this very clear to his mother and to me. Again, Mr. O'Farrell, this is a very delicate situation."

He swallowed hard.

"I have been informed that my son is dating a Caucasian girl at the university. I know that you may think that I insist that he marry within his race. This is very true, but that is not my problem. I have been hearing stories that this young girl may be interested in my son for reason of monetary gain, and not of matters of the heart. I have heard she was or is married, and perhaps she has worked as a prostitute in her past. I do not know for sure."

I could tell that this whole business was eating Mr. Wang up inside. He rubbed his stomach like he had acid indigestion.

"As you can imagine, I can't start looking into this matter without my son finding out. Plus my two assistants lack the social charms to extract information without bodily harm to others. Likewise, I cannot imagine them following this girl without being noticed. Jimmy tells me you are an excellent investigator and discreet. Please look into this matter for me, Mr. O'Farrell. All I ask is that you ensure that my son or his young lady friend never find out about this. If she has ulterior motives, my wife and I need to know so we can deal with it."

I tossed out a question.

"What if she is a gold-digger? What will you and Mrs. Wang do?"

Jimmy squirmed in his chair, as if I'd asked the wrong question.

Mr. Wang smiled.

"That is a fair question, Mr. O'Farrell. If this young woman is simply looking for money, we will give her what she wants and make her go away."

Mr. Wang sat at his desk and crossed his arms.

"This young woman is not a competitor of mine. I will not deal with her harshly. You have my word on that, Mr. O'Farrell."

Mr. Wang stood. "I must prepare for my luncheon. Mrs. Wang is woman not to be kept waiting. Again, thank you for coming and I wish you good luck." We shook hands, and off he went through the side door.

Jimmy went to the booze cart and poured a couple of drinks. He handed me a glass of scotch. It was very good scotch.

We took a slug of our booze. "Nice leather chair behind that big desk, Jimmy. See yourself in it someday?"

Jimmy smiled. "The last three gees who thought they could take over the Wang Empire are missing and presumed dead. I don't plan to join them, I'll simply wait for the Wang's to retire, thank you very much." He paused. "Mr. Wang doesn't talk money, Sean. What do you get?"

"Fifty bucks a day, plus expenses." I said.

"Mr. Wang will pay two hundred and fifty a day, plus expenses."

"For the love of Mike, Jimmy," I said.

"I know, Sean, it's a lot of dough, but don't squawk. I told Mr. Wang you are the best. It makes him feel better that he is getting the best by paying the best."

"Just so we are clear, Jimmy, if there is any crime business in this, I will walk and walk fast."

Jimmy held up his hand like a traffic cop telling me to stop.

"Sean, take my word, the old man is aboveboard on this one. This is personal for him and his wife. If it were business he would use his own people."

I took a swallow of the scotch.

"All right, Jimmy, I'm in. But if the dame is clean, I won't paint her any other way."

"Don't worry, Sean. Mrs. Wang is in full and complete control of this operation, and that includes Mr. Wang. They are both off for some charity event, but she came in here not to remind him, she came in here because she wanted to get a look at you and approve of his choice. That's what the nod was for."

"Well, I'll be damned," I said.

Jimmy's face got very hard and his voice lowered a little.

"Don't kid yourself, Sean, about Mrs. Wang. A couple of months ago at some Chinatown charity event, some local guy from the neighborhood had too much to drink and made a pass at Mrs. Wang. He said some pretty disgusting things to her. It was vulgar. He said he wanted to put his penis in her mouth. He put his hand on her ass."

"Jesus, Jimmy, you can't blame any guy, she's a looker."

"Sean, they found the guy in an alley with his hand cut off and his dick in his mouth."

"So what you are telling me, Jimmy, is don't cross Mr. Wang. It could be very unhealthy."

"Think again, Sean. Mrs. Wang had it done."

"I get it. So tell me, Jimmy, you ever had your hand on the vivacious Mrs. Wang's ass?" I said.

"I like my hands and my dick right where they are," Jimmy said. "No thanks, Sean."

CHAPTER THREE

Jimmy gave me three pictures of the son, Kuai, and a couple more of the girlfriend. Dorothy was her name. He also loaded me up with Kuai's apartment address, phone number, class schedule, and the places where he studies. He spent a lot of time at the main branch of the library on Larkin Street. I thought my school schedule was packed, but this boy was just plain goofy. I found the kid coming out of his first class and followed him all day. He took classes from eight in the morning until five in the late afternoon. A double load. He crammed in a fifteen-minute lunch and a fifteen-minute dinner on the run before he hightailed it to the library. He met the girl there. They studied together, how romantic. At nine thirty they shut the place down and caught a cable car up to Hyde Street and his apartment. She stayed for thirty minutes or so, then he walked her to her place over on Chestnut. He went straight back home and the lights stayed on at his place till one. Man, this kid was bing. No one could keep up this kind of schedule. If she was a chippy, I don't know where they were finding the time.

After two days of this nonsense I decided he wasn't going to alter his schedule at all, and if he did it would be on the weekend. I might learn something on Saturday morning.

So I gave it a rest on Thursday and went to the library on Friday, to see if the kid was on schedule. Like clockwork, the kid showed up at 5:30 p.m. on the dot. The girl arrived at six and they went to a large table in the reference section. Some skinny kid showed up and asked for help with math homework and the kid was generous with his time. From a distance I could tell the kid was a good teacher, patient, and thoughtful.

I was reading a book when I noticed the kid looking over at me. I never made eye contact. It was time for me to move away so the kid couldn't notice me again.

I was reading a collection of short stories by Mark Twain. Great stuff, but I needed to check it out and bring it with me if I was going to finish it.

A mean-looking broad was manning the checkout desk. She was about sixty, but looked about eighty. She had frazzled gray hair on top of a pruney puss. When I was in the Navy, I had a chief petty officer that worked for me who looked like he could pull a battleship out of the water and on to a dry dock all by himself. He killed and ate junior officers for lunch. You didn't talk to that bird unless you had to. This must have been his wife.

A little kid of about seven was ahead of me in the line. He slipped the book and library card onto the desk. The little old lady shuffled through a card index and held up a yellow card.

"You have a fine on file for five cents. You can't check out any books until you pay your fines." She kind of spit it out at the poor kid and she had a wicked smile.

The poor kid was quaking in his shoes.

"I'm sorry, I'll pay the fine, but I need this book for a school assignment and I really need to check this out," he said.

The old lady showed no mercy.

"What makes you so special, young man? Do you think we can grant special fee waivers to everyone? You need to go home and tell your mother—"

I butted in before the witch could throw the poor lad into a boiling cauldron and slapped a nickel on the counter.

"And just who are you?" she said.

"I'm a guy with a nickel. Cut the kid a break. He needs the book for school."

You could see the wheels turning in her head; she was reviewing her librarian's playbook trying to figure how to work this one.

"Are you his father?" she said.

"No.".

"Well, you can't pay his fines, then." She was pleased with herself.

I took the nickel off the counter and handed it to the boy.

"Here you go, young man. Here is a nickel, and you do anything you want with it," I said.

Now it was the kid's turn to think. After a moment of deep contemplation he delicately placed the nickel on the counter.

"I do believe I have a library fine to pay," he said.

Apparently the old lady didn't have this covered in her list of rules. She looked at the kid, then gave me a dirty look, picked up the nickel, pressed the five-cent key on the cash register and slammed it down. She gave me a dirty look as she checked the book out to him. He grabbed it, told her thank you and skedaddled. He called over his shoulder, "Thanks a lot, mister."

Now it was my turn. The old lady took off her glasses and put her flat hand under her hair and lifted it slightly. She smiled at me, and it was creepy.

"Hey you know something, handsome. You're pretty good-looking."

"Well, that makes one of us," I said.

It took a moment for the insult to sink in. She reached under the counter and slammed a POSITION CLOSED sign with an arrow pointing at the next station. She got on her broom and stormed off.

The next station had seven people in it. Nice going, O'Farrell. You're a real charmer, pal.

I lit a Lucky and started reading in line. It took ten minutes to reach the counter. When I got there the librarian stuck a jumbo-sized amber ashtray under my beak.

"Mr. Carnegie doesn't like it in the library," she said.

I snuffed the butt and got a good look at this librarian. She was a knockout. She was in her early thirties and tall, maybe five nine or ten.

When you are six feet two, you don't meet many women that are tall. She had red hair pulled tight into a bun and the prettiest green eyes hiding behind large framed tortoise-shell glasses. She was wearing a paisley dress with a lace collar, kind of plain, subduing her figure a little bit, but you could tell there was plenty of motor under the hood. She had long, elegant fingers, covered with shiny red fingernail polish.

She also had an absolute necessity for old Sean O'Farrell: she didn't have a wedding ring, or a line on her ring finger to indicate there had been one there before.

I slid her the book and she gave me ever so slight a smile.

"I was wondering if you got the new Hemingway book yet?" I said.

She brightened up.

"For Whom the Bell Tolls. I've read the reviews, but it doesn't hit the bookstores until next week. We should have it in about two weeks. Would you like to add your name to the reserve list?" Now she gave me a real smile.

"Yes please," I said.

I was starting to wonder if she was wearing red anywhere besides her nails. She wrote down my information on a card and again on a piece of paper.

"So what does a librarian like you do when you are not checking out books?" I felt like an idiot the moment I said it. A pimple-faced freshman could be smoother than that. Come on, O'Farrell, get in the game.

The mood was instantly destroyed. The wicked witch of the west returned from her break and came right over.

"You still here, bub?" She turned to the pretty librarian. "Don't take any grief from this creep. Give him his book and move him along."

The redhead drummed her fingers on a large open dictionary. The smile was long gone.

"Here is the information you requested. Sir."

She slammed the dictionary shut and slid the book, library card and paper to me. She lowered her head and was back to work. I told her thank you. "Good evening, sir," she curtly replied.

I went down the steps, lit up a butt, and went over to a bench at the far end of the pavilion. I was far enough away from the front entrance of the library that when the kid and the girl came out I could pick up the tail and they wouldn't notice.

There I was sitting on the bench, feeling sorry for myself. It was long time since I flirted with a young lady. Apparently it went over like a lead balloon. Real smooth, O'Farrell, nice and clumsy. That redhead did everything but push you down the stairs. I really was out of practice.

It was a beautiful evening, the just-beginning sunset golden and orange, and casting warm and refreshing rays. The air was fresh with a breeze from the sea.

I returned my attention to Mr. Twain and the short story called "The First Lie I Told and How I Got Out of It." It seemed like appropriate material for the private eye or a lawyer to know.

There was a slip of paper in the book. It had a reference number for the waiting list for Hemingway's new book. But in the corner in very neat writing was her name. Kaitlin O'Doherty. And a phone number, and a note: Call me later.

Well, not too clumsy after all. I was in love.

CHAPTER FOUR

I was bored out of my mind. The two lovebirds went to the library on Saturday and Sunday, from opening to closing. The only break they took was going outside to eat sandwiches. All this high-flying living was starting to get to me.

Since I was living at the library, I was on the lookout for Kaitlin O'Doherty. But apparently she had the weekend off. I called her twice. No answer. I left it at that. I didn't want to seem too eager.

On Monday, I followed Dorothy from class to class for about two hours. There was no doubt about it that she was on her schedule and likely to remain so. I decided to pick up the tail after classes later this afternoon, and headed to my office.

The Russell Building is a swell place for an office. It's not all that fancy, but it is functional. It was built of steel and marble after the big earthquake. Only twelve floors, but expansive, taking up the entire block. I also had a great view of Union Square and the rent was right. More importantly, the building was teeming with law firms. It was like being the in-house gumshoe for nine firms. The lobby was tall and grand. Marble tile and pillars soared up forty feet. There were four elevators and a pair of bathrooms.

On the left side of the middle of the lobby was a niche with a custom newsie and coffee stand. Marty Durrant was the owner and operator. Old Marty was three days older than dirt. He spent thirty years on the San Francisco police force before he was injured in the line. He took a round in his left leg that damaged the knee and compromised the thigh muscle. Marty walks with a limp and on damp, rainy days he uses a cane. He spent a few years on the Chinatown beat and knows who all the players are.

With bathrooms in the lobby and Marty's top-drawer tonsil varnish, there was always a steady cop presence. The cops loved Marty and he enjoyed being kept in the loop. Once a cop, always a cop. He had newspapers, magazines, pulps, gum, butts, and of course coffee, pretty good Joe too. Behind the counter Marty kept a side-by-side Greener shotgun. It was the old-fashioned kind with two triggers. It was like a portable cannon. Not that he would ever need it. It just made the old bird feel protected, I guess.

To top it all off, Marty had a part-time job: busting my chops. I, of course, returned the favor.

"Deck of Luckies, Mike," I said.

"You know something, O'Farrell? You are tooting the wrong ringer, gumshoe," Marty said.

He tossed a deck of Camels on the counter.

"Hey, I asked for Luckies." I tried to act offended.

Marty tapped his fingers on the glass display case.

"You're something of a sleuth, O'Farrell. When you start getting my name right, I might start getting the butts right."

"Okay, Marty, can I please have a deck of Luckies, please!"

Marty gave me a phony condescending smile. "There, that didn't hurt coming out your mush, did it, O'Farrell?"

Marty slid the smokes across the glass counter. He flipped me a pack of matches to go with it and with his large paw, he collected the Camels and the dime off the counter.

"So what's shaking, Sean?"

I lit a butt. "I got a case in Chinatown for a big wheel named Wang."

Marty straightened right up.

"Jesus Christ, Sean, you watch yourself. The Wang's are meaner than any junkyard dog you will run into. Any story that may have heard about the Wang's, no matter how mythical it may sound, chances are it's true."

"Come on, Marty. They can't be all that bad."

Marty refilled his coffee cup and looked around the lobby, like he was making sure no one was listening in.

"Back in '09, they found that one of their people was feeding dope to the cops. The inspector that was handling the case went to meet his contact in the Tenderloin district, outside of Chinatown. The contact didn't make the meeting. The dick went home; his wife and kids were asleep in the house. When he opened the garage the informant was hanging upside down with tongue cut out. A little calling card and reminder to all in Chinatown what happens when you start talking."

"Holy shit," I said. "They don't fool around, do they?"

Marty checked his pocket watch in his vest and gave it a few winds. He smiled and shook his head.

"That's not all, Sean. The next morning when the inspector went to the precinct, he opened his desk drawer and the informant's tongue was in there. The Chief went ape. They talked to every cop, inspector, janitor, and suspect that was in the building. They never did find out who put the damn thing in his desk. These people don't mess around, Sean, so why the hell are you screwing around in their business?"

"Marty, I can't really talk about particulars," I said. "But I can tell you this is a personal family affair and is no way associated with their business interests. I wouldn't have taken the case if there was anything illegal going on. Their youngest kid is involved."

Marty folded up a newspaper into a perfect roll and tossed it underhand to a young lawyer coming into work. Simultaneously, the kid tossed a nickel to Marty and he caught it. It was in the cash register in a flash. Marty regarded me again.

"Old man Wang is a real piece of work. I hated the guy while I was working Chinatown, but I respected him after I left and I still do."

"Do you know anything about the two gorillas that follow him around?" I said.

"I don't know their names, but I have seen them around and I know what they look like. About three years ago, when I was about to retire, there was this dumb rookie that told those two apes to move the car from the front of that social club. They were waiting for Mrs. Wang to come out. He told them to move it now and he started to get tough with those two. He swung his billy club at one of them and the gee stopped it with his hand, one inch from his face. He took the club away from the kid and broke it in half over his knee, then he handed the two pieces back to the kid. I stepped in before anything else could happen."

Marty smiled, refilled his mug, and went to work on it.

"The funny thing about the Wang's is the way they do things, they always seem to know everybody everywhere and have lots of friends. When I got the rookie back to the precinct, there was a brand-new billy club and an apology note from Mrs. Wang to the kid. I don't know, Sean. There is a kind of mystery or mystique about them. They run Chinatown, don't you ever forget that. Whatever happens here in San Francisco it is just that, San Francisco. The same rules don't apply in Chinatown and they sure as hell don't apply to the Wang's."

As Marty and I were talking, a young beat cop entered the lobby and waved to Marty. He went into the bathroom and came back for a cup of Joe.

"How are you this morning, Mr. Durrant?" he said.

Marty gave a theatrical sigh. He took a mug and filled it with coffee.

"Look, rook. It's Marty or Sarge. Don't get all formal on me. Here, have some coffee. There is a chill in the air."

The kid almost blushed. "Thanks, Sarge."

Marty jerked a thumb in my direction.

"Tommy, this is Sean O'Farrell. He is a private eye who works in this building, so you'll see him around. Sean, this is Tommy D'Amato. He just started this beat last week."

The kid had a good firm handshake and a genuine smile.

"Nice to meet you, Tommy, welcome to the neighborhood. How long you been on the force?" I said.

"About nine months, Mr. O'Farrell. I started out in the Embarcadero and the ferry terminals."

"Tommy, call me Sean. This town is full of people that don't like cops, so you need all the friends you can get."

"Amen to that," Marty piped in.

"Thanks, Sean." The rookie took a pull on his Joe. "Do you mind if I ask you a professional question?"

"Sure, shoot."

"My sergeant says you have to read people, and one of the things he said was you got to know when a gee is carrying a rod. I can't tell if you are or not," Tommy said.

"In my line of work, Tommy, I don't need to carry a roscoe with me wherever I go, but frankly, I usually do. Right now I have on a suit and an overcoat. Overcoats make it real hard to tell if a man is packing. I'm a private eye, I have to look sharp. My suits are cut specifically to allow for a double shoulder holster. I can carry twin .45 caliber automatics. I always carry two, you can't be too careful. As a result, you can't tell if I have a rod or not even without an overcoat.

"Most of the criminals you will run into are lowlifes, and they got a bulge in their coats you can see for a block. When you get near them you will see them lower their shoulders and they will touch their rod on the outside of their coat and make sure it is tucked away. It's a reflex action, its fear. They can't help it," I said.

Marty piped in. "Tommy, the day is coming you will instinctively know when a bum is carrying a gun. You know to brush your teeth before you go to bed. You don't have to look on a map to find your way home, you know where it is. It's the same thing: you'll walk down the street you'll get one look and you'll tell him to stop and he'll make a run for it. Guaranteed, you are going to know."

The rookie drank in the advice and the coffee. "I got to get back on the beat. Thanks, gentlemen." The kid reached in his pocket, but I cut him off.

"You beat cops don't make enough to buy free advice. The coffee is on me, Tommy."

"Thanks, Sean. Thanks, Marty." Tommy said with a smile and spring in his step as he went through the revolving door and back onto the street.

I handed Marty a dollar bill. "I'm buying the kid's coffee for a month, Marty. He's going to be a good one."

"Like you have to pay for his coffee, O'Farrell. Cops drink free at this joint."

"Yeah, I know, but it's a privilege to buy coffee for a kid like that."

Marty put the bill in the drawer.

"He's a great kid, Sean. His sergeant is a guy named Mulligan, he's an old buddy of mine, and he stops by to check on the lad. He likes him too, but he has the same concern I do."

"What's that?" I said.

"He is such a nice kid. What I worry about is when the moment of truth comes, when he has to pull his service revolver and pull the trigger, will he hesitate?"

"Maybe he will and maybe he won't," Marty said. "What he might do is get himself or another cop killed. That's why they moved the kid to here, more of a business area. No violent crime here. Mulley asked me to look after the kid."

"Well Marty, I'll keep an eye on the kid too. I worried that the poor kid is going to die of poisoning from this cheap tonsil varnish you serve here."

"Hit the bricks, Dick Tracy. Go to the bathroom and look in the mirror, you can tell your wise comments to someone who cares." Marty said.

I turned my back on Marty and headed to the elevators with a smile.

CHAPTER FIVE

I got to my office, turned the light on and took off my trench coat and placed it on the hat tree, along with my fedora. I opened the shades and turned on my newly battered desk lamp. It was still foggy and it seemed earlier than eight thirty. I got the coffee pot to perking and took out the morning paper for the Seals score from last night. They lost to the Rainiers up in Seattle. It just wasn't the same as it was when Joe DiMaggio was playing for them. They sold Joey to the New York Yankees for $25,000. Lefty O'Doul was the manager when Joey hit in sixty-one consecutive games. Damn it, without Joe, the Seals were just another baseball team.

The smell of fresh coffee filled the office as I picked up the phone and dialed the main library number. I had a lump in my throat as I asked for the reference desk.

"Good morning, reference desk, Miss O'Doherty," Katlin answered.

"Good morning Miss O'Doherty, Sean O'Farrell calling. I was calling to see if Hemingway showed up yet?" It was a lame line, and there was a long pause.

"I'm sorry, did you call me this weekend, Mr. O'Farrell?"

There was no hiding on this one. "Yes, I called a couple of times but there was no answer."

"I'm very sorry. There were several people sick this weekend. I had to fill in at the Richmond branch one day and the Chinatown branch the other. I didn't have much a weekend. I'm sorry I wasn't around to take your phone call."

I let the air out slowly. "Well maybe I can take you out to dinner this Saturday night, if you are available."

"I get off work at five on Saturday. Shall I meet you?" Her voice was tight and nervous.

"I'll meet you at the library, and I'll take you to North Beach for Italian."

As I was formulating how to conclude our conversation, a woman walked into my office.

"I have to go, a client just walked in. I'll see you Saturday." She gave me a friendly goodbye and the line clicked off.

The woman was quite a looker. She was tall and blonde, fit and trim with a narrow face. Legs that wouldn't quit, and brother, she was stacked. All that, and her makeup and fashion sense was impeccable. Her smart gray business suit matched her long skirt, black high heels and purse.

"Good morning, can I assist you, Miss..." I asked.

"Actually, it's Mrs., Mr. O'Farrell. I am married. But rather, it is Doctor. Doctor Constance Morehouse, M.D. You have been recommended to me by an associate."

She wasn't looking at me. She was looking at the pictures on the wall and walking around.

"Tell me, Mr. O'Farrell, who is this, a picture of?"

"That would be Jasper O'Farrell. He was the surveyor of San Francisco and designer of the 'grand promenade' that is today's Market Street. O'Farrell Street here in Union Square is named after him."

"Is he a relation then?"

"No relation that I know of. He's just another Irishman made good in our fair city. Won't you have a seat, Dr. Morehouse. How can I help you?"

She strolled over to the client chair and carefully sat. It was quite a production. She smoothed her skirt out and adjusted her sleeves, then slowly took off her black gloves and opened her purse. She placed the gloves in the purse and placed a pair of wire-frame eyeglasses on her nose and carefully placed the temples on her ears. Next, she removed a handkerchief and dabbed the corner of her eye. She was holding it all together, but barely.

"One of my nurses, Wilma Wellington, recommended you, Mr. O'Farrell. She said you were very good and discreet." She gave me a knowing look.

"I remember Wilma quite well." I left it at that. I didn't want to discuss another client's case.

"Wilma was destroyed by the fact that her husband was a cheat," Dr. Morehouse continued. "She told me you investigated and confirmed the fact for her. I believe I need the same."

She was on her feet again, pacing in a circle around the office. She couldn't look at me while she told me her story.

"My husband, Randall Morehouse, and I have been married for twelve years. He has been a wonderful husband and provider. He is an architect and civil engineer. His firm was the designer of support structures for the Golden Gate Bridge. He is the architect of the Oakland Bay Bridge, as well as another bridge project in Sacramento. He travels there every week on business for an overnight trip."

"How does he get there?"

"He takes a riverboat from the Embarcadero, every Monday evening at six thirty p.m. and arrives in Sacramento at five thirty a.m. He meets with clients all day, then returns at six thirty p.m. from Sacramento and arrives at five thirty a.m. He goes directly to the office and works all day. He leaves the office at five p.m. and is home by five thirty p.m. You could set your watch by my husband's comings and goings. He is never late, never alters his schedule or habits for any reason what so ever. Until..."

Her voice cracked, and she dabbed her eyes again.

"Eight weeks ago he started coming in late, then later. Missing dinner, staying in Sacramento longer. He started coming home like he slept in his suit of clothes. Two weeks ago his office started calling the house looking for him. His employees played it coolly. The truth be told, they didn't know where he was for days at a time. Suddenly I have had to keep putting money into our household account. He is flying through money. He refuses to talk about it, and brushes the entire affair off as my being paranoid."

"Doctor, I know you have suspicions," I said. "What do you think is going on?"

Her voice was firm and she had a face of stone. I guess it's the kind of demeanor you would expect from a surgeon, but something about her was just a little too cold and steely for me.

"My husband is screwing another woman. A wife can tell these things. My guess is he is seeing a woman in Sacramento and maybe another here." She delivered this news to me like she was cleaning out the cupboards, without an ounce of emotion.

"Tell me, Doctor. Does he have lipstick on his collars, the smell of another woman's perfume, hotel receipts, receipts for flowers, gifts, things like that?" I asked.

She gave it some thought.

"I'm not your average housewife, Mr. O'Farrell. I am a surgeon, and I too keep a busy schedule. I have a household staff to do laundry, so I don't know about lipstick and perfume. I can tell you there are no receipts at the house. I simply don't know what to do."

The tears were really flowing now.

"Doctor, this is going to be very hard for you to hear. But please, consider this," I said. "It may be something else entirely. If I look into this and you are right, it may mean the end of your marriage. But if I look into it and you are wrong, you will feel guilty for the rest of your life. So, you have to ask yourself what is worse: knowing or not knowing."

Dr. Morehouse opened her purse and took out a gold cigarette case. She fumbled with the lighter and couldn't get it to light. I got up, walked around the desk, and lit a match for her. She inhaled deeply and relaxed slightly.

"Mr. O'Farrell, every time my husband comes home hours late and crawls in my bed, I feel like there is another woman in there with me. I have to know, one way or another. If I am wrong, I will tell him and suffer the consequences, but I have to know."

"Doctor Morehouse, I'll take your case. I'll follow your husband to Sacramento this evening and report to you on Wednesday. Where can we meet?"

"Please come to my home. I am off on Wednesdays and frankly I'd prefer that my office staff not know what is going on. I suggest you follow my husband to his office Wednesday morning, and then you can come to my home."

She handed me an ivory business card. On the back was her home address and phone number. She fumbled in the purse for her wallet and handed me two photographs of her husband.

She had a vacant look on her face. "He is quite handsome," she said. "I know I am very busy and not the perfect wife, but I can't imagine him running to another woman. It just doesn't make sense." You could tell she was questioning herself more than her husband. She was shifting around in her chair, she smoothed the bottom of her skirt. She was straightening her appearance, but she was a mess inside.

"Doctor, sense has got nothing to do with it," I said. "Years ago I was in the Navy, stationed at the Brooklyn Navy Yard. I was in charge of the base military police force. I was called to a Navy commander's home. He was killed in New York City. He had a wife and three lovely children. He was going into the city at night and hiring prostitutes off the street. One of them slit his throat with a knife for five bucks. There was no reason at all for any of it. I had to tell his wife what had happened. She blamed herself for not being a good enough wife. Sometimes, there are simply no reasons and no good answers."

She nodded. "What is your fee, Mr. O'Farrell?"

"I get fifty dollars a day plus expenses. I am working another case, so I will prorate based on when I am working on yours. I will give you a complete accounting."

Dr. Morehouse stood up, shook my hand and slowly walked out the door. She was good-looking from the front, but there was something about those long legs and the stockings with the seam up the middle of the back of her legs that really made her look even sexier. If Mr. Morehouse was screwing another woman on the side, he needed to have his head examined. I looked at his picture, and I was sure the guy was bing. I watched the good doctor walk down the hall to the elevator. Easy Sean, she's married, she's a client and you don't do that.

Jesus, I needed a cold shower.

CHAPTER SIX

After the doctor made her exit, I decided I needed to watch the lovebirds for a few hours before I faded from town. As I was leaving the building, Marty waved me over.

"Hey, Sean, did the looker with great-looking gams find your office?"

"You're all class, Marty. Yes, the lady doctor found my office," I said.

He laughed, but he suddenly became sullen.

"Sean, I've been a cop for over thirty years before they put me out to pasture, and I know people. That dame is no good. She may look all sugar and spice, but that broad is all about calculation and manipulation, I know the type. You be careful, kid."

Normally, Marty is one joke after another. This time he was serious, and I took it as such.

"Thanks, Marty. I'll watch my back." I said.

As I started to walk away, Marty opened a box of donuts and flashed them at me.

"Take a look, O'Farrell. Boston cream, your favorite." He gave a sinister laugh.

"You bastard, you really know how to hit a guy low." I grabbed a napkin and a doughnut and left.

It was another exciting day of watching the lovebirds living their charmed lives. After today, I could hang a sign around my neck that said PRIVATE DETECTIVE PLEASE IGNORE, and those two kids would walk right by it. When they were together, I was starting to get the impression that they were simply friends. After I got back from Sacramento, it was time to see Mr. Wang and fill him in on the big goose egg I had collected.

THE HALFWAY TO HELL CLUB

As soon as the lovebirds entered the library, I ran home and packed an overnight bag. Since I didn't know what I was getting into, I packed a shirt, underwear, and socks, and put on the double shoulder holster with the twin .45s. I tossed four extra loaded magazines in the leather bag. I threw in a couple decks of Luckies, a shave kit, and my library book

I timed it just right. I caught a cable car heading back to Union Square. I jumped in my car and headed to the Embarcadero and arrived at 5:50 p.m. I parked, grabbed my bag and ran for the boat.

At the California Transportation Company office, I stood in line to buy a ticket. With Mr. Morehouse's picture in hand, I started looking for my subject and I couldn't have been any luckier. The guy was three places ahead of me in line.

He bought a round-trip first-class ticket on the steamboat Delta Queen for three bucks. Boarding was about to begin at six. After purchasing my ticket, I hung in the back of the waiting room until boarding began.

Morehouse was tall, about six feet, and broad-shouldered, with a thin mustache and wavy brown hair. He kept taking off his grey fedora and running his hand through his hair in a nervous manner. He looked more like a banker than an architect. He was reading a newspaper, but I got the feeling he was reading something behind the newspaper he was trying to hide. His eyes darted around the room, and at the door, like he was looking for someone. I've seen guys do that before, looking to prevent anyone from coming up behind them.

The double doors leading to the gangway opened and the waiting room emptied to the sternwheeler's main deck. I stayed behind Morehouse as he went straight to the dining room and got a table. I went to the other end of the room and ordered the special: chicken-fried steak, mashed potatoes, gravy, and peas, with rolls. It was great. I had been on the run all day, and the only thing I had eaten was that donut from Marty's. I followed dinner with a piece of apple pie and a glass of milk, and was halfway through my after-dinner Joe and butt when Morehouse got up to leave. The steamboat was only two hundred and eighty-five feet long, so he couldn't get lost, but I wanted to see if he went right to his room.

He walked up the grand staircase and stopped by the purser's office to yap with him. I was close enough to see him reach for his room key, and I caught the number: 211. Then Morehouse leaned in close and the purser whispered to him. Morehouse nodded, then slipped the purser five clams. I doubted it was for a sneak peek at the breakfast special.

Morehouse hightailed out of the lobby and flew up the stairs like a little kid running to a candy jar. I had trouble keeping up with him. He went to the top deck, all the way forward, near the pilot house. He looked around and knocked twice on a door. He whispered something and ducked in. The room number was 420. The wooden shutters were closed and I couldn't see inside.

I waltzed over the rail and lit a butt, and pulled out that collection of short stories by Mark Twain. Before that I had read Twain's Life on the Mississippi. There was a passage about being on a steamboat at sunset. I was living that passage at this very moment. I was as close as I could be to the pilot house without being there. The sunset was orange, red, yellow and gold, with a kiss of purple. The breeze was light, and the flag on the jack staff slapped lightly in the wind. I was as far forward as possible, but I could still hear the steady, rhythmic sound of the paddlewheel churning up the water of the Sacramento River. A man and woman, arm in arm, strolled the deck near me heading toward the stern and the paddlewheel. The water was like glass, and the only evidence of our movement was the small wave created by the high bow of the Delta Queen. I was as if I was on an oversized birthday cake sliding through the water, silently and gracefully.

The steamboat was full of people everywhere, except where I stood, alone. It was how life is for a private detective. People who read the pulps and dime-store detective novels think that every day is a gunfight or a fistfight. It couldn't be farther from the truth. Most of the time you are waiting, watching, and sitting around. Most of the time it's cold, raining, muddy, cheap, and uncomfortable. You spend your days and nights waiting for that five seconds that the man you are shadowing reveals himself. Just like now, standing and waiting for a guy behind a closed door. At this time and place the sunset was warm, and beautiful. For once, I didn't mind the wait.

As I was watching the sunset, I heard out of the quiet: "Hey buddy." I looked around and couldn't see who called. Then he called again. I looked around again, then up. It was the captain sticking his head out of the window of the pilot house.

"Hey, Mack, usually they send a waitress up here with coffee. Could you find one of them and bring me a cup of Joe?"

"Sure, how do you take it?"

"Black."

I left my station and went looking around for a crew member, but there was none to be seen. I went down two flights of stairs to a bar and asked the bar keep for two coffees: one black and one with cream. He delivered the mugs, and I hurried back up and found the small steep stairway to the pilot house.

The pilot on duty was grateful. "Thanks, pal. It's starting to cool off up here, and the Joe really hits the spot."

The view was magnificent. The pilot house itself was a sight. The mahogany wheel must have been ten feet across. A gleaming brass engine-room telegraph was nestled between cherry, mahogany, oak, and other exotic woods in the cabinets and window casings. The view was fit for a queen. Along the back of the pilot house were two elevated leather couches for guests to view the river. The pilot pointed to one.

"Pull up a seat on the lazy bench, enjoy the view."

"Thanks, Captain. I was in the Navy; we didn't have bridges like this one."

"Oh yeah, I was in the Navy too. I was a boatswain's mate. The name's Charlie McCoy."

"Sean O'Farrell. Don't hold it against me that I was an officer."

Charlie laughed. "This sure beats destroyer duty."

Charlie moved back and forth, from side to side adjusting the big wheel. He was short and round, the kind of guy you would want on your side in a bar fight in Singapore. I liked him instantly.

I sat for a bit, but I needed to get back to my post.

"Hey, Charlie, I have to fade and meet a guy."

"Sean, you coming back?" he asked.

"I should be back on board tonight."

"I'll be on watch from six to midnight. Come on back up. The lazy bench is always open for fellow sailors."

We shook hands, and I descended the stairs from the pilot house and took up my spot again. After a few minutes, I decided it was time to walk a little bit. As I said, it was all about waiting, and sometimes luck is a big part of being a private detective. I had walked down to the stern and turned around when a girl with a tray full of drinks passed me. I followed. I was in luck; she stopped at 420 and knocked on the door. The door opened wide and she went in. Again I was lucky; they left the door open wide, and as I walked by she was handing out drinks. It was a poker game, and Morehouse was sitting there were a pile of chips in front of him. It was only a glance; I couldn't stop and take a good look. Morehouse had been in there for two hours. The one thing that I could see from the quick glance that I got was that Morehouse had fewer chips than anyone else at that table.

It took just a five-second glimpse into a small stateroom to answer all of his wife's questions: Randall Morehouse had a gambling problem.

CHAPTER SEVEN

In the morning, in my stateroom, I shaved, showered, packed up, and had a quick breakfast of fresh eggs, toast, bacon, and fresh coffee. The Delta Queen had been tops; even the cream for the coffee was fresh.

The boat would be tying up in Sacramento in fifteen minutes. I had a hunch about Morehouse, and played it. I went by his stateroom, number 201, and the cleaning staff was in there. It looked as if it had never been used.

I took a spot on the top deck near the stern. There was a table and chairs there. I had an unobstructed view of stateroom 420 at the other end of the boat. I didn't have to wait long. The pilot blew the whistle, and the door to 420 opened. The poker-game participants piled out of the tiny door. The last to leave was Randall Morehouse, looking like he had been dragged from the bumper of a car. He looked more than tired; he looked beaten, destroyed, and humiliated. He didn't walk; he shuffled his feet to the gangway like a man in disgrace. It was hard to watch.

I followed him to the gangway and he tossed his room key in a wicker basket. He didn't clean up, eat breakfast, shave, or do anything at all. He just lumbered off the boat like a dead man.

He didn't go far. At the end of the pier was an old flophouse. He paid four bits for a room, climbed the rickety outside staircase to the second floor, opened a door and went inside. The door did not close. I quietly went up and looked inside. Morehouse was face down on the mattress, fully clothed and out like a light. The room smelled of body odor, cigars, and vomit. It was the kind of hotel where chippies rented space by the hour. It was more than I could watch. I slipped back down to the lobby.

I waited until eight thirty to ensure that offices were open for business before I started making calls. There was a phone booth in the lobby of this dump. It was the kind of hotel where even the rats knew better than to set up shop. I jumped in and played a hunch. I opened the phone book and looked under state agencies. When I found the State Building Standards Commission, I wrote down the number and the name of the director, Gerald Ramsay.

I dialed the number.

"Gerald Ramsay, please."

"I'm sorry, Mr. Ramsay is out of the office this morning and won't return until two."

I said thank you and hung up. Then I got the operator and called long distance to San Francisco. I called the main offices of Morehouse and Wheeler Architects. The phone rang only once. "Good morning, Morehouse and Wheeler."

I cleared my throat. "Randall Morehouse, please."

There was a long pause. "I'm sorry, Mr. Morehouse is not in. May I take a message?"

"I certainly hope he is not in. This is Gerald Ramsay of the state of California Building Standards Commission, Mr. Morehouse was due at a hearing here in my office in Sacramento thirty minutes ago. He has rescheduled this meeting three times. Now if you people want your license to operate terminated let me know right now."

"Hold please." The receptionist was probably peeing and running at the same time. One minute later a new voice picked up.

"Good morning, Mr. Ramsay. This is Jonathan Wheeler, Mr. Morehouse's partner. I had no idea that Mr. Morehouse is due in Sacramento today."

"I'm not going to waste any more time here, Mr. Wheeler. It is now eight thirty and we are adjourned until after lunch. Your partner better be here at one thirty and ready to testify." I slammed the phone down.

THE HALFWAY TO HELL CLUB

I left the hotel and went to the park bench across the street right near the Delta Queen's pier. It was a bright and sunny day, and I returned my attention to Mr. Twain.

At eleven thirty, a Packard touring car drove quickly up the street and, with a squeal of brakes, stopped in front of the flophouse. A young man in a check double-breasted suit with a bow tie and white fedora jumped out of the car before it stopped and ran up the stairs. He flew into Morehouse's room, and a minute later dragged Morehouse out and down the stairs. The kid took the beleaguered architect to the bar next to the flophouse and started pouring coffee into him. I slid into the joint and took a place at the bar. It was lunchtime, and the soup-and-sandwich crowd was in. A couple of men were drinking drafts at the bar. The place was a real hole. The kind of place where the whiskey is used to clean car parts, first.

The kid was working as hard as he could to bring Morehouse to life. I slipped back over to the hotel and used the phone booth again to call Morehouse and Wheeler. Wheeler picked up the phone.

"Mr. Wheeler, Gerald Ramsay here. One of the commission members' children has been in an accident and we will have reschedule Mr. Morehouse's testimony for another date, two or three weeks from now. We are sorry for the inconvenience."

Old Wheeler was all apologies, and promised that Mr. Morehouse would meet with the commission on time in the future. I slipped back into the bar and watched the action.

Morehouse fell asleep at the table, and the kid went to the bar and asked for the telephone. The barkeep gave him some crap, but the kid slapped a ten-dollar bill on the bar, and the keeper slammed the phone on the bar. The kid started dialing.

"Mr. Wheeler, its Child, sir. Yes, sir, I know sir. Yes sir, he looks like he was up all night again, and yes sir, he's drunk and hung over. I didn't know anything about a meeting at the commission, sir. No sir. Yes sir, he is the worst I have ever seen him. Sir, something has got to be done, the Eighth Avenue bridge project is worth millions, and he is not getting anything done on it. Yes sir. I'll get him to a hotel, clean him up, and put him back on the boat at six thirty, yes sir. Just a minute, sir."

The kid went over and patted down Morehouse and took out his wallet. He returned to the phone.

"All he has is a return ticket for the Delta Queen. He is tapped out. Don't worry, sir; I'll put him on the Queen this evening. I recommend that Michaels or Linderman meet the boat at five thirty and get the old man to the office. Yes sir, I will." He hung up.

I was leaning on the bar while the kid tried to wake Morehouse. There was a back office in the rear of the bar. A short fat bald guy with an open vest and a cigar came out. He was flanked by two torpedoes. They were your garden-variety muscle. The fat guy walked up to the kid.

"Let's get something straight, sonny. Your boss owes me a bundle of dough. Either he pays it, or you pay it, or he doesn't come home to mama. You got that?"

"Yeah, I got it." The kid was a little flippant in his response.

The little guy slapped him with the back of his hand. "Look, kid, I know you just work for the guy, but get this straight. He is out of time, and so are you." The squirt and the two gorillas returned to the private office and slammed the door.

The kid was embarrassed. He picked up his hat, put it on, and got Morehouse on his feet. He shuffled his boss into the car and away they went.

The bar was so dirty that I saw cockroaches running for the exits. Needless to say, I couldn't trust the food. But I had to risk it. There was a guy sitting at the bar nursing a beer and having a bowl of soup. It was potato, according to the barkeep, but it looked like it could bend the spoon. I ordered an egg-salad sandwich and a beer. I gave the bartender a dollar and told him to keep the change. "The little guy has a temper, doesn't he?"

The bartender shrugged. "Little Joey Patrone is pretty much angry all the time. Forget to pay money you owe him, and he can be downright ugly."

I was barbering with the bartender when what had to be the ugliest woman I had every laid eyes on squeezed in between me and this guy eating a sandwich.

"Hey good-looking, buy me a drink?"

"Another time, lady," I said.

The bartender chimed in. "Beat it, Alice. We have had enough fights in here with you. Fade."

"Screw off, Arthur. You just tend the bar, you don't own it. Little Joey does and he don't mind me being here." She turned her attention to me.

"What do you say, good-looking? Want a date?"

I wasn't in the mood, but I wasn't looking for any trouble.

"Come on, lady. I have to go back to work. Leave me alone."

She called me a cheap no-good rotten son of a bitch and slapped me in the face as hard as she could. I had to hand it to her, it was a pretty good slap. I felt it good.

"Easy, sweetheart, that's your money-counting hand."

The old broad grabbed an empty beer bottle from the bar and expertly broke it on the edge. Screaming at the top of her lungs, she swung her arm and the jagged neck of the broken bottle. Destination, my face. It was about six inches from my nose when I blocked it with my left arm. The bottle flew out of her hand and I gave her one stiff punch right in the snot locker. She folded up like a cheap deck chair, her eyes rolling around in her head. She had enough steam left in her boiler to tell me I was a cold-hearted bastard before she passed out on the floor.

She was right. I was.

CHAPTER EIGHT

I left the bar and flophouse, and wandered through the downtown area. I knew Morehouse would be back on the Delta Queen for his return home. I had six hours to kill. I found a nice little drugstore with a lunch counter. I reordered lunch: burger and fries, with a Coke. I was eating because I was hungry and I didn't know if I would get a shot to eat on the boat. That was all up to Mr. Morehouse. Would he sleep? Would be gamble again? Or would he find a honey to snuggle up to?

Ever since I got in the private-eye game I have always known that violence can walk right up and smack you in the kisser at any time. I have pulled a .45 eight times. I have never had to fire. Not yet, anyway.

I had always believed I could talk my way out of any fight. When you throw a punch, all reason is gone. And more than that, your ability to control a situation is gone.

I was still beating myself up for hitting that broad back at the bar. If I hadn't cracked wise to her, maybe she wouldn't have gone for the bottle and broken it. I could be in a hospital having multiple stiches in my face.

I hit her once, only once. It was as much as was needed. I didn't haul off and beat her for five minutes. Even the barkeep told me afterward that I did less than any guy would have. Men who hang around in those kinds of bars carry blackjacks or worse. Still, I did feel like a coldhearted bastard.

My old man told me from day one: "You never hit a women, you protect them, and you honor them, your treat them all like they were your mother or grandmother." He would really get all worked up about this subject. "The lowest kind of skunk hits a women. When they do, boyo, you straighten them out." He said.

I knew what that meant. When I was thirteen, my pop's younger sister Martha, my Aunt Martha, was married to a cable-car gripman. He was a big strapping Scotsman named Brown. He was over six feet tall, and huge like a weightlifter. My old man was only five feet six and wiry. He was a baker, he wasn't real big but his hands and arms were strong. He still kneaded bread by hand, and he was a kind and gentle man.

One Sunday after Mass I walked with Pop to my Aunt Martha's house. The old man had a loaf of sourdough bread for his sister. We heard the screaming and yelling a block away. All the neighbors were on the sidewalk, wondering if they should get involved. The old man pounded on the door. My Aunt Martha opened the door. She had a split lip that was bleeding, and she was sobbing uncontrollably. Uncle Ian was yelling at my Pop to get out. Pop ignored him and went into the kitchen got a cold towel and helped my aunt calm down. We were there for a good hour. He helped her to bed and quietly closed the bedroom door.

I was sitting in the living room as my Uncle Ian was towered over Pop.

"Go home, you bug Irish prick," he snarled, "and worry about your own wife and your own business, why don't you."

Pop kicked Uncle Ian in the leg, and he went down to his knees hard. Pop started kneading Ian's face like soft dough. Fifteen socks to the puss later, my old man was whispering in his ear.

"Don't you ever hit my sister again, or I'll shove a bagpipe so far up your ass every time you fart it'll play 'Scotland the Brave.' So help me God, I'll ship your body back to Glasgow if you touch her again. And one more thing, Ian: don't ever call me a bug Irish prick again." He popped Ian one last time and my uncle went down for the count.

As we were walking back, Pop spoke.

"I've told you before, Sean. Never hit in anger, never get down in the gutter with your enemy. But always remember, there are some men in this world that need a little straightening out every now and again. That would be your Uncle Ian."

He never spoke of it again. All I know for sure is my old man never laid a hand on my mother. From that day forward I was pretty sure Uncle Ian never did it again to Aunt Martha.

I knew I did the right thing, popping that broad at the bar, but I still felt awful. Oh well. I had another Coke and pulled out my library book and read for a while. I finished a couple more stories and the book was almost done. Mr. Twain never disappoints. I paid for lunch and picked up a Sacramento Bee and a San Francisco Chronicle for the ride back. I was at the register when I looked out the window and saw that the blue Packard had pulled into the bank across the street. The kid with the bow tie got out and opened the door for Morehouse. He was cleaned up, all right. He was wearing the same suit, but the kid must have gotten it cleaned and pressed at the hotel.

Morehouse went into the bank, and walked out two minutes later counting money. He had a butt dangling from his lip and his fingers were counting away. He piled back in and the kid drove him the three blocks to the Delta Queen. I had twenty minutes before we boarded.

I strolled the street to the piers. The pilot I met on board, Charlie McCoy, was about ten steps ahead of me. Past him, a kid in a three-piece suit and white fedora was walking toward me, reading a racing form and smoking a butt. He bumped into Charlie. That's when I called to Charlie. He turned around and waved. I raised my left arm and yelled hello.

When the kid with the white fedora was even with me, I clotheslined him with my left arm. His legs went straight out and he landed flat on his back. He was stunned and tried to get up, but I put my foot on his shoulder above his left arm.

"Easy cowboy, don't make me get tough."

A street cop came running up.

"I saw that, pal. What did you hit the guy for?"

The kid started to protest. He raised his left arm and pointed at me. I grabbed the kid's hand and twisted his arm.

"In two seconds, punk, I'm going to twist this arm off and beat you to death with it," I said. "Give him the wallet back."

The kid reached into his inside left suit pocket and handed Charlie his wallet. Charlie was stunned.

"Hey, that's my wallet."

"The kid's a grifter. He picked you clean when he bumped into you a second ago." I addressed the kid. "Nice pull, Junior."

The kid smiled with pride. "Thanks, mister."

The cop asked Charlie if it was his wallet. Charlie checked and said it was. The cop kicked the kid in the side as hard as he could, then kneed the kid in the stomach and clamped the nippers on him. When he was sure he was secure, he took his billy club and raised it over his head. He was going to split the kid's melon open. He swung through, but I caught the stick halfway.

"Come on, pal. The kid's handcuffed, and he's defenseless."

The flattie was honked that I stopped him. He thought about it for a second and he knew I was right. He got the kid by his arm. Charlie put the kid's hat on his head.

The kid said thanks. He looked at Charlie for the hat, then at me for saving his puss a workout. The copper hauled him away. Charlie and I watched him shove the kid down the street.

"Sean, how did you know the kid swiped my wallet?"

"I'm a private eye, Charlie. I know these things."

"Well, I never knew he got my wallet."

"Don't worry, Charlie. That makes two of you."

"Two of you, what do you mean?"

"As the kid was getting handcuffed, he lifted the cop's wallet. And while he was at it, he got the flatfoot's keys. They are in his left hand."

Charlie laughed. "How do you see all that stuff?"

I shrugged.

The boarding had begun and Morehouse was already on board. I told Charlie I had to work for a while, but I would bring hot coffee to the pilothouse and fill him in.

I made my way to the top deck. The whistle blew and we slowly started to back away from the pier. When we were one hundred yards away and picking up steam, I looked at the street and saw the young pickpocket running as fast as he could go in spectator shoes, holding his white fedora with the black band. That cop was chasing him on foot, but you could tell that he was out of breath, out of gas, and about to give up.

The door to 420 opened, and sure enough, old Morehouse was in there again. If nothing else, this bird was consistent.

CHAPTER NINE

I knew Morehouse would be at that table all night. There was no sense standing outside that door and not getting a good night's sleep. I decided that I would run below, have a nice dinner, then join Charlie in the pilothouse for coffee and watch the sunset.

There was a wait for a dinner table, so I chatted with the purser about the boat. The Delta Queen and her sister, the Delta King, were only a couple of years old. They were the most expensive and elaborate sternwheel steamboats ever built.

The hostess called my name, and I descended the grand staircase and took my table. Since the good Dr. Morehouse was paying, I ordered a steak, baked potato, and green beans. I'm a real steak snob; my favorite place for a steak or chops is John's Grill, over on Ellis Street in San Francisco. It would be hard for the Queen to beat them, and they didn't, but they came damn close. I ordered two cups of Joe and made my way to the pilothouse.

As it turned out, Charlie had been at the Brooklyn Navy Yard while I was there. He finished his twenty and came west. He was a tugboat captain in Suisun Bay, but he joined the Delta boats when the California Transportation Company opened for business. He started as the first mate and became a pilot within a year. It was a little slice of heaven in the wheelhouse. It was quiet, peaceful and the scenery was world-class. It started to rain, ever so slightly, cooling things off and making the air fresher than normal.

Charlie asked what I was up to on board. I told him about the cake eater I was following in room 420.

Charlie laughed.

"That game has been going on ever since these two boats went into service. There are big rollers that ride this boat just to get in that game. Every Monday night and the Tuesday return."

I went back two more times for coffee. It was a beautiful evening, just like the one before. Charlie was going to be relieved at midnight, so I said my goodnight.

I went by room 420 and sure enough, you could see the lights through the wooden shades. It would be another long night for Randall Morehouse.

In the morning I had sourdough toast, grapefruit, a soft-boiled egg, and coffee. The boat pulled in at exactly five thirty as scheduled. In a repeat of the previous morning, here came old Morehouse. My favorite daisy boozehound was ready for another day of work. He was a little bit better than yesterday, but not by much. He tried to throw his key in the basket, and missed, of course. He was walking like a sailor at sea on a rough night, weaving and bobbing, trying to walk straight but unable to manage it. As soon as he was on shore, two suits grabbed him and starting walking him toward the Financial District.

Doctor Morehouse was out of her nut if she thought this tool was fooling around on her.

I walked over a block to the parking area at the Embarcadero. My Ford was waiting for me. I mentioned before that I have always had a thing for cars. Last year I finished a big case for a law firm, Donaldson, Donaldson, and Drake. Their client had been embezzled for more than two hundred large. It turned out it was an employee was skimming the bank accounts. The dope kept the cash in shoeboxes in his closet. I waited till the gee was out living it up with his girlfriend, then I got into his house and took the illegal proceeds. I gave the money back to the client. They paid my fee and gave me a thousand-dollar bonus.

I own the house my parents lived in; I have no debt or bills. So I spent eight hundred and fifty clams and bought my baby. She was maroon, with a gray interior. A 1937 Ford Coupe with the three-point-six-liter V8. I do love her so. There is nothing like dropping her into a high gear and driving across the Golden Gate and driving around on a clear day in the country.

I paid the twenty-five-cent overnight parking fee and headed to the office. Marty was just opening up. He tried to lure me with a donut, but I was full from eating on the boat.

I opened the door, flipped on the light, and opened the bills and more bills that were scattered on the floor below the mail slot. I hung up my coat and made for the phone. Phyllis at Acme Answering gave me the rundown.

My sister Margie called from Los Angeles. Mr. Wang called looking for an update. Father O'Connell from my church called; please call back. Let me translate that for you: he wants something, he wants something fixed, he wants something done, he wants help, he wants money. In other words, call him back, because it's all of the above. And last but not least, Kaitlin O'Doherty called. My heart skipped a beat.

I called her home number immediately. It was only seven thirty, but I thought I might catch her before work. The phone rang a couple of times and she picked up.

"Good morning. Sean O'Farrell returning your call. I hope I am not calling too early. I just got back in town."

"No not at all, thanks for calling. My shift was changed today; I don't work until one this afternoon. How would you like to go to lunch?"

I tried to remain cool, but it was hard. "Sure what time and where would you like to go?"

"How about Sears at eleven thirty?" she said.

"I'll be there." She said goodbye and hung up.

Am I free for lunch? She must be kidding; I'd cancel an audience with Pope for a chance at lunch with her.

I first called Mr. Wang and left a message with Jimmy: that I would meet him tomorrow at ten a.m. with a complete report. Next, I gave the good Doctor Morehouse a call. I told her I had a report; when could I see her? She had a tennis lesson, followed by a match. We agreed to meet at her house at three.

I drove home, grabbed a quick shower, shaved and put on my best suit and tie. I went into the dining room and opened the top drawer to the linen chest. It's where I keep my gun-cleaning supplies. I also keep two cleaned ready-to-go M1911 .45s. Every Saturday morning was gun-cleaning time for two hours. In addition to the two .45s on my person, I had two spares in the drawer, one hidden in the kitchen under the sink, one hidden under the fireplace mantel in the living room, one in the night table next to the bed, one between the mattress and the box spring, one hidden in the door panel of the Ford, two in the office, and I keep one extra at Marty's, behind a loose kick panel on the glass display case.

After I got out of the Navy, I received a crate. It held the parts for twenty M1911 .45s in a wood box. It was from a gunner's-mate chief that worked for me, and knew I was a .45 fan. A private eye can never have enough firepower around.

Every Friday, I bring the office guns and the one from Marty's stand home to clean on Saturday, and return all three on Monday. The .45 is a great handgun, but if you don't take care of it, it won't take care of you. If you don't clean and properly oil your .45, it may not fire during the moment of truth. I heard horror stories about guys having their guns jam and at the cost of their lives in World War One. It wouldn't be happening to me.

The chief was a hillbilly from Tennessee named Hartfield. He used to kid me endlessly about how particular I was about my .45. He use to chide me with that Southern drawl and say: "You know, Lieutenant, that pea shooter ain't any more dirty than it was the last time you cleaned it, yesterday." I wasn't that bad, but the chief had a good chuckle over it at my expense.

We went to the range to do the military police semi-annual

qualification. After everyone had qualified, the chief and I got into a friendly shootout. We were dead even after three magazines. On the fourth, the chief's .45 jammed. I put all of my rounds in the black for a perfect score. I imitated the chief's drawl.

"You know, Chief, that pea shooter ain't any more dirty than it was the last time you cleaned it last year." The entire group of guys howled.

All the chief could muster was a humble "sumbitch." I wasn't sure he was talking to me or his .45.

Happy memories. I put the two fresh .45s in the holsters and I left for lunch. Yippee!

CHAPTER TEN

Sears Fine Foods is one of those restaurants that make San Francisco what it is. I eat there a lot because the food is excellent and the service is fast. It is a block away from my office and it's right on the Powell Mason cable car line. It just opened a few months ago, but it will be around for years to come. They serve this new breakfast called Swedish pancakes. The line is up the block on weekends, but you can still find a table during the workweek. I got there early.

I had a table by the time Kaitlin O'Doherty entered Sears. She was wearing a lovely emerald green dress that made her red hair and green eyes stand out even more. When you are trying not to look nervous you usually are anything but. But the second I laid eyes on her, I relaxed.

Her smile could melt the North Pole. So effective was her smile that I was about to call Santa and tell him to clear out while he could.

I didn't know how to start things off, but she seemed to have an agenda as the waitress brought us coffees and menus.

"Mr. O'Farrell."

"Sean, please."

"Okay Sean. I asked you here to tell you something. I am looking forward to dinner on Friday, but I wanted to clear the air so to speak so that there is no misunderstanding."

I kept a smile on my puss, but it wasn't easy.

"I am going to tell you a little bit about myself and my past. If you don't like what you hear, I won't blame you for taking a walk. Lots of men have."

I sat there and smiled like an idiot and nodded.

"My family is from Boston. I am thirty-two. How old are you?"

"Thirty-two."

"Well, I have been engaged to be married twice. The first guy was a lawyer from a prestigious family name. My parents were thrilled. The night before the wedding I got word that he got one of his family maids pregnant. The lout told me not to worry about it, that it would never happen again. Thank goodness I broke it off, I found out a week later it was not one pregnant maid, but two.

"Speed forward four years and I am engaged to a wonderful young man. His father is a U.S. congressman and he is a fast-rising attorney. My maid of honor came to see me, this time a week before the wedding, and told me my fiancée made a pass at her brother. I confronted him and he didn't seem to think that it was a real problem. After all, dalliances with men isn't really cheating, like it would be with a woman, he said.

"Then there was the handsome young doctor from New York. After dating for two months, I just knew he was going to pop the old question. One evening he came over to our house, my parents were out. He was dressed in evening clothes; I asked where he was off to. He told me it was none of my business, and he proceeded to beat me to within an inch of my life. Three weeks later I got out of the hospital and my father informed me he had been offered a promotion in San Francisco. I told him to take it, and along I came.

"That was four years ago. I live at home with my parents. If you think the police are tough in an interrogation, wait till you meet my mom and dad. One meeting with them and you are going to feel like you have been worked over with a rubber hose. I'll give you a heads-up: they aren't going to like you. They are overly protective, overbearing, surly, and downright inhospitable. I should also mention that my mother hears my reproductive clock ticking and sees her chances at grandchildren slipping away, so she may want a blood sample and a fertility test, any questions?"

She gave me a wry smile.

I shrugged, taking it all in.

"Do you like baseball?" she asked.

"I beg your pardon," I stammered. "Do you like baseball?"

"I'm from Boston. Of course I like baseball. Are you daft?" Her look was serious.

"No, I used to play, and I like a gal who likes baseball," I said.

"Let me guess: by the way you are drinking your coffee, I would say you are left-handed. You are well over six feet, so you are too big, too clumsy, and too slow to play shortstop or the hot corner. My guess is you are a one-bagger, probably a switch hitter." She had a calm poker face with no smile.

I acted with mock displeasure. "It takes a great deal of talent to play first base."

"With a glove the size of garbage-can lid, how can you miss?"

I leaned over the table and gave her a serious look.

"Let's get down to it, shall we?"

"Let's," she eagerly responded.

"Oaks or Seals?" I asked.

"Seals, they are much closer. However, I hold it against them for selling off DiMaggio. He went to those thieving Yankees. Imagine if he had gone to a good team in the bigs like the Red Sox. His career might have a chance. His little brother Dominic might be smarter and play for Boston." She took a drink of coffee and winked at me.

"Sure, then the Red Sox can sell him for boatload of cash to the Yankees, just like the Bambino," I said nonchalantly.

It was a surefire score for points. It was a major hit for points with that comment. The corners of her mouth formed an ever-so-slight smile. She took a drink of coffee and smiled.

"My, we are a wee bit of a smartass, aren't we?" she said.

"I attempt to provide thoughtful social commentary where needed."

"Like I said, a wee bit of a smartass."

"We do our best. Maybe we should catch a game soon."

"I'd love to," Kaitlin said. "I'll explain what all the different positions on the field do. Plus, I'll teach you how to keep score properly." She laughed.

"And you called me a wee bit of a smartass. Well, then, after our first real date and then a baseball game, we ought to get married. Don't you think?"

She fell quiet.

"I'm being serious here, Sean. I'm afraid. I haven't been out on a date in four years. The men I have met have all been with were disasters. I am not kidding; my parents are a handful. Not to put it all on them: I have a terrible temper and it gets the best of me sometimes. I feel sometimes that my parents peddle me like a product. They are constantly trying to get me to go to charity events, church affairs, and dances. It is never to have fun; it's to marry me off. It's depressing." She looked out the window.

I cleared my throat.

"When my mother was alive, she was constantly trying to find the right woman for me. In her mind any woman, regardless of looks, smarts, or disposition was eligible, just so long as she was fertile. Every date brought on the inquisition. What was she like, do we know her parents, and is she seeing anyone, does she want children? My father referred to it as the O'Farrell Captive Breeding Program. You are cordially invited to marry our son Sean and deliver unto us grandbabies. I know exactly where you are coming from. What do you like to be called?"

"My family and my friends call me Katie."

"That's great, but what do you want to be called?"

"Kaitlin was my late grandmother's name, I have always fancied it," she said with a sense of pride.

"From now, on you will be Kaitlin to me," I said.

She blushed, and it was a wonderful blush.

"Thank you."

"My mother named me Sean Patrick O'Farrell, and when she was on the warpath I heard all three names. It was my cue to hide in another country."

She laughed. "I'm sorry, I feel like this is a job interview and I am pumping you for information. But, do you go to church?" Her expression was one of hope.

"Born and raised Catholic. I go to St. Peter and Paul's in Columbus Circle. I am a member of the Knights of Columbus. I go to confession and everything," I said.

She let out a little breath of relief.

"From the sound of letting out a breath of relief, I would venture to guess that you are too?" I said.

She nodded. It was clear she was greatly relieved.

"Well, I'll bet you don't want me to meet your parents in the future and tell them I my parents are looking forward to our wedding in the synagogue."

That got a real laugh out of her.

"You don't talk about yourself much, do you?"

"No, I am saving myself for your parents. I am sure you don't want to hear all the salient facts twice."

The waitress came. Kaitlin ordered eggs and toast, and I ordered oatmeal and toast.

"I have one more question, and I am sorry for being nosy," she said.

"Go ahead."

"I'm sorry, but are you married?" She looked at the bottom of her coffee cup.

"No," I fired back quickly.

"Have you ever been married?"

"Yes," I said tersely.

"Divorce?" She was looking at me now.

"No, Kaitlin, I'm widowed. I'll tell you all about it one day, but not now." It was my time to look away and out the window.

Our order came and we ate in silence.

"Sean, when you were at the library, I noticed you were wearing a shoulder holster. Are you a policeman?"

"Gees, you don't miss much, do you, young lady? No, I'm a private detective."

"My mom won't like that. It sounds dangerous."

"Life is full of risks. I don't generally take risks that put me and others in danger. I try not to be afraid of what the future will bring. Except meeting your parents, of course."

"Most cops and private eyes I have met don't have your vocabulary or know who Hemingway is, or check out books by Mark Twain."

"I really don't read any of that stuff. The words are too big for me. I just did that to impress you. I mostly ready comic books and the funny papers."

"I have one final question, and it's an important one. It is what they call a deal breaker as far as I am concerned."

"Go ahead, you are on a roll."

"You have to tell me the truth here. You said you lived in New York. Are you a New York Yankees fan?"

I smiled broadly. Wow. Single, sexy, smart, educated, funny, Catholic, and she talks baseball. My dream girl!

CHAPTER ELEVEN

I drove to Pacific Avenue in Pacific Beach. It wasn't Knob Hill, but there were views that you couldn't beat. The Morehouse residence was your run-of-the-mill Georgian mansion, with a cramped seven-car garage that was four times the size of my house. It was a masterpiece of Classic architecture, with all the bells and whistles: grand crown moldings, pilasters, entablature, massive windows, and a front door big enough to drive a car through. Speaking of cars, in the circular driveway was a 1938 Cadillac LaSalle. Momma, what a car: a two-door convertible, canary yellow with red interior. The top was down and covered with a Tonneau. The LaSalle had two trumpet horns on the sides of the hood that were three feet long. It had a large V8 and everything about this car said, "I'm rich, and don't you think otherwise."

I rapped my knuckles on an oak door so heavy that it looked like it would take three guys to open it. Connie Morehouse answered the door in a skimpy white tennis outfit and white sneakers. Her hair was pulled back, but she still looked rather fetching. I had to keep my mind on the game.

"Good morning, Mr. O'Farrell. Won't you come in?"

She led me up the stairs to a large glass-enclosed family room. A pair of French doors led to a patio. In the back yard was a pool and expansive patio with a table, umbrella and chairs. They looked comfy. She sat down and crossed those fabulous legs.

"What have you learned, Mr. O'Farrell?"

I filled her in on my trip. "It also looks like he owes a lowlife in Sacramento a lot of money, gambling debts," I concluded. "There may be others. There usually are." I lit a smoke and tossed the used match in the ashtray.

"That's great. Randall never could handle liquor. As far as I know, he can't play cards either. "

"Oh, he knows how, all right. He just doesn't appear to know how to win."

She looked a little stunned by that statement. The Doctor had a pretty good poker face but she was showing signs of stress in her face. She composed herself.

"I want you to do two things. One, keep digging on the women angle. I know he has a girlfriend. Second, please find out who he owes money to. If I am going to bail him out and pay off his debts before it comes back to ruin us, I need to know who to pay. I don't know if our marriage is going to survive this, but I will give him every chance to set things straight. It's time for him to straighten himself out and start being a man. If I set him adrift, I will at least have tried to help him out. I am getting sick and tired of being married to a screw-up." She forced another smile. "Jesus, I don't know about you, but I need a drink."

She went to a serving cart near the door and brought over a tray. It had all the fixings for a martini. She asked me if I wanted one. I nodded. After all, the sun was over the yardarm. I was ready.

She went to work. She poured the gin out of the bottle and into a jigger, watching every drop. She emptied the booze into the jumbo-sized shaker and measured out the vermouth. With silver tongs she added the ice cubes one by one. She closed up the shaker and then, well, she started shaking. Both the shaker and her body. Every move was like watching a ballerina glide across a stage. She had it all: grace, movement, flow, and sex. Lots of sex. She was wearing a bra, but her breasts were pretty actively bouncing. Needless to say, she had my undivided attention.

She poured the shaker into a slender glass pitcher and stirred it with a long glass spoon. She then filled each martini glass, and lightly tossed in an olive and a pearl onion on a sword toothpick. She handed me one.

It was the best I ever had. The moment it hit my mouth it ran straight to my brain and hit it like a hammer to a nail. Dr. Morehouse took her olive and ran it around the rim of her glass, then took a drink and giggled. She then expertly pushed the olive into her mouth and smiled. As she refilled our glasses she had a look that said making perfect martinis was not her only skill. She then said she would be right back, and stepped through a set of French doors that did not lead to the living room.

"Take your time Dr. Morehouse," I said.

"Please, call me Connie."

For ten minutes, I watched the pool like an idiot. It was a beautiful afternoon and I kept telling myself that this was work, that I was reporting to a client. I wandered around and came to a table with pictures on it. Pictures of Connie, with her husband. Them sailing together, her holding a cute little baby and smiling.

I kept checking my pockets for my lighter, I must have left it in the car. I opened an end table drawer looking for a book of matches. It was crammed full of lipsticks, compacts, and all kinds of lighters. I borrowed one, lite a butt and put the back where I found it and closed the drawer.

Then it occurred to me that my heart and mind were racing, I dragged on the smoke hard. My mind wondered I started wondering who the Seals were going to pitch on Saturday when the Oaks came over from Oakland. I was hoping that the Seals would start Jumbo Carlson. Jumbo was a huge-shouldered kid they found in the logging country of Oregon. The kid could throw four pitches for strikes. He featured a nasty fastball, but he could also throw an Uncle Charlie at any time in the count for a strike, plus he could mix in his other two pitches…

The French doors opened, and I just about passed out.

The good doctor was wearing a white bustier, with sexy white nylons and a floor-length sheer white robe. Her hair was down. There was a string of oyster fruit around her neck, and she was wearing white high-heel slippers. She was the best-looking croaker I croaker I had ever seen. There was little left to the imagination, and I have an excellent imagination. She strolled over to the table and refilled her glass; she then bent over close to me and re-filled mine as well. I got a good look, point blank, at Connie Morehouse's assets. Trust me, this broad had absolutely no liabilities. I was lightheaded. She retook her chair and smiled.

"Doctor Morehouse," I said hoarsely. "I don't sleep with clients, and I really do not sleep with the married clients."

"Really" was all she said. She gave me that look that said liar. She worked on her drink and stared at me.

A moment later, she got up from the table and announced she was going to take a shower, and would I like to come along and scrub her back and other places. She started toward the French doors, sliding the robe off her shoulders. I watched as it cascaded to the patio deck. She walked that walk into her bedroom, and left the French doors open as an invitation.

I have always said that flexibility is key to being a good private eye. I crushed out my smoke, downed the rest of my drink and started to manufacture another pitcher full of martinis, but my hands were trembling as I fumbled with the pitcher. I poured two fresh ones and headed for the French doors.

Then it hit me like a sledgehammer. Three quick thoughts ran through my feeble brain.

First it was Marty's words that came back to me. "That dame is no good. She may look all sugar and spice, but that broad is all about calculation and manipulation, I know the type, Sean. You be careful, kid." I could hear the words echoing in my head, over and over. "That dame is no good." Marty was too good a judge of character to be wrong.

Secondly, I live by a set of rules, personally and professionally. And one of those rules is never sleep with a client. And Dr. Constance Morehouse was not only a client, she was a married client. And her husband was in trouble. I'm supposed to be part of the solution, not part of the problem. I wasn't going to be the last straw that pushed this gee over the edge. With all his troubles, the poor schmuck doesn't need another guy using his wife like a party favor.

The third thing hit me harder than anything. I had a lump in my throat. How could I ever go out with Kaitlin O'Doherty and look her straight in the eye?

I put the martinis on the serving cart, took it on the heel and toe, and faded. A few minutes later, I was hitting all eight as I drove across the Golden Gate Bridge to get my head on straight.

CHAPTER TWELVE

I got back home about eight. I was never clearer in my mind that walking away from Connie Morehouse's bedroom was the best move I ever made. All that hard thinking had made me hungry. I had stopped at Molinari's Deli and got the last couple fresh sourdough rolls and some genoa ham. At home, I raided the ice box for provolone, lettuce, olives, and some sweet Italian mustard. There was a little pasta salad left from yesterday, and I made a meal of it with an ice-cold Coke. I'd had enough booze for this day. Hell, this month.

I walked over to the bookshelf and grabbed the first book that my mitt touched. It turned out to be The Scarlet Letter. I shoved that back where it came from. My next grab was Two Years Before the Mast, by Richard Henry Dana, Jr. Okay this would work for tonight. I read for two hours and was out like a light.

In the morning I decided to watch the lovebirds until I had to head to Chinatown and meet Mr. Wang. I grabbed sourdough toast with peanut butter and drove the Ford over to the campus. Young Wang had an eight a.m. class. I ate my toast and waited.

When the lovebirds arrived at seven twenty, it was not the same old. There was some heavy-duty action. They both got to the engineering building and the show was on. They were fighting like two cats in a bag. There was loads of finger-pointing, yelling, and foot-stomping. I couldn't hear much of it, but I heard the girl scream, "When will be the right time to tell them?" It ended with Wang entering the building, and her sitting on the steps and crying. After a while she blew her nose, got a determined look, and started walking off campus. I left the Ford in the parking lot and started on foot after the girl.

She grabbed a cable car. I hopped on as well. She held onto a leather strap and stared out the window all the way to the ferry terminal at the Embarcadero. She paid her fare and got on the Eureka, headed for Sausalito. The nice thing about shadowing someone on a ferry is you don't have to keep sight of them. You just have to let them get off first, and you easily pick up the tail.

I went to the second-deck coffee stand and got a cup of Joe. They didn't have cream, only milk. That is absolutely barbaric in my book. I bought the morning paper and pulled up a seat. I had to be careful, because the ferry was almost empty. All the traffic would be coming into San Francisco, not leaving it. I didn't want the girl to get a good look at me.

She came in ten minutes later and got hot tea. She sat directly behind me with her back to me. The best thing I could do was sit still. I heard her sniffling and shuffling her feet.

When the ferry docked, she hightailed it to the ramp. She was the first off the boat, moving at a pretty good clip. I'm tall and take large strides, but this girl was almost running. She went through the small town and along the walkway near the water, fifty paces ahead of me. I was keeping up, barely. Abruptly, she crossed the street and climbed a set of concrete stairs. At the top was a large home overlooking the water, a Queen Anne Victorian with a large turret. From across the street, I saw the girl ring the door. A man and woman came out and started hugging her. They talked for about a minute. Let me rephrase that: the girl talked a mile a minute and her parents—I assume—did the listening. The girl broke down and collapsed in her mother's arms. The older woman dragged her into the house and the father hugged them both, then bolted. It looked like he was late for work. I wrote down the street address and watched the father head for the ferry. My guess is that the kid would not be coming back out anytime soon. The father was probably a better lead. I followed him to the ferry and we both got onboard.

The guy was an average-looking Joe, wearing a gray pinstripe double-breasted suit. He wore a gray Hamburg and his shoes had a good-quality shine on them. He carried a very expensive black Italian leather briefcase, the kind that opens at the top and expands. He looked like a banker to me. He put on some black frame reading glasses and started reading the latest edition of Black Mask. What a nance!

I went out on deck and had a butt. It was windy, but you could really smell the salt air from the sea. It's that salt air that makes San Francisco sourdough bread taste so good, unlike any other in the world. I took a deep breath; my head was not hurting at all from all the booze yesterday. I thought I would follow this guy to his office and find out who he is. Then I would find the office of Morehouse and Wheeler and see what was going on there. I was running over in my head what I was going to say to Connie Morehouse. I decided to call and see if she wanted me to continue, though after yesterday, she might not want me anymore in any capacity. But I had to give her the benefit of the doubt: she was hurt, lonely, and feeling betrayed.

The ferry docked and I followed the guy to the Financial District. He stopped at a flower shop and got a white carnation for his lapel. Up Market Street, he stopped at a newsie and asked for the latest edition of Modern Detective magazine. I wanted to puke.

The strolling continued until Wells Fargo headquarters. I figured this was where this bird perched. But I was wrong. He went to a teller and cashed a check, and went back onto Market.

He walked to the new Federal Building between Hyde and Leavenworth. It was only a couple of blocks from my office at Union Square. In the large marble lobby, I looked up at the building directory until he got in an elevator. He was the only one to enter the car. I ran over and watched as the arrow went up and stopped on the fifth floor. Another car opened and I asked the elevator operator for five.

"I'm sorry, sir, but that is a restricted floor. Authorized personnel only."

I said I needed to consult the directory; that I might have gotten the wrong floor. I got out of the car and re-checked the directory. There were agencies and names everywhere, but I didn't see any listed for the fifth floor. As I was gawking at the directory, a postman came huffing and puffing into the lobby with two leather mailbags one on each shoulder. He went to the box below the mail chute and with a large key, unlocked the box and started scooping envelopes into the bags.

I went over to bother the guy after he was all loaded up.

"Hey buddy, what time do you pick up here?"

"Every two hours starting at eight a.m. till five, Monday through Friday."

"I was trying to deliver a letter to the IRS on the fifth floor, but the operator said it was restricted up there. Do you know what address I use to send them a letter?"

"You got it wrong, pal. The IRS is on three, not five."

"Well, I was sure the gal said the fifth floor. What's up there on five, then?"

"Buddy the IRS is on three. The Attorney General and the FBI have offices on five."

"Are you sure? The directory says the FBI is seven?"

"The fifth floor is some special office. It's called the Organized Crime Federal Task Force. They are trying to run the mob out of Chinatown, can you believe that? Like that is ever going to happen." He pulled the straps higher on his shoulder and headed for the revolving door.

A bolt of lightning ran through my heart. I went to the elevator and told the operator to take me to seven. At the reception desk was an older brunette, the kind of broad Hoover handpicked for the assignment because she looked tough. As I approached, a couple of agents were leaving.

"Hey, Judy, you need anything? Coffee or something?"

"No thanks, Phil. I appreciate you asking."

She looked at me.

"Hi, I'm Sean O'Farrell from the fifth floor. I was wondering if you had a reverse directory I could use. We don't have one down there."

"Sure, sweetie, I keep telling the big cheeses that you guys don't have enough equipment down there," she said. "That's what happens when they quickly set up these task forces."

She handed me a reverse directory for San Francisco and Sausalito. I looked up the address of where the girl went and got the name: William Broadcreek, Sausalito 5143. I handed back the directory with my thanks and faded out as quickly as I came.

I went to the phone booth in the lobby, looked up the number for the FBI, and dialed. Judy answered the phone. "Good morning Federal Bureau of Investigation, San Francisco."

"William Broadcreek, please."

"Deputy Attorney General Broadcreek is at another number. Fairview 1244. I'll connect you."

"Extension 1244" was all the voice on the other end said.

"William Broadcreek, please," I said.

"I'm sorry, Mister Broadcreek is in a conference. May I tell him who is calling?"

"Yes this is Jeffrey Gunderson from the San Francisco Chronicle. We were wondering if Mister Broadcreek would be willing to sit for an interview about the investigation that is ongoing in Chinatown?"

The phone went dead. I instantly dialed the number again. I got an operator.

"I'm sorry that number has been disconnected."

I hung up. Chinatown. I'll be damned.

CHAPTER THIRTEEN

I walked over to Union Square and checked in at the office. I gave Marty a wave and told I would be down and fill him in.

First order of business after I opened up the office was to call Mr. Wang. I told Jimmy something was hot with the kid and I would have to see Mr. Wang later. I told Jimmy that I knew Mr. Wang was not the kind of guy to be kept waiting, but there were developments and I needed to follow a hot lead. Jimmy understood and told me he would smooth things over with Mr. Wang.

Next I dialed Doctor Morehouse at her office. Her nurse told me she was with a patient, but she was waiting for my call and wanted to speak to me. She said she would call back shortly. Shortly was two minutes.

Connie Morehouse was stammering on the phone.

"Mr. O'Farrell, please forgive me, and please let's forget about yesterday, please," she said.

"All right, Doctor, There was no harm done."

"Randall never came home last night," she said, her voice quavering. "At two a.m. I received a call from a man named Patrone. He told me that my husband owes him over five thousand dollars, and he better pay up or else."

"I know this gee, Doctor. He's a lowlife in Sacramento. I'm sure your husband owes him the money. I am also betting he owes of a lot of other people as well. You need to face the fact that your husband is a degenerate gambler and he may be an alcoholic as well. One problem is feeding the other. It may be time to confront your husband and find out how many people have the hook into him. This is starting to get pretty serious, Doctor. These types of guys like Patrone don't take no for an answer."

There was a palpable silence.

"All right, Mr. O'Farrell, I believe you, but I want you to follow him tonight and see if you learn anything more. I am going to contact my family and see if I can get a large amount of cash to make these bloodsuckers go away. I don't know if my marriage is going to survive this. My husband has got to grow up and act like a man. It is very hard being married to a screw up."

Her voice cracked. I had been pretty hard on her, and I felt sorry for her. But that didn't mean I could completely trust her.

"I want you do something for me, Doctor. I want you to go home and pack a bag. Check into a hotel. Make it a nice one. You can register in your own name, it will be okay. I don't think these people will come to your home, but I don't want to take the risk. If you talk to that riverboat-gambler husband of yours, tell him you have to go out of town on business."

She agreed and hung up. I was about to go see Marty and fill him in when the door opened and two suits walked in. They were trying to look tough. I slid the middle right drawer open.

"You O'Farrell?" The suit on the left demanded.

"Check the door, pal. I'm pretty sure there is a name on it in gold leaf." I said.

"Look what we got here, Brian, a real honest-to-goodness smart-aleck gumshoe," he said. "On your feet, wise guy. You're going downtown."

"What's the rumpus?"

They just gave me a blank stare.

"Just a curiosity question: Where do you go to finds suits that cheap-looking?" I asked. "It must be a popular place, seeing how you both shop there. You two monkeys got some kind of ID?"

They practiced this a lot in front of a mirror, I could tell. They whipped out their black leather credentials folders and flipped them open with their arms fully extended.

"Special Agents Ashwythe and Dunderbeck, FBI."

I opened my wallet and displayed my ID in the same way.

"Sean O'Farrell, Book of the Month Club. FBI, huh? Well, that explains the really cheap suits. They must have a cheap-suit-buying seminar at FBI finishing school. I'll bet your mommies are real proud." I broadly smiled.

"On your feet, O'Farrell. Get your hat. We're going downtown," Dunderbeck said.

"I know all the local FBI guys around here. How come I don't know you two mutts?" I said.

"Let's move it, O'Farrell. You are going downtown with us on own your two feet or on a stretcher. It doesn't make any difference to us." Ashwythe said.

"You two must be part of that Federal Bureau of Idiots special task force that Broadcreek is heading up?" That got their attention. They were stymied for a moment.

I leaned over my desk and lowered my voice like we were exchanging a secret.

"I know you boys are new to town, and you don't want to look bad in front of all the other little agents on the playground, so let me give you a little tip. Just between the three of us, okay? This is Union Square. WE ARE DOWNTOWN."

Dunderbeck had his fill and he was coming around the desk with a sap in his hand. I drew a .45 from the drawer.

"Listen, boys, unless you have an arrest or material-witness order signed by a judge, the only place you are asking questions is right here," I said.

"Do you know you can get ten years for pulling a roscoe on a FBI agent?" Dunderbeck said.

"You know when I was in Boy Scouts, we use to sing a song about a butcher named Dunderbeck." From his adverse reaction, he had heard it too. I smiled.

THE HALFWAY TO HELL CLUB

I started singing the song in a really exaggerated German accent and bobbed my head from side to side: "Oh Dunderbeck, oh Dunderbeck, how could you be so mean. To ever had invented that sausage-meat machine." Dunderbeck cringed and turned crimson.

"What do you say we make a quick phone call before we go?" I picked up the phone and dialed Danny O'Day's office. The phone was answered on the second ring.

"Good morning, office of the San Francisco U.S. Attorney General."

"Hi, Lois, Sean O'Farrell here. Is that good-looking and pithy Deputy Attorney General of the United States of America in?"

She laughed. "Hold on, Sean."

A moment later: "Hey, Sean, what's shaking'?"

"Hey Danny, a couple of quick items," I said.

The two FBI guys were looking at each with a look that said What the hell did we get ourselves into?

"Father Mickey called from the church," I said. "It seems the number-one hot water heater has had it. I called Tony Balducci and he thinks he can fix it by installing a new pilot light. Father Mickey wants a new one and he wants the Knights of Columbus to buy it. I'm just the treasurer, you are the Grand Knight, so this baby is all yours."

"All right, Sean. I'll put in on this week's agenda. We can't wait long on this thing," Danny said.

"Next item, speaking of Tony Balducci. He is trying to weasel out of being the fish-fry chairman. I did it three years running, you did it two years running. This is Tony's first year, so no dice on bailing out."

"Okay, I'll talk to Tony and smooth things out. What else?" Danny chuckled.

"I got two FBI agents here in my office that want to haul me in for questioning." I smiled and looked at the two agents.

"What are their names?" Danny's voice became all business.

"Ashwythe and Dunderbeck." I said.

"Those are special task-force guys. Call me as soon as they clear out."

He hung up.

I slowly hung up the phone and kept my hand on the receiver. I didn't say a word. Two minutes later when the phone rang, the two agents jumped.

"Sean O'Farrell, Private Investigations," I said.

"Good morning, Mr. O'Farrell, this is Deputy Attorney General William Broadcreek. May I please speak to Special Agent Ashwythe?" Broadcreek's voice was stiff.

I put the phone over my chest. "Is there a Special Agent Ass Wipe here?" I said.

Ashwythe held out his hand for the phone. I whispered to him, "I think he's upset." I gave him the phone.

"Special Agent Ashwythe. Yes sir, no sir, yes sir, I completely understand sir." He handed me the phone and the pair walked out my door and never looked back, until…

I started singing that song again with a German accent.

"Now long tail rats and pussy cats will never more be seen, they all been ground to sausage meat in Dunderbeck's machine. Oh umpa, umpa, umpa, umpa."

If looks could kill I would be on the slab. Dunderbeck wanted a piece of me real bad. He stood there in the doorway and glared at me, his hands in tight fists. Ashwythe knew the score and wanted to clear out.

"Come on, Dave, let it go." Ashwythe pulled Dunderbeck by the arm out the door. Dunderbeck's eyes were locked on me as the door quietly closed and the catch of the doorknob clicked shut.

I called Danny back the minute they were gone.

"Jesus H. Christ, Sean. What the hell is going on? This guy Broadcreek has got some real juice." Danny's voice was shaken, but took a breath and regained his composure. "He has been here a year, but they keep to themselves down there on the fifth floor. A pal in DC tells me he is tight with FDR and may be the next Attorney General. They know you are working for Wang, and one of the agents saw you shadowing his daughter. Jesus, his daughter, Sean! This whole thing is getting out of hand. Broadcreek is taking this very personal. He is baying for your blood. What the hell are you into?"

I cleared my throat. "Danny, I never discuss my cases with anyone, but I will with you this one time. You can't tell Broadcreek, okay?"

Danny quickly agreed.

"The Wang's hired me to get background information on the girl their youngest son is dating. This kid is clean as a whistle and not involved in the family business. He is an architect and engineering student. The Wang's want to make sure the girl isn't a gold-digger. Danny, the girl is Broadcreek's daughter."

"Holy shit in a country handbasket," Danny said. "I see why you don't want me to tell Broadcreek. He called, by the way, and is coming up to see me in an hour, I'll keep quiet. You better watch your step, Sean. Broadcreek is pissed and he wants to break you open and bust you into little pieces like a fortune cookie."

"Yeah. I ate Chinese the other night. My fortune cookie said, 'Get the hell out of the detective business.'"

CHAPTER FOURTEEN

It was going to be delicate, how I handled this with Wang. I made the intelligent choice and decided to work on the other case.

I'd been following Randall Morehouse for a few days, but I didn't know where his office was. I got out the phone book and looked up Morehouse and Wheeler. Son of a bitch, there they were, big as life: Morehouse and Wheeler, Architecture and Industrial Design, Inc. Union 4599, 300 Post Street, Suite 355. My building, six floors down.

I took the elevator down to the third floor. The hallway walls were full of pictures of projects Morehouse and Wheeler had designed. In the middle of the hall was an oak and glass case with a model of a bridge. The Oakland Bay Bridge. It had a sign above it: OAKLAND BAY BRIDGE, RANDALL R. MOREHOUSE ARCHITECT AND DESIGNER. It had an additional note: BRIDGE OPENED NOVEMBER 12, 1936, FINAL ACCEPTANCE AND PROJECT COMPLETION SCHEDULED FOR JUNE 1, 1938.

There were many pictures of Morehouse with San Francisco's elite. He worked on several projects with Julie Morgan, who designed the Fairmont Hotel and designed that monstrosity of opulence and self-aggrandizement, Hearst Castle, for William Randolph Hearst, local millionaire and muckraker. She was considered the preeminent architect in the area. From the pictures, it looks like Morehouse worked with her a great deal. There were photos of many of the best homes on Knob Hill and Russian Hill. There were extensive drawings of City Hall and the main branch of the library. There was a photo of Morehouse and Andrew Carnegie. I think the good doctor was little remiss in calling her husband a screw up, as there were newspaper articles describing Morehouse's designs as brilliant. Could this be the same cat that staggered off the Delta Queen? One thing I noticed in all the backslapping items on the wall was no mention of Wheeler or his designs. Kind of strange.

I walked to the end of the hall and peered into the office. Morehouse walked ten feet in front of me, going the other way down a hall with a cup of coffee in his hand and three young guys on his tail. Two of them were the guys who met the boat here in San Francisco. The third was the guy named Child who cleaned him up in Sacramento, then brought him back on the boat.

I turned and went back to the elevator, not wanting to be seen. I heard the door open, and footsteps. From inside the office, I heard a gal call out.

"Mr. Wheeler, Mr. Gladstone called. I told him you would call him later," she said.

"Thanks, Gladys," he said. "I'll be about ten minutes."

I pushed the call button for the elevator and leaned against the wall. Wheeler looked like a college athlete. Young, good-looking, tall, athletic, and broad-shouldered. He didn't have a wedding ring on. He definitely looked like a boy toy to me. He was dark-complected, and he sure as hell didn't look like a Wheeler to me. There was a mirror next to the elevator and sure enough, Pretty Boy admired himself in it and straightened his four-in-hand.

I got on the elevator, so did Wheeler. I told the operator, lobby and that was where Wheeler was headed. I was lucky it was a fill-in operator who didn't know who I was or call me by name. I let Wheeler get out first. He went to Marty's and grabbed a deck of Luckies. Marty saw me and I put my finger to my lips. Marty nodded and didn't even look at me. Wheeler paid and off he went.

"Hey, Marty, what do you know about that gee?" I said.

"Name's Wheeler, he's an architect upstairs, if that is his real name. Real ladies' man. He moves on anything with a skirt, married or otherwise. He's the kind of guy you give him a ten-dollar bill and he'll give you change in threes and fours."

"Gees, Marty, don't hold back your opinion of the guy."

"You know Johansson, the CPA on four?" Marty asked.

"Yeah, the bookkeeper that looks like a lumberjack," I said.

"His wife came in to meet him. She goes upstairs then she comes down and is getting some mints here at the counter and Wheeler moves in. Next thing you know, they are over the corner barbering and before you know it they leave together. I walked out the door and watched them; they went straight into the St. Francis. He came back in an hour looking like a cat that just caught a mouse." Marty smiled.

"Holy moly," I said.

"That guy wears a path out between here and the St. Francis, three, four times a week, and it's always with a different broad," Marty said. "It's a wonder the kid gets any work done, lucky bastard. That guy lays more pipe than a union plumber."

"Thanks, Marty. I could have lived without that thought in my head."

"What are you working on, Shamus?"

"I'm still working for that doctor you don't like."

"The one with the great gams?" Marty said.

"Yes, Marty, that would be her, and I'm working away on that Chinatown case too."

"Those two G-men that came up a little while ago … they aren't the only people looking for you, pal." Marty gave me a serious look.

"Really, who else?" I asked.

"A single guy. Five feet four, round like a bowling ball. This gee is a real dick, all right. Soft-soled shoes, suit one size too big to cover the roscoe, and he never made eye contact with anyone. He ran his finger over the directory, stopped at your name, went up and came back down."

"When was this?" I asked.

"Yesterday, while you were out. This guy was a pro, Sean. I can't put my finger on it, but this guy was real smooth."

"Swell, this Chinatown thing is getting real hot. I may be under FBI surveillance, now I got a PI on my tail. You looking for a new partner, Marty?" I asked.

Marty smiled.

"You may need a guy to go halves with you," I said. "I need a new line of work where I am not so popular."

Before Marty could respond, Morehouse came out of the elevator and lit a butt. He walked right past us and out the revolving door. It was time to shadow.

"Get to work, you worthless bum. You are scaring away the paying trade." Marty smiled broadly. "I'll keep an eye out while you are gone. When you get where you are going, call me here and I can tell you if you picked up a tail."

"Thanks, Marty," I said.

I followed Morehouse across the square. He nearly got ran down by a cable car as he bolted into the St. Francis Hotel.

In my opinion, the Fairmont and the Mark Hopkins are the two best hotels in the city, but they're on Knob Hill. The St. Francis is in their league, with a quiet elegance. The lobby features a Magneta grandfather clock that controls all the other hotel clocks so that they're are perfectly synchronized. The St. Francis has always appealed to upper-crust partygoers and nightlife lovers.

Morehouse got on an elevator and I watched it stop in the twelfth floor. I got on the next car and before the door could close, Jerry Ronkowski got in. He is the St. Francis house detective.

"Sean O'Farrell, as I live and breathe. You working, pal?"

"Yeah. I'm following a husband that has a zipper management problem."

"Crap, I hate those kinds of cases. You have a much stronger stomach that I did, Sean."

Jerry was a contemporary of Marty's. He got shot twice in year on the job, and his wife laid down the law. He left the cops and got this swell job here at the St. Francis. It was a sweet deal.

"Is this guy meeting a broad?" he asked.

"I didn't see him with anyone. He got off on twelve."

"Your boy play a little cards, does he?" Jerry asked with a wry smile.

"As a matter of fact."

"It's against the law to gamble, as you know. But that doesn't stop some big wheels from meeting on the twelfth floor for a friendly game once a week."

"What room do they play in?" I asked.

He laughed.

"You are going to love this, Sean. They play in room 1219. Can you believe that?" Jerry gave me a knowing look.

The infamous room 1219 was the party room where Roscoe Conkling Arbuckle's life came crashing down. Old Roscoe was better known as Fatty Arbuckle, Hollywood funny man. Back in September 1921, Fatty was throwing a party. Some bit actress named Virginia Rappe became ill at the party and died four days later, and Fatty was charged with rape and murder.

It was the crime of the century. And it was the sham trial of the century. San Francisco DA Matthew Brady pressured witnesses to lie. He was making a run for governor and needed all the favorable press he could get. Conservative groups called for Fatty to be executed. Movie studios ordered their stars not to stick up for Fatty because it was bad for business.

What would yellow journalism be without William Randolph Hearst? He sold millions of papers and made a bundle of greenbacks printing false stories about Arbuckle and fueling the flames. There were three trials; the first two ended in hung juries. In the third, in 1922, he was found not guilty.

The trial was so bad and the evidence so flimsy that the jury demanded to release a statement at the verdict. It took five minutes to read the letter of apology to Arbuckle.

But the damage was done. Arbuckle's movies were banned. He owed about a million dollars in legal fees. He lost everything: homes, cars, his good name, everything and anything of worth. He was box-office poison. The studios would have nothing to do with him. Buster Keaton got him some work as a director, using the pseudonym William B. Goodrich. Will B. Good, what a name. He died in 1933 of a massive heart attack in his sleep. Ever the optimist, he was mounting a comeback in Hollywood.

There I was, outside the very door that destroyed the life of Roscoe Arbuckle. Inside Randall Morehouse was destroying his, one hand at a time.

CHAPTER FIFTEEN

I left the office and grabbed the Powell Mason Line and headed up the hill. If someone were following me, they'd find it hard to do on a cable car. On California Street, I got out and waited for a California Street cable car to come downhill. I was standing on the corner of the University Club, only two blocks from Chinatown, but I wanted to make sure I didn't have a tail.

The California Line cable car came and I rode it till Grant Street and got off. I had about three level blocks down Grant Street to get to Wang's place.

As I was walking down, two tiny Chinese guys came running up the street. Behind them were two beat cops with their billy clubs out. The guy in front was young and fast, but the other guy was older, fat and slow. The two Chinese guys went down a set of cement steps into a cellar and slammed the steel door. The young cop was just about to head down the stairs when I grabbed his collar and pulled him back. He landed on his can and tried to get back up, loaded for bear.

"What's the idea, Mack?" he hollered.

"You go down those stairs, junior, and you'll break your neck for sure," I said.

"Huh?" The young cop looked bewildered.

The older cop finally arrived, out of breath.

"Thanks, mister, you saved the rookie's life," he puffed, out of breath.

The kid got to his feet and dusted himself off, still upset.

"What do you mean, Sarge? I'm not clumsy."

"You are new to Chinatown, kid," I said. "You better learn the rules don't apply here. This is Chinatown, and everything you look at may not be what it seems."

I grabbed the kid's shoulder and started him down the stairs.

"Take a look. The threads of the stairwell are curved. They all look alike. Now take a closer look. They get progressively smaller as you go down. Now look at the riser. That's the part of the step that determines the height. It varies in height every step, some taller, some shorter. This was done on purpose. Every cellar stairs in Chinatown is rigged like this. It took a lot of planning and coordination to make that happen. It works great for a little Chinese guy with little feet; it is not so easy for a big white cop with big feet. They run, you chase, and you fall melon-first down those steps. They are long gone, kid."

The older cop took over. "It's okay, kid, it happens, it's your first week. There are a million more little tricks like this that makes this place different. Let's get back on patrol." He looked at me. "Thanks, pal." The kid's color started returning to his face.

"Anytime." I said.

The kid would learn that this place was like betting on the ponies: there was no such thing as a sure thing.

I walked another block to Wang's club and asked the doorman to get Jimmy for me. He disappeared inside and Jimmy popped out a moment later.

"Come on in, Sean," he said.

We took an elevator to the top floor. There was a leather bar up there along with a class restaurant. Jimmy ordered a Harbin beer, and I did the same. It was pretty good stuff.

"What's up, Sean? Mr. and Mrs. Wang are all over me for a report," Jimmy said.

"I have a report, Jimmy, and you don't want it, Mr. and Mrs. Wang don't want it, and I don't want to give it," I said.

"Come on, Sean, it can't be all that bad," Jimmy said.

"First order of business is if I tell you, you keep your mouth closed. You can't tell the Wang's, period," I said. "This could get messy and thing are already messy enough."

"All right, Sean. I'll keep mum," he said.

"The kid's girlfriend isn't a hooker, she isn't a gold-digger, and she has never been married. It's a lot worse than that." I said.

Jimmy took a slug of beer and shrugged.

"The girl's name is Dorothy Broadcreek. Her father is William Broadcreek, Deputy Attorney General of the United States. He is in charge of the organized crime task force looking into shutting down your boss in Chinatown." I gave him a hard look.

I found out what Jimmy would look like as a Caucasian because he turned white before my eyes.

"Don't even make jokes Sean, this is…" Jimmy said.

I cut him off. "This is on the level, Jimmy. No joke, these two love birds are the center of the storm. Her folks don't know either."

"Holy crap" was all Jimmy could say.

"We have other pressing matters. First, the FBI caught wind somehow that I was working for your boss, then I was spotted following the girl. Now I got G-Men following me around. Next it looks like there is private eye nosing around about me too. Did your boss have some else shadowing me?" I asked.

"No way, Sean. If he did, I would know."

"How about Mrs. Wang?" I asked.

"Same thing again. The Wang's are a lot of things, but underhanded and deceptive they are not. They would have said something to me."

"Let's start with this," I said. "I don't want you lying to the Wang's. That could be trouble. You tell Wang that I am a hot item and the FBI is tailing me, that they may have bugged my phones. I wouldn't put it past them. I need to keep a low profile for a while and stay away from Chinatown. I'll call you directly from a pay phone. If I'm bugged, you can bet they are bugging your phones as well. If I call, you answer, then hang up and go over to the Telephone Exchange Building and I'll call you there. Are there any guns at the club?"

"There are a couple of handguns. One is Mr. Wang's."

"Get them the hell out of there. The Feds could come with a search warrant. Now that Broadcreek is in a lather, he may move up any actions against the Wang's. This is now personal for him. I haven't worked this part out yet. I'm going to tell both Mr. and Mrs. Wang and Mr. and Mrs. Broadcreek at the same time, in the same place together. I'm going to need Righty and Lefty to be there."

"Righty and Lefty?" Jimmy looked confused.

"You know, the two big guys that are always with the Wang's."

"Oh, you mean Chin and Loc. What are they for?"

"To keep the Wang's from doing anything stupid."

"Who is going to keep the Broadcreek's in line?"

"I got a couple of FBI agents in mind."

"Sean, you are nuts. How do you expect to make this work?"

"Working on it, Jimmy, working on it."

I finished my beer and left the club. My old pals Ashwythe and Dunderbeck were on my tail. I wasn't going to fool around anymore with these two cats. I took the direct approach.

I turned on my heel and walked right up to them. "All right, boys, we need to clear the air and fast," I said. "Let's go somewhere and talk. I'll buy."

Dunderbeck was still steamed. "So you can call our boss and turn us in taking a nip during working hours, wise guy?"

"I'm sorry I went too far. Let's go somewhere and talk. You will be glad that you did."

We walked to the California cable car and went up to the Fairmont. I headed for the lobby bar and the FBI guys followed. I ordered a beer, this time American, and they did the same.

"Look, I know I can be a real smartass, I thought you guys were coming over for a standard shakedown. You both need to know everything. The first thing I have to ask you is that not tell Broadcreek."

"Come on, Shamus. You know we can't do that."

"All right, here's the deal. I'll give you the full crop, then you have decide how much, if any, to tell your boss."

They looked at each other and nodded.

"I got hired by the Wang's for a personal matter. They wanted to find out about the girl their college-age son is dating. It's a white girl named Dorothy Broadcreek."

Ashwythe and Dunderbeck both looked like they got kicked in the gut by a mule.

"Holy shit, is that the reason you were shadowing the kid?"

"Yeah."

"Does Wang know his kid is dating the Broadcreek kid?"

"Nope."

"Oh my God, what a mess" was all that Dunderbeck could say.

Ashwythe chuckled. "This isn't funny, but old man Broadcreek loses his mind when one the secretaries brings back Chinese food for lunch. Can you imagine how this is going to play?"

"That's where you guys come. I am going to set up a meeting with the Wang's and the Broadcreek's. I'm going to tell them everything together."

"Oh, man, O'Farrell, you sure have a twisted sense of humor all right. Where do we come in?"

"I'll call you with the meeting place and time. All the parties will be there. I have a couple of guys from Wang's team along to control them. You two take care of the Broadcreek's. I'll make sure there are no rods in the room. I'll have a retired cop watching the door and checking for the roscoes.

Dunderbeck was chuckling now. "Gees, if I could tell everyone in the office, I could sell tickets to this event."

"You boys have got that right. And one last thing, there will be plenty of booze for afterwards."

"The old man is a teetotaler. But he just might have a nip following that clambake."

"Sorry, boys. I wasn't thinking about the Broadcreek's or the Wang's. I'm thinking about us."

Both agents looked at each other and nodded again.

"We're in, O'Farrell. This whole thing is so farfetched it has to be true. We won't say anything. Are you going to tell anyone else?"

"Yes, I am going to fill in Danny O'Day. It's his neighborhood. I told him I would keep him in the loop, no one else."

"A couple more things, O'Farrell. Call me asswipe again and I'll clean your clock. Second, are you expensing these drinks?"

"Oh course, wouldn't you?"

"What can I tell you, O'Farrell? Things can't get any stranger? We just agreed to keep secrets from our boss with a private eye that we have under surveillance. And while we are at it, we just had a drink during working hours and it was paid for by Wang. If it gets any stranger than that, you be sure to let us know. We'll be waiting for your call."

CHAPTER SIXTEEN

I bummed around the office on Friday and did as little as possible. I got to the office at seven a.m., nervous about my date with Kaitlin. With all that I have on my plate, you would think I would be worried about Broadcreek or the Wang's. No, I was worried about a date.

About eight, I went down to Marty's for a donut and a paper. His place was a beehive of activity. As I waited in line, Morehouse came in through the revolving door. Holy crap. I left him at the St. Francis yesterday at noon. Now here he was, walking through the door in the same suit, almost twenty hours later. He was sober, however. He wasn't stumbling, but he looked like he was a street bum shatting on his uppers. At least I didn't spend the whole night hanging out at the St. Francis, waiting for this duck to fly home.

I looked across the street and I saw the short fat guy that Marty had described. I put on my hat and walked out the door. There was a newsie on the other side of Union Square. I walked over and the bowling-ball-looking guy stayed put. He was good. He didn't make the usual mistakes that PIs make, being too eager and following too quickly. You let your mark get a head start.

Then he made his mistake. While I was in line at the newsie, he reached into a flivver's jockey box and got a fresh deck of butts. It was probably the only mistake this bird was going to make, so I decided I'd better make the most of it.

I strolled back to the office and stopped at Marty's.

"What the matter, O'Farrell. Wasn't I working through the line fast enough for ya?"

"The round fat guy is across the street, Marty. I went to the newsie, and he tipped his mitt and showed me which car was his. I'm going to go check it out."

Back in my office, I dialed police headquarters and asked for Inspector Vincent Castellano.

Vinnie Castellano and I have been best friends since grade school. He lived at the extreme end of North Beach, though closer to Fisherman's Wharf than my neighborhood near Columbus Circle. Vinnie and I were altar boys when we were kids.

I'm careful not to ask my cop friends for loads of favors. Lots of the Irish and Italian kids in my neighborhood became cops. Since I am a private eye, I see them a lot and work with all of them at one time or another. It's a fact of life that cops don't like private eyes; they think we are lowlifes who get paid way too much for what we do. In reality, I don't think we get paid all that much, but compared to a cop walking the beat I make a king's ransom.

Vinnie growled on the phone. "Hey paisano, what do you want? You must want something?"

"Easy, Vinnie. This is a personal call. I'm working a couple of cases and I am mixing it up with a couple of G-men. Yesterday I picked up a tail. As far as I can tell it's not related to any case that I am working on. I'm mixed up in a case in Chinatown, and things are getting ugly. I want to know who this bird is; he may be in danger and not know it."

"What can I do, Sean?"

"I have the guy's license number. Can you run it for me? It's California N1334."

"I'll call you right back, pal."

I was working the crossword puzzle in the Chronicle, a favorite pastime for all private eyes, when the phone rang.

"It was an easy find," Vinnie said. "The car is a 1933 Ford, registered to the Pinkerton National Detective Agency in the Flood Building." He chuckled.

"Well, well" was all I could say.

"Sean, are you dating anybody yet? It's about time, pal."

"As a matter of fact, I have a hot date with a librarian tonight."

"Good for you, Sean, good for you. Hey, Gina and kids would love to see you. Why not give me a call at home and you can stop by for a meal."

"Thanks, Vinnie."

I called down to Marty's.

"Hey, Marty, look outside and see if there is a black '33 Ford with the fat guy in it down there, will you."

After of couple of minutes, Marty came back. "He's sitting in the car working the crossword puzzle."

"Thanks. I'm coming down the back way."

I grabbed my hat and took the back stairs that emptied into the alley off Market Street. I walked around the building and came up behind the Ford. I had my .45 out, hidden in the paper, as I opened the passenger door and got in the Ford. The fat boy was caught off guard and stunned. I stuck the .45 in his ribs.

"Reach for the sky, pal."

"Go ahead, take the wallet, I don't want any trouble."

"Save the act, Pink. Let's get to hitting all eight over to your office. I want to meet your boss. Hands on the steering wheel, pal." I reached in and pulled his .38 out of the shoulder holster.

The guy was smooth under pressure. "I won't give you any heat, pal. Safety the roscoe."

"All right, pal, you're on." I clicked the thumb safety and the guy relaxed. I told him to drive. We didn't have far to go. We could have walked there faster than driving. The Flood Building is at the end of the Powell Mason cable-car line on Powell Street. The front door was just off the turnaround.

The Flood Building is an odd building. It is the shape of a long triangle. It was one of the only buildings to survive the big earthquake in 1906. The all-marble lobby makes my building look like a tar-paper shack.

We took the elevator to the third floor. The fat boy wasn't saying much. Not much to say when you got a rod in your ribs.

We got off the elevator and came to suite 314. It had that logo on the glass, the never-blinking eye. Well, one of their ops was just caught blinking. The fat guy opened the door. The place was crawling with operatives who stopped whatever they were doing and stared.

"Morning, boys. Who is the head Pink around here?" The fat guy was nervous and sweating.

"That would be me. You O'Farrell?" A tall redheaded guy with a Van Dyke walked over with his thumbs hitched in the straps of his leather shoulder holster.

"That would be me. Here." I tossed him the fat guy's roscoe.

"Your buddy here kept dropping it on the ground. I took it from him before it went off." I put my .45 back in my holster.

The redheaded guy gave the fat guy a dirty look and nodded toward his office. "You want some Joe?"

"No thanks."

We went into his private office and he closed the door.

"My name is Powell, take a seat. Bertie is generally a good op. How did you spot him?"

"I didn't, it was a retired cop that works in my building. He put me wise to your boy. I went out for a stroll and he reached into his car for a butt. I ran the plates and here we are."

"Nice work, O'Farrell. I told Bertie he better be extra careful shadowing a PI, a detective is a detective. You got to have your A game going."

I nodded. "When I was in the Navy a few years back, I worked a missing-kid case with one of your ops, a guy everybody called Slim."

"Oh, yeah, that's Sam Hammett. He's out of the detecting business. He came up lame as a lunger, couldn't work anymore."

"Shame. He was a sharp op. What he doing now?"

"You must live under a rock. He's going by his middle name now, Dashiell Hammett. He writes pulp about detectives and makes us all look exotic."

"Gees, that's Slim?"

Powell shrugged and gave me a bewildered look.

"Who hired you guys?" I demanded.

"Come on, O'Farrell, you know I can't tell you that. Why don't you blab to me all about your cases? I'm sure your clients won't mind. Much."

Good point. He leaned back in his chair and puckered his lips and sucked air through his teeth. It was an irritating sound.

"Look, Powell, I will tell you I am working on a couple of cases. One involves the mob in Chinatown and the other involves gamblers and big-time debts. The FBI is tailing me and both of these babies are getting out of hand. There have been death threats. I get the feeling that your shadow job isn't related."

"You might be right about that, but then again, you might not." Powell sucked through his teeth again.

"Well, that's clear as mud, Powell. If your boys are going to follow me around they better be a lot smarter than this Bertie. I have enough trouble keeping myself alive on these two capers; I don't want one of your guys to take the big dirt nap while shadowing me. That's not a threat from me. There are some bad hombres in this deal and they are definitely wrong gees. Make sure your boys are on their game and everything will be Jake. I don't want anybody getting hurt."

I got up and stated to walk out.

"O'Farrell, your rep around is pretty solid. Everybody I talk to says you are a standup gee. If you ever want to join up, we got a spot for a smart guy like you. I sorry, I wish I could help you out."

I believed him. I opened the door. Powell hit the button on the box on his desk.

"Hey, Sharon, will you bring me the number of hours that Bertie has been following this O'Farrell guy. Mr. O'Doherty wants a complete accounting." He folded his hands on the blotter and smiled, then he sucked air through his teeth again. Man, that sound was maddening. I gave him a nod, then I faded.

CHAPTER SEVENTEEN

I walked back to the office and checked in with Marty. I asked him to be available for the meeting between the Wang's and the Broadcreek's. I didn't have anything set up yet, but he was willing to stand by.

Back in my office, I called the library and asked for the reference desk. As luck would have it, that old battle-axe librarian answered the phone.

"Main Library reference, Mabel speaking." She had the voice of a Mabel, whatever that sounds like. It was like a fingernail against a blackboard. I asked for Kaitlin O'Doherty.

"Oh, it's you, handsome. I've been waiting for you to call or come by. You want to talk to Katie?"

"Yes, please," I said.

"I'll bet you would like that." She slammed the phone so hard that my eardrum rattled around in my head like a maraca.

Being a determined cuss, I called again. This time Kaitlin answered.

"Good afternoon. I was calling to see what time I could pick you up?"

I heard that old biddy in the background telling Kaitlin to hang up on the worthless bum, meaning me of course.

She giggled. "We are going to North Beach?"

"That is correct, my dear."

"Meet me here at five and we'll take the cable car there. It's going to be a beautiful evening."

"I'll be there right at five."

"Be careful, Mabel works till six. She'll be here."

"Don't worry, I'm a licensed private investigator and everything. I'll bring a gun to protect myself."

She giggled and hung up. She had the best giggle.

I walked over to the St. Francis and asked the front desk to find Jerry Ronkowski. They sent a bellboy who came back in a few minutes with Jerry in tow. We met near the grandfather clock.

"Hey, Sean, what's up?"

He sunk into a couple of lobby chairs. "I need a favor, Jerry. I need a meeting room where I can stick two big wheels and their wives for a meeting."

"That's no problem. Anything special I need to know about?"

"Yeah. One is the Deputy U.S. Attorney General in charge of the special task force to bring down the kingpins in Chinatown."

"Okay, and the other guy?"

"The kingpin in charge of Chinatown."

Jerry leaned forward in his chair.

"You putting me on? You're putting Chin Wang in a room with the U.S. Attorney, and their wives?"

"That's the plan. I'm bringing along two FBI guys to cover this Broadcreek guy, and two bodyguards that work for Wang to cover them. I got Marty Durrant watching the door and checking roscoes."

"Oh, you can count on me to be there to back up Marty. Are you expecting trouble, Sean?"

"This is a personal matter, not business. But the subject of business may come up. That's why I have the wives coming and the bodyguards for both sides. Plus, I'll be in the room."

"We got the Borgia Room. It used to be the chapel. It's small and close to the elevators, so we can keep a lid on the place. I'd take it you want to keep the newshawks from getting a whiff of this?"

"That would be a disaster for everyone involved. We have to keep this quiet," I said.

I thanked Jerry and headed for the library. Kaitlin was right: it was a beautiful afternoon and it would be an even better evening. I mounted the steps and looked for the reference desk. It was 4:58 p.m., right on the money.

Mabel was at the desk. I tried, "Good evening, Mabel, and how are you?"

"Shove it in your pie hole, pal."

She was a real charmer, all right.

"Don't you worry about little kids hearing you talk that way?" I said.

"Why don't you do me a big favor and go lie down in front of a cable car," she countered.

Kaitlin came out of the back room with her sweater and purse, ready to go. "Good night, Mabel." She smiled.

"Good night, Katie, I hope you have a wonderful time and a wonderful dinner."

She then looked at me. "You, I hope you choke to death on a meatball."

We started across the library. It was hard not to laugh. Kaitlin was starting to smirk and giggle. She couldn't hold it much longer. Then I said, "All that charm and looks too."

We made it to the steps before we started laughing.

"This is good training for me meeting your parents one day."

"Mabel is one tough old gal. She lost her husband in a shipboard fire," she said.

"Navy?" I asked.

"Yes, he was a chief petty officer. She's got a heart of gold, but she never lets anybody see it. For some reason, she likes me."

"Well, she hates me. I make it a point to keep an arm's length away from her. My guess is she has a blackjack under that counter, and she knows how to use it."

"Give her a break, Sean. She'll warm up."

We got to the cable car turnaround and were able to hop right on. That is not usually the case on a Friday night, right after working hours. We grabbed a seat and enjoyed the warmth of the sun. It was at moments like this that I appreciate living in San Francisco. I loved New York City, but it was not the same as home.

I asked her, "Do you miss Boston at all?"

"I don't miss the cold weather," she said. "But I miss good New England clam chowder, New England boiled dinner, and the Red Sox. My father misses red flannel hash and eggs, he swears no one here knows how to make it here. But, I left some bad memories in Boston. I like it better here. I just wish we had the bigs here."

I looked up the hill. "My kid sister got married to a great guy and moved to Long Beach," I said. "They live in an area called Los Cerritos and have two great kids. He's a city councilman. They love where they live, but my sister has to come home every so often and eat the sourdough bread and seafood. She misses it."

The cable car turned hard left onto Jackson Street. When it did, Kaitlin slid over close to me. She smelled great. It had been so many years since I had been out on a date; I hardly knew how to carry on a conversation with a woman. It's one thing to quip at her in the library, but it's another thing when the chips are on the table and you are out on a date. We traveled along for a few minutes, listening to the cable car rattling and groaning.

"Where are we going to eat?"

"Gino's Italiano and Bocce on Mason Street. You better get yourself ready for Uncle Gino and the gang."

"Uncle Gino. You're related?"

"I grew up three doors down from Uncle Gino. My dad and Gino were friends as soon as my folks arrived in San Francisco. My old man built a bakery. He baked bread, cookies, pastries, and he had a little espresso machine. His place was a neighborhood hangout for the guys. My old man was one of the first bakers to mechanize. He put every penny into new equipment and started making a pretty good living. He provided all the bread and desserts for Uncle Gino's and lot of other restaurants."

"Is the bakery still around?"

"I sold it to Uncle Gino's son, Peter, we call him Petey. He should pay me off in another twenty years. The place is still running and the old retired guys hold court there. Petey does a great job with the place. If I don't have anything going on Saturday mornings I go in and help Petey make bread. Saturdays are big bread days because the restaurants are extra busy that night. My old man always told me that if a man can make bread, he can feed the world. There is something about kneading dough and cutting them into loaves."

We got off the cable car and walked the half a block to Gino's. Uncle Gino's youngest, Fredo, was at the podium outside the front door. He came out from behind with his arms open wide.

"Sean, it's been weeks since you have been by. The old man and Grandpa Mario have been looking for you." He gave me a big Italian hug, complete with the back slapping. He looked at Kaitlin and was taken aback. "Sean, and who might this be?"

"Cousin Fredo, this is Kaitlin O'Doherty."

Fredo gave her the same treatment. "It's so nice to have you both here. Let me get you a nice table. I'm going to warn you, Kaitlin, your table will probably be invaded by family, so be ready. Come on, come on."

He waved his arms and found us a primo table near the indoor bocce court. There were about eight older men on the court, arguing about which ball was closer. Every one of them had a glass of red wine in their hand. They always did at Gino's. It may not have been the most expensive Chianti in town, but it was pretty good, there was plenty, and it went well with the meal. All of the old guys stopped arguing long enough to say hello to me. I pulled the chair for Kaitlin, and in the background I could hear, "O'Farrell's got a date, can you believe it?"

I had just gotten settled into my chair when I was bear-hugged from behind. It was so crushing that it brought me out of my chair. It is a good thing I didn't have a gun on, or I might have broken a rib. It was Uncle Gino.

"Where have you been, everyone has been asking about you?" He filled our wine glasses and, with a swift move, he pulled a chair for himself and pulled a wine glass from his apron pocket.

Gino Chiconis was short, round, bald, and funny. He was the Italian version of a leprechaun. He didn't serve people in his restaurant; he worked the room like he was half comedian, half politician. When the church or a civic organization needed money, no one was tougher to turn down then Uncle Gino. He'd work you over like a tough guy with a blackjack. I'd seen it time and time again: some poor guy taking out his checkbook and writing a check to get Gino off their back. He is a good egg.

"I've got an idea, Uncle Gino. Why don't you pull up a chair and join us?" I said.

He gave me that look that said, Shut up, smart guy.

"Don't worry, Sean, I told the family to leave you alone for a while. I am not going to bug you and this lovely young lady while you are dining. I wanted to let you know that Fredo told everyone Kaitlin's name. He even went upstairs and told Papa, he is listening to a baseball game on the radio. He'll be down and he is going to try to pay you. Beware. Now you two lovebirds look over the menu and I'll be right back to take your order."

Uncle Gino danced away to another table.

Kaitlin was all smiles. "Wow, what a character. What's this about Papa paying you?"

"Grandpa Mario is a fisherman. He has been fishing six days a week forever. He owns a beautiful little Monterey Clipper fishing boat, the Sun Dancer. When I was starting high school, Mario's wife got very sick and was in the hospital for several months before she died. It turns out she had cancer. Mario didn't have insurance and he borrowed against his house and the Sun Dancer. After she died, the bank moved in to take both. The kids all pitched in and saved the house. There was no money left over, so the bank was about to take the boat. My old man stepped in and paid off the note. The deal is, Mario pays one percent of his profits to my old man, and now me.

"Even though on paper I own the boat, it's still Grandpa Mario's as long as he lives and he fishes Monday through Saturday. When he is shorthanded I go out with him as a deckhand. It's beautiful on the bay. You forget all your worries."

Uncle Gino returned with a pad and pencil.

"Sean, the clams and mussels are excellent today. The veal parmesan is to die for. Your Aunt Celia made a pan of lasagna tonight, its excellente. The sweet basil is very fresh. Make sure you leave a little room, I saved you the last couple of cannoli from the case for dessert. Now what would you kids like?"

Kaitlin was studying the menu and was lost.

"What do you recommend for a small appetite?"

"Why don't you let me bring you a small piece of lasagna and some spaghetti Bolognese with Celia's meatballs? Would you like a cup of minestrone or a salad to start?"

"A salad would be great."

Cousin Fredo came by with a basket of sourdough bread right out of the oven and placed it in the middle of the table.

"How about you, Sean?"

"Bring me the same thing, Uncle Gino. I have to leave room for espresso and cannoli."

Out through the kitchen double doors came Aunt Celia. She was short, round, full of life, and not a woman you wanted hunting for you. When the Chiconis family is happy, there are hugs all the way around. When they are fighting however, they are like a cage full of wolverines. I wasn't sure what I was in for with Aunt Celia.

"Sean, where have you been? I only see you at church anymore, and you live just down the block."

It was a big bear hug, so I was all right. The real purpose of her visit was to inspect and grade Kaitlin.

"So you are the girl Petey was talking about. I'm Aunt Celia, and don't let this one fool you into thinking I am mean, it's not true."

I laughed. "Aunt Celia, I hadn't had a chance to tell her how mean you are yet."

She slapped me on the back of the head with an open hand. It was a loving slap, the same as she does to her own kids. It felt like my brain was going to come out my nose.

"You be quiet, you're already in the dog house for not coming around. By the way the Altar Committee met this morning and Father Mickey wants that hot water heater fixed. Get to it."

She gave me a big hug and gave Kaitlin one as well.

"We are proud of you, Sean. It was about time." She dabbed her eyes with a hanky and headed for the kitchen.

Kaitlin gave me a funny look. "About time for what?"

CHAPTER EIGHTEEN

Kaitlin had a sly smile on her face.

"Okay," I said. "Let's start with this: When were you planning on turning the parents loose on me?"

She gave a more genuine smile and sipped her Chianti. "Well, I am supposed to invite you for dinner at the house on Sunday."

"Supposed to?" I said.

"I've been told to be coy and not let on that you are going to be grilled over cocktails."

I laughed. "Well as long as there is a drink or two that goes with the meal, I can't say no to that. I'll tell you what: Let's save all the family questions for the Sunday night inquisition. I won't have to repeat myself. Who is going to be a tougher sell, your mother or your father?"

"One will be absolutely impossible, and the other will be harder than that."

Uncle Gino delivered our salads and mixed the dressing at the table. I cut up some fresh sourdough bread. Fredo came along and deposited fresh Romano cheese on the salads.

Kaitlin was impressed. "Is the service always this good or are they putting on a show for me?"

"This is Uncle Gino's place, it is always like this. The food is great, but the people who come and the people who run it are better. It's always fun here. Wait till Uncle Gino and Aunt Celia get into an argument in the kitchen."

As I said that, an argument broke out on the bocce court. Joeseppi and Michael got into a beef over whose ball was closer. Mike called me over to settle the dispute. I waved my hands and indicated there was no chance of that. Uncle Gino had to settle in Joeseppi's favor. There was lots of talking, lots wine drinking, and then it was time for a new game.

Kaitlin was having a ball. "This beats the movies by a mile," she said. "Not quite a baseball game, but fun just the same."

"I have been meaning to ask," I said. "I have two tickets for the Seals and the Oaks, at noon. You still want to teach me how to keep score?"

"No doubt you learned how to keep score; you just didn't learn to do so properly."

I smiled. "That sounds like an acceptance and a challenge, all at the same time."

"You deserve a little fun before I feed you to my parents. Are you baking bread in the morning?"

"As a matter of fact I am."

"Well, I'll meet you at the bakery then at ten thirty."

The parade of food began. Uncle Gino delivered the platters, and the food was wonderful. We asked for small portions, but Aunt Celia just couldn't lay off. It was the best, as always. Petey came over and gave me a hug. He went to work singing "O Sole Mio." He has a great voice. Kaitlin was blushing; she is so beautiful when she blushes. Petey finished and the placed erupted into applause. He took his bows like Caruso.

I shrugged and smiled. "They are really pouring it on, and we haven't made it to cannoli yet."

Kaitlin winked at me. "It's better than going to a wedding single. For some reason every woman in the place turns into Cupid."

The cannoli and coffee arrived. It was heaven. I have to watch this dating business. I could gain weight. I gave Kaitlin a stern look. "If you think the evening was hard, now comes the really hard part: getting a bill out of Uncle Gino."

It was as described: he was insulted, you're family, etc. I got the bill anyway and paid. There were lots of hugs all around. As we were making for the door, Grandpa Mario made an appearance, shuffling my way as fast as he could

"Sorry I am late, Sean, the Giants lost to the Cards. What's the world coming to? That bum Frenchy Bordagaray hit a ninth-inning bases-clearing triple for the Cardinals. Slick Castleman had a no-no going until he walked three guys with two outs. Frenchy did the rest. How do you lose a one-hitter in the ninth, I ask you?"

To my surprise Kaitlin answered for me. "What are you talking about? Frenchy is on a twelve-game hitting streak. Check out Slick Castleman's stats, he's lost his last four in the eighth and ninth innings. He better learn to lay off that fastball in the late innings. The big hitters are waiting for it."

Grandpa Mario was all smiles, ear to ear.

"Sean, who is this beautiful young lady, and when are you available for a date, my dear?"

"Easy, Grandpa. This is Kaitlin O'Doherty, and she already booked for the next Seals game with me."

Grandpa Mario was undeterred.

"Bob Joyce is going tomorrow for the Oaks."

Kaitlin was not asleep at the switch. "Lefty O'Doul is going with Bill Shores. His stats only look fair to good, but the real story is that he is serving up three to five double plays a game. I'll go with Shores."

Grandpa Mario was really pouring it on.

"What time are you picking me up for the game?"

I had to cut in here and save the poor girl. "Sorry, Grandpa, this swim is just for the kids. Are you going to be at the bakery after you fish tomorrow?"

"Is Kaitlin going to be there for coffee? It's always a pleasure to talk baseball with a woman that knows her stuff. "

"She'll be there at ten thirty."

Grandpa Mario gave us both a big hug. "You two have a ball; I might see you in the morning. Kaitlin, it was a real pleasure to meet you. If you get tired of this guy, give me a call."

We made our exit. I pointed across the street to the bakery. "There it is in all its glory, Grimaldi's Bakery."

"How come you don't call it O'Farrell's Bakery?"

"My pop bought it from Mr. Grimaldi when I was little. He never changed the name. This is North Beach; it's an Italian neighborhood. An Irish bakery wouldn't quite fit."

I had a key to the bakery and opened it up to give Kaitlin a look. While I was fumbling with the keys, I saw them. It was dark and they were staying in the shadows but I saw them: a short guy and a tall guy, rain oats, fedoras, hands in pockets. FBI guys? Pinkertons? All I, and they, knew was that they were made.

Inside, I turned on the light and reached under the base of the bread-kneading table for an extra .45.

Kaitlin noticed. "Worried about a couple of loaves of bread getting out of line?"

"Kaitlin, I am working on a couple of cases where there might be trouble. I doubt it, but I want to be ready just in case."

"I'm not trying to be a killjoy, but its eight thirty and I'll bet you are getting up extra early to bake bread. Why don't you give me a lift home?"

"I like a sharp girl. How did you know my car is here?"

"You're just too organized not to have a way home."

"True, but I can walk from here, how about you?"

"I'm not that far away. I'll show you how to get to my place for Sunday night."

The Ford was parked up the block. I helped Kaitlin with her sweater and we walked to the car. No shadows. Either they were very good, or they gave up for the night.

"Where to?" I asked.

"Up Mason, and I'll guide you there."

I was heading up Mason when Kaitlin asked an odd question. "How's the transmission on this Ford?"

"It's fine, do you hear something funny?"

"No, turn right here on California and go up."

That's what she meant. The Ford was roaring up California, where its steep, and it's pretty hard to shift and clutch it in gear if you come to a stop. Luckily we made it to the top of Knob Hill where California goes flat for a while. We passed the Mark Hopkins, the Fairmont, Huntington Park and Grace Cathedral.

"Take a right here on Taylor," Kaitlin said. We passed the Pacific Union Club on our right.

"This is it," she said.

I was in the middle of the most expensive real estate in San Francisco. This is where the big wheels of the city, and some say the country, live. Nestled on the corner of Taylor and Sacramento streets was this little bitty shack at the top of the Knob.

"This is your abode?"

"Be it ever so humble," she said.

Humble, my backside. It was at least four floors of Italianate mansion, with a Rolls Royce in the circular driveway. The lamps at the front door were gas, and gave the building a real sense of grace. It was really quite daunting to look at.

"Let me guess, the owners are broke and they take in boarders."

"No, Sean, just me and my parents."

"Gee, where do they find room for you?"

"Believe it or not, there is an apartment in the basement. Three bedrooms, kitchen, separate entrance. I come and I go. My parents stopped waiting up for me by the front door a long time ago."

I smiled, "That may be true, but why do I get the feeling that if I kiss you good night, three or four tough guys will come running out the front door and clobber me?"

"You are over-exaggerating, Sean. It would only be two guys. I guess you are just going to have to find out if it's true aren't you. Remember you do have a gun."

I pulled her close. I kissed her gently on the lips, once, twice, and again. It was the best kiss I had had in years. It left me wanting another.

She wrapped her arms around me. "Survive my parents on Sunday, and there's more where that came from."

We kissed again. She opened the door and waved good night. I walked her to her door and kissed her again. I could get used to this real fast. She went in and closed the door.

I got into the car and I noticed a figure on the second floor looking out through the curtains at me. I fired up the Ford and slowly left the driveway.

I figured I'd better fade before someone came and chased me away from where the better half-lives.

CHAPTER NINETEEN

It was three a.m., and I had one job to complete before I headed for the bakery. On the back porch was a garbage pail filled with sand. I removed the lid, emptied six .45s, and make sure they were safe and locked in the open position before I went into the dining room where everything was all laid out. When I was in the Navy, this type of bucket was called a "clearing station." You always make sure your weapon was empty before you entered the armory.

I had a wool blanket on the dining room table, covered with an old bedsheet, and a flathead screwdriver, a toothbrush, a wire tube cleaner, a can of gun oil, and a bottle of Hoppie's gun cleaner. It was time to begin, one at a time; the same way every time.

One, ensure the weapon is properly unloaded and clear. Two, engage the slide lock. Three, remove the front barrel bushing. Four, remove the slide lock. Five, next remove the slide itself. Six, remove the firing pin. Seven, remove and clean the extractor. Eight, clean the breach plate. Nine, position the barrel lock. Ten, reinstall the slide assembly.

I do this little act every Saturday morning before I go to bake bread. I do it once, then twice, then a third and so on, until all of the guns that I have in the house are cleaned and ready to go. Every once in while during the week I get a head start; I listen to a program on the radio and clean a gun for relaxation.

It always comes back to that old adage: take care of your gun and it will take care of you when needed.

Once I finished, I jumped into the Ford and got to the bakery in five minutes.

Petey was hard at work. Peter was a good-looking young kid: twenty three, olive complexion, large sensitive brown eyes, and a smile that would melt a girl's hearts. Boy, did they melt. When Petey was in high school he was busier with girls then homework and sports. He was quite a playboy, then in his senior year he started going steady with a girl named Roberta. He called her Bobbi. I thought it was pretty serious, and so did Petey. After graduation, she suddenly broke it off and married another guy, a guy who wasn't even from the neighborhood, my Aunt Celia would say. Petey shrugged it off, but five years later, he still hurts. Love is not a game for the weak.

Petey was working a two-foot ball of dough fresh out of the mixer. "Hey, Sean," he greeted me. "Wash up and take this, will you? This is my third ball and my arms are going to fall off."

I washed up, grabbed a flat scrapper, and went to work. The dough had been kneaded in the mixer, but now came the hard part. Kneading and cutting into loaf shapes without overworking the dough. It takes years to perfect the proper technique. My old man had me up to master-baker level by the time I was ten.

I cut the big ball into quarters and kneaded that section flat with my hands. Without even thinking, I cut that section into thirty portions. I did the same to the other three sections.

Next came the shaping. Petey had his racks greased and filled with dough ready for the oven. He opened the oven door and stuck his arm in for ten seconds, then pulled it out. "Three fifty on the nose, Sean. We are ready to go." I could go over to the wall, take off a portable oven thermometer and check the oven, and it would be three fifty. When you do this every day, you can tell what the oven temperature is by waving your palm over the closed door. It's a guarantee when you check it like Petey did.

I had one hundred and twenty square cuts of dough. I threw some flour on the table and started shaping. You take the dough with both hands, put it into a little flour, and roll it into a ball. When it is the size of a softball, you take scissors and cut an X in the top, take it over to a tub filled with corn meal. There, you cover the bottom with it, shake it, then place it on a greased rack to rise.

Petey and I did all one hundred and twenty in ten minutes. All the racks were filled with bread; all they had to do was rise. That gave us ten minutes to clean up, then it was breakfast time. Petey was washing a few last items in the deep sink. The water was so hot that the steam was billowing up into his face.

The stove was hot and ready. I took a sauté pan and drizzled a little olive oil in the pan. While the pan was getting hot, I scrambled four eggs in a bowl. A pinch of salt and pepper, and into the pan they went, sizzling the moment they touched the cast iron. With a spatula, I glided the eggs back and forth in the pan so they wouldn't stick. Opening the refrigerator, I took out a block of Roma cheese and grated it over the eggs. I beat the grater with the palm of my hand to ensure that all the cheese was put to good use.

Finished with the dishes, Petey went over to the espresso machine and made two cappuccinos to go with the breakfast. I flipped the eggs over in the pan, it sizzled again. I waited a minute and onto plates the eggs went. I pulled a loaf of sourdough off one of the cooling racks and cut it into six thick slices. Heaven on a plate. Petey brought the cappuccinos over and a plate with butter.

I was pretty hungry, but Petey must have been starving; he swallowed two eggs in two bites. He poured a little olive oil on the plate and soaked it up with his bread.

"Pop tells me you came in with a looker last night. Time to give, Uncle Sean."

"Not much to tell, Petey. Her name is Kaitlin and she's a librarian."

Petey gave me a look. "Come on, Unc, you are going to have to do a lot better than that. People in this neighborhood been waiting a long time for you get back into the game."

"I had no idea that my dating life was such a point of concern for everyone."

Petey shrugged. "Come on, Uncle Sean. It's been a few years. Everybody wants you to be happy again."

"Petey, I'm happy right now."

"Quit changing the subject, tell me about the librarian, is she cute, you seeing her again, you know…"

I swallowed a piece of bread. "You are turning into a little gossip, Petey."

"What are you taking about? Momma, Papa and Gramps talk about two things: the weather and when are we going to get Sean a girl. I'm not gossiping, I'm just asking."

I took a slug of espresso. "You will get to meet her at ten thirty. Yes, we are going out again, today. We are going to a baseball game. She is very nice, very attractive, very funny, very bright, and apparently she was not scared off by the family. Of course she hasn't met you yet, paisano, so that could change everything."

Petey gave a mock laugh.

"Ha ha, ha, you should have been a comedian, Uncle Sean. I'm looking forward to meeting her. She can't be all that bright, though, if she's going out with you a second time."

There was a baseball-size piece of dough on the table; it was in and out of my hand in two seconds. It was covered with flour and exploded into a cloud of white dust when it hit Petey right on the forehead.

"Okay, Uncle Sean, you have this rule. No grab-assing in the bakery, I believe." Petey pointed to his face. "This would be considered grab-assing." He stood with his hands on his hips when I threw another piece of dough. This time he caught it in midair and returned it. He caught me right in the mush, and flour went everywhere. I couldn't see real well.

"You are slowing down, old man. Now I believe this also," Petey said, "would be considered grab-assing, if I am not mistaken?"

"Okay, Petey, we're even. Since there are racks of rising dough everywhere, I won't take your life at this particular time, but that time is coming and soon."

The door opened and the bell rang. It was Kaitlin. She looked great. Her hair was tied back and she was wearing a Seals cap. She was wearing a white cotton dress with orange and black trim that matched the Seals home colors. She wasn't dressed up by any means, but she looked great in whatever she was wearing.

The ovens were ready to go and the bread smelled great. Petey opened the doors and starting loading bread into the oven. He put about seventy-five loaves in at once.

She was all smiles. "Are you sure you want to see a baseball game? You two look like you are having a lot of fun right here."

"Kaitlin O'Doherty, this little trouble maker is Peter Chiconis. I hate to admit it, but this is Gino and Celia's youngest."

It didn't take Petey long to pour on the charm. "So this is the fair Kaitlin everyone is talking about." He ran over and gave her a big family hug. When he was through, Kaitlin has as much flour on her face as Petey and I did.

"Nice work, genius." I slapped the back of Petey's head.

Kaitlin dusted the flour from her face and smiled. "Come on, Sean, the gates open in forty-five minutes. We need to get going. Then she surprised me by giving Petey a hug and telling him it was great to meet him. Petey beamed, and they dusted themselves off a second time.

I grabbed my coat and opened the door. Kaitlin went through the door, then turned around and threw a ball of dough at Petey; she had grabbed it off the table when she gave him the second hug. Petey was caught off guard, he didn't see it coming. The dough hit him in the middle of his chest and made a tiny dusting in the air. Petey laughed and waved goodbye.

I opened the car door for Kaitlin. She slapped me on the back of the head, the same way I hit Petey. "Be nice, don't hit your Cousin Petey. He's a good kid."

CHAPTER TWENTY

We arrived at eleven twenty, forty minutes before first pitch. Seals Stadium was an unusual ballpark for many reasons, some good and some not so good. It was the only ballpark that I know of that was built with three locker rooms. One for the home team, the Seals; one for the visitors; and one for the Mission Reds. The Reds were also part of the Pacific Coast League, but they folded after the 1937 season. Seals Stadium could seat 18,500 fans, which is pretty good-sized for a ball field. Ebbets Field in Brooklyn, New York, where the Dodgers play, holds about 25,000. I'm sure Kaitlin would remind me that Fenway Park holds 35,000 and Yankee Stadium holds a whopping 72,000. I went to Yankee games when I was stationed in New York. It was a great baseball atmosphere, but it was like watching ants run around on a green piece of bread. I'll take Seals Stadium any day.

The grandstand was uncovered. In the summer, we don't get a great deal of rain, so San Franciscans prefer to sit in the sun in the afternoon or see a game under the stars at night. If it rained, which was rare in the summer, you were expected to tough it out as a loyal Seals fan.

After we got our tickets, we bought a couple of scorecards and started looking for seats. Kaitlin seemed to know where she wanted to go. We made our way along the first-base side and went right up the middle of the stadium to right below the scorers' box. This is my favorite area as well. I like it because you can see the pitches coming in to the batters, plus you can tell where the ball is going in a big hurry. Kaitlin said she liked it because she could better judge field play by the infield and see all the outfielders. For a true baseball fan, this is the best seat in the house.

Kaitlin had a soft book bag. From it, she took a clipboard and put her scorecard on it. She had a portable pencil sharpener and a bundle of rubber-banded pencils. She took one and handed the other to me. She then removed an envelope from the bag; it was filled with hundreds of clippings from the newspapers. Old Seals game box scores. They were all categorized and organized a certain way: by opponents; lineup charts, stats, and several pages of personal notes on player tendencies. This was no time to make any Yankee jokes; this gal had come to the office to work.

I pointed out to Kaitlin. "Look, Jumbo Carlson is warming up in the bullpen."

She glanced up from her notes. "He better get that fastball down in the strike zone or it's going to be a short day for him."

"Give the guy a break, he's warming up. First, a pitcher has to find the strike zone and consistently hit it, then you start to work on location. Besides, it's his curve that sets up that fastball. He hasn't thrown one yet."

Just as I said that he fired off the deuce, and baby, it was pretty. It got Kaitlin's attention. "Woo, that one is going to freeze some batters today. That was pretty."

"Are you a peanuts or popcorn gal?"

She gave me a stunned look. "Peanuts are for baseball, popcorn is for the movies." She smiled and reached into her book bad and brought out a small brown paper bag. She opened it and placed it between us on the deck beneath our feet. "For the shells. I hate a mess during a baseball game."

It was about ten minutes before first pitch. The Oaks and Seals were done with infield practice, and the managers were about ready to trade line up cards and cover the ground rules with the umpires. When Lefty O'Doul walked out onto the batter's circle, there was a loud round of applause. Lefty doffed his cap and acknowledged the crowd.

Fifteen rows down was a vendor selling peanuts. It would be a while before he made it to the top, so I told Kaitlin I was going to run down and buy a couple of bags before first pitch. I got to the bottom of the stairs and purchased two bags.

I smiled and turned to run back up the stairs. A guy sitting on the end asked for two bags. He handed off his dime and got two bags. It was Righty, with Lefty. I froze for a second; I looked up and saw that Kaitlin was still sitting where I left her. My heart skipped a beat. I had left my .45 in the trunk of the Ford.

"Are you two following me for some reason?"

"Relax, boss, we are off today. We're Seals fans, came to see Jumbo hurl," Righty said.

I relaxed just a little. "Enjoy the game."

"The redhead, she your wife?" Lefty asked.

I was suddenly guarded again. "No just a date, why?"

Lefty looked over his shoulder at Kaitlin. "You're a lucky man, boss. I should be so lucky."

I gave them a smile. "Got to get back, we'll see you later." They gave a salute with one finger. I couldn't quite put my finger on it, but I was starting to like those two guys.

I got back to my seat and Kaitlin asked. "Who are the two huge guys you were talking to?"

"A couple of guys I know through work. They are tough customers."

"I've seen them here at the park pretty regular. They seem like good fans to me."

Who would have guessed, a couple of Chinese strongmen working for Wang, and they were baseball fans. Go figure.

Jumbo had the stuff that day. He only gave up six hits, but the Oaks hit into five double plays. He mixed up his pitches well and had them guessing all day. On the other hand, the Seals didn't hit the ball that hard, but managed eleven hits and seven walks. They won this day, seven to zero. Watching Kaitlin keep score was like watching a master. A couple of times the official scorer in the box above us stuck his head out and asked Kaitlin how she scored a call. He went with her both times. The second call was a questionable play by the first baseman, very close. It could have been called a base hit or an error by the one-bagger. She called it an error. My sympathies lie with the first baseman, but I have to admit that he should have made the out and she was right.

As we left the stadium we were holding hands. I don't know who reached for whom first. It may have been simultaneous, I don't know. All I know is it felt right and I was happy for the first time in years.

CHAPTER TWENTY-ONE

I took Kaitlin home because I had to take care of some Knights of Columbus business. I spent the remainder of the day, and most of the evening, helping ten other men wrestle a hot water heater out of its place so Tony Balducci could squeeze his little body into a small space to replace a pilot light. It took hours of wrench-turning to remove all the pipes to get the tank ready. We were all covered with soot and grime. It only took Tony fifteen minutes to install the new light, but it took six hours to heft that beast back into place and re-attach the pipes. At eleven thirty, the tank was fired off. It came to temperature in less than an hour. We all staggered out of the church basement at one a.m.

Vinnie Castellano and I looked like a couple of coal miners. I opened the trunk of the Ford. Inside I had an old bedsheet and a clean pair of work gloves. I was so dirty that I wrapped the front seat with the sheet and put on the gloves for the ride home. When I got home I got right in the shower and watched half a pound of coal dust go down the drain.

At five a.m. the alarm went off. I shaved, dressed in a suit and tie, and zipped back to the church. My job this Sunday was adding up the collection plate for all four Masses. Mass was offered at 6:30, 8:00, and 10:00 in the morning. The big Mass of the day was the 11:45 in Italian; it's usually standing-room-only.

By the time all the collections were counted, it was two in the afternoon. It was like a full workday at the church. Dinner was at six at Kaitlin's, but I was hungry so I had a little sandwich and an espresso at Molinari's.

I went home and shaved, again. I decided to go with the Navy blue suit that I just got back from the cleaners on Friday. A crisp white dress shirt and silk tie, I was ready to go. I ironed a white pocket square and checked myself in the mirror.

I picked up a bottle of red wine as an offering. I don't know much about wine, so I went strictly by price: expensive.

I arrived at three minutes to six. I parked the Ford behind the Rolls-Royce and strolled to the front door. I rang the doorbell. It sounded like a carillon going off.

Kaitlin answered the door. She was a sight for sore eyes. She was wearing a floor-length velvet-green dress, and her hair was down, red and flowing. She looked like an angel from heaven.

Then I saw them at the end of the hall, motionless and expressionless, eyes were locked on me like a beam of light. Not one hair moved. I was being observed, sized up and evaluated, and they both didn't like what they were looking at. I could see the hate in their eyes. Kaitlin slowly held my right with her left hand and laced her left arm in mine. The two pairs of eyes burned at me. Then they went insane.

The barking and growling started and did not stop for one minute. Then Kaitlin told them to stop and they did. Before me stood a matched pair of West Highland White Terriers. They seemed a little confused; they looked at each other, then me.

"Sean this is McGregor and McTavish. They are my dogs, they love and protect me."

I kissed Kaitlin on the cheek and they lost their minds again. Kaitlin told them to behave and they stopped instantly.

Kaitlin looked at me.

"If you are going to love me, you have to love my dogs."

She looked at me, hard, for a moment. "Well?"

"I'm thinking about it," I said.

She mockingly gave me a punch on the arm.

I leaned over and addressed the dogs.

"Hi boys, let's get something straight. When we get married, you two get to live in the back yard in a dog house."

I sensed they understood what I was saying, because they lost their minds collectively. I got the full show, complete with teeth and growling.

From the end of another hall I heard a male voice with an Irish brogue call to the dogs. "Lads, that's enough."

Joining the dogs at the end of the hall was Shamus O'Doherty, Kaitlin's father. He was in his late fifties, I guessed. He was dressed in a smart tweed suit, with knickers, a four-in-hand made of tartan, with brown and white spectators. He walked down the hall like a man with confidence. He shook my hand and about broke every bone in it. I did my best to return the favor.

"Mr. O'Farrell, I am Shamus O'Doherty. Welcome to our home. I see that you met the lads. Do you like dogs, Mr. O'Farrell?"

I looked at Mr. O'Doherty, then at the dogs.

"I do if they are properly cooked," I said.

The dogs lost their minds again. This time they barked so hard that they were rocking back and forth between front and rear legs. Mr. O'Doherty called to them.

"Enough, lads, Mr. O'Farrell was just pulling your leg." He looked right at me. "You are right, my dear, a wee bit of a smart ass. I like him."

I gave Mr. O'Doherty the wine.

"Excellent choice, I'll serve it with dinner. Why don't you come in the parlor and have a drink."

The parlor, as he called it, was the size of Uncle Gino's restaurant, and his place seats two hundred. When we entered the room, a beautiful, gracious woman was sitting on the sofa. She rose as we came in. It was clear where Kaitlin got her looks from.

"Mr. O'Farrell, may I introduce my wife, Catherine O'Doherty." She warmly shook my hand. She was the same age as her husband, but had gray and silver hair. She wore it in beautiful Gibson Girl style from the Victorian era. It was old-fashioned and outdated, and it looked perfect on her. Her full-length gown was royal blue and it made her hair even more stunning.

Mr. O'Doherty poured his wife a sherry, and followed with three generous scotches and handed one to Kaitlin, and one to me. He took a chair facing me. Kaitlin was seated next to me on a sofa. Mrs. O'Doherty was seated in a large wingback chair. She appeared to be settling in for the show. I sensed the questioning was about to begin.

"Why don't you tell us about yourself, Mr. O'Farrell."

"Please call me Sean."

"All right, Sean. I know Katie has probably warned you that we would probably grill you prior to dinner. I figure we should get to know each other a little. I know, for instance, that you and Katie are the same age."

"I was born here in San Francisco. I grew up in North Beach. My father was a bread baker and my mother stayed home and raised my sister and me."

"Katie tells us that you are a private detective. Did you get into that game after high school?"

He was a smooth old buzzard, all right. "No I picked that up in the Navy."

"Oh, so you enlisted after high school, then?"

Kaitlin was enjoying the serve and volley.

"No, I went to the University of San Francisco. I was a criminology major. I was a Navy ROTC candidate and became a commissioned reserve officer; I was the base security officer in charge of the Shore Patrol at the Brooklyn Navy Yard, where I did my first police and investigative work."

"So, you got out of the Navy and became a private eye then."

"No, I went to law school at San Francisco University. After I passed the bar, I went to work for a small law firm. I was doing routine pleadings and business contracts when they needed an investigation done on a client's business partner. I wrapped that up in week and I was hooked. I opened an office a week later and have been very busy ever since."

Mr. O'Doherty was impressed. "Well, I would have loved to have you interview for position at my company."

"You did, Mr. O'Doherty, I interviewed at Standard Oil of California. You were in the conference room when I was interviewed."

He was a little taken aback. "I'm sorry I don't remember. I wish we would have offered you a job."

"You did, Mr. O'Doherty. I had to decline because of a family emergency."

A maid came in and placed a tray of canapés on the coffee tray. She straightened up and let out a small scream.

"Lieutenant O'Farrell. My God, lad, it's you." I stood and hugged her. It was Maureen O'Reilly, who I knew from my days in the Navy. She started to cry and told me how sorry she was, and how she prayed for me and my family. She was so overcome by emotion that I walked her out of the room and put my arm around her. I took her to the kitchen and sat her on a stool. She lowered her head into her lap and wept. Several of the ladies in the kitchen surrounded her and gave her support. I was getting embarrassed; I told her she did nothing of the kind, and returned to the parlor.

Mrs. O'Doherty and Kaitlin was a little shaken and concerned. "Is she all right, Sean? What was that about?"

I knew this moment would come.

"Might I ask what happened?" Shamus asked politely.

"Mrs. O'Reilly was my housekeeper in Alameda. She also helped my wife with our baby daughter."

The words hung in the air; I had to let it out.

"My wife and one-year-old daughter were killed by a drunk driver. My wife Barbara was walking our daughter Susan in a bassinette; the Packard was going forty-five in a twenty. They were both dead on impact."

I didn't mean to drop this on them; I was hoping the Pinkerton's report had included that information. But apparently Shamus didn't know. I guess they weren't very efficient.

Mrs. O'Doherty had tears streaming down her face. I knew she understood my pain.

"God almighty lad, I'm so sorry. I feel like a fool for asking. How could things be any worse than that?"

"That was bad enough, but that evening my father died of a heart attack. My mother died two weeks later. She had cancer and we never knew it."

The room was quiet for several minutes. Kaitlin developed a perplexed look on face, then it turned to anger. I was getting a good look at Kaitlin O'Doherty about ready to explode.

"Daddy, I never told you that Sean and I were the same age."

Shamus O'Doherty looked like a cat with a mouth full of canary, he was cornered. He had that look like a kid caught with his hand in the cookie jar. He started to hem and haw.

Kaitlin's voice was rising.

"Daddy."

I cut in.

"I'll tell you how he knew, Kaitlin. He got the report on me from the Pinkerton National Detective Agency. It probably came today."

Mrs. O'Doherty was on her feet.

"Shamus O'Doherty! You promised me that you would never do this type of thing again. You said you would not poke and pry into Kaitlin's private affairs."

I jumped in."

"Mrs. O'Doherty, please." I put up my hand a motioned for her to sit down, and she did so gracefully.

"I'm a private detective, I don't get into much trouble with my work, but you and your husband don't know that. But if I was in your husband's shoes, I would wonder how safe my daughter is with this guy. I lost my wife and my daughter. I can never change that. I would give anything to have been in a position to protect them. Your husband is in charge of a multinational corporation. He needed to know who I was and if I am worthy of the opportunity to gain your trust, and more importantly, if can I be trusted with Kaitlin. I would have done the same thing."

Mrs. O'Doherty was satisfied, but gave Shamus a cold hard look. "We'll discuss this matter later, Shamus" was all she said.

Oh, I bet they would. And Kaitlin might have something to say about this also.

Mr. O'Doherty was on his feet.

"Let's eat." The women walked out first. Shamus O'Doherty hung back a little. He slapped my back as we went out.

"You really are a silver-tonged devil, another fast-talking lawyer. Well, son, you saved my butt tonight, thank you."

I smiled broadly. "Next time, hire somebody good. I made the Pinkerton on the first day."

Shamus and I both chuckled as we drank the rest of our scotch, which had to be thirty year or older. It was the best I ever had.

CHAPTER TWENTY-TWO

Dinner consisted of roast beef and Yorkshire pudding, with garlic green beans and fresh rolls. Dessert was lady fingers, cherries and kirsch. It was great. Mr. O'Doherty opened the wine I brought, and opened another halfway through the meal. Kaitlin painted her parents as tough customers, but they were actually very nice, just protective. In many ways, they were like my parents, only richer.

The conversation was light and humorous. The O'Doherty's were wonderful and gracious people. I liked them; I was hoping the same was true in reverse.

When it was time to go I thanked them for the wonderful evening. We shook hands and Kaitlin showed me to the door. She walked me to the car.

"How did I do?"

"Well, I think they like you, and that's saying something."

I put my arm around her waist and pulled her close. I gave her a kiss. She returned my kiss and asked me to call her soon.

As I was getting into the Ford there was a note on my windshield: MEET ME AT THE TOP OF THE MARK IN THIRTY MINUTES, SHAMUS.

Well when the Irish Pope says come to a meeting, you go see the Irish Pope.

I drove a couple of blocks over to California and parked in front of the John Hopkins Hotel, across the street from the Fairmont Hotel and the Union Pacific Club.

The kid running the elevator was pleasant. "Which floor, sir?" he said.

"Top of the Mark, please."

I have been to the Mark a few times. It offers the best view in San Francisco, a three-hundred-and-sixty degree view of the city. This evening was clear as a bell. It was so clear you could easily see sailors walking on the deck of a tanker in the middle of the bay. The Top of the Mark was empty, not a soul in the place.

I went over to the bar and took a stool. The bartender came over and placed a cocktail napkin on the bar in front of me.

"Good evening, sir. Welcome to the Top of the Mark, what can I prepare for you?"

"I'm meeting someone here for a drink. I'll wait for him, if you don't mind?"

"Not at all, sir. Mr. O'Doherty should be along in ten minutes."

"How did you know I am meeting Mr. O'Doherty?"

"Sunday evenings are quiet here; things slow down after brunch. Mr. O'Doherty is here every evening at nine p.m., almost every night."

I heard the elevator door open and out came Shamus O'Doherty. He had the dogs on a leash. He strolled right in and released the dogs' leashes. They both sat and waited. Mr. O'Doherty went behind the bar and pulled something out from the lower shelf. It was a large, cushy-looking dog bed. He walked over to a corner and waved for me to join him. He put down the bed, and the two dogs ran over, got in, and laid down.

I looked at the bartender. "He's a regular, I assume?"

He smiled and laughed. "Yes, sir. He drinks scotch, neat. What would you like?"

"I'll have the same."

I sauntered over to the table. The dogs did not even look at me funny.

"Pull up a chair, Sean." Shamus looked at the dogs in the bed, then me. "Don't worry about the lads. All that barking at the house was just a show for Katie and her mother."

I didn't quite follow him. "Excuse me?"

"Katie thinks these dogs are hers. They are sort of; they would give their lives to protect her. But in reality they are mine, they have testicles, and they know where the bread is buttered, so to speak." He took out a couple of dog treats from his jacket pocket. The pair eagerly snapped them up and sank back down.

"I asked you here, Sean to lay my cards on the table. I am a no-nonsense plain talker. I am going to speak my mind, but I wanted to do without the women around. Man to man. I hope you don't mind?"

"Not at all." I said.

The bartender delivered the drinks.

"Thanks, Patrick, you are a good lad." Mr. O'Doherty took a short pull and carefully considered his words.

"I know you look around my house and think I was born with a silver spoon in my mouth. My parents, God rest their souls, came to this great country with nothing but a dream. They worked hard and both died young. My older brothers and sisters raised me and kept the family together. I worked hard every day from the age of ten. I sold papers, delivered coal, moved furniture, and loaded cargo on ships, even shoveled shit at a horse paddock. I worked hard in school, but God was good to me and he gave me a skill. I was a boxer, a good boxer. With good grades I got a scholarship to Harvard. I made good use of my time and did very well; I graduated with a degree in mechanical engineering and geology.

"After I graduated, I got a job with an engineering firm and worked my way up. I was designing of all things, a sewage treatment plant, when Mr. Rockefeller's Standard Oil Company came a-calling. They hired me away and I managed to catch on at the right time. Better than that, I became rich."

"Sounds pretty perfect to me," I said.

"It was almost perfect. I was at a Harvard Club society do one Christmas and my eye caught a beautiful young thing. She was the most beautiful woman I had ever laid eyes upon. The same thing went for every other available man in the room. Catherine O'Shea was a sight. She was handsome, bright and a wonderful dancer. I fell in love with her the moment I saw her. Well, I made up my mind right then and there that I would marry her one day."

"I'm going to guess that you achieved that goal, Mr. O'Doherty."

"Knock off that Mr. O'Doherty stuff. Call me Shamus. You should know right here and now that I like you." Shamus took another tug on his scotch.

"I asked for a dance, and I believe she was smitten as well. Mr. and Mrs. O'Shea, on the other hand, had long ago decided that their daughter was going to do better than me. They had narrowed the families she might marry into down to two, and one did not include poor Shamus O'Doherty, the Southie boy from Charlestown. I think they thought since I was poor and from Charlestown, I was a gang member. Her father refused to allow me to see her, but I was persistent. It took me three years until I think they figured I had won her heart and they weren't going to stop us. So we married."

"I can sure see where Kaitlin gets her looks."

"Well, she is a beauty like her mother. But Katie is stubborn like a mule and hot-tempered like I am. You need to know several things, Sean. I don't want to appear to be forward, but you have to know certain things so you understand why the O'Doherty's are the way we are.

"After we were married for a year, my Catherine became pregnant. Kaitlin was born, but she was a twin. Her brother was stillborn. My Catherine started bleeding and they couldn't stop it. She was in surgery for six hours, and she lost a great deal of blood and she slipped into a coma. I found out in the surgery she lost her ability to have any more children. But that was the least of my problems. I had a new baby daughter and a wife in a coma. I nearly lost my mind."

Shamus teared up. It was thirty-two years later and it still brought out strong emotions. I put my hand on his shoulder. He quickly pulled himself together.

"After eight days God shined upon me and my Catherine came back to me. She spent three weeks in the hospital, but a cloud came over her for a year. She was so depressed for so long. When she brightened up again and became her old self, she became a wonderful mother. She has never spoiled Katie, but she is very protective of her. She is all we have left. Has Katie told you about some of her past suitors?"

"Yes, she has. She was pretty upfront about it all."

"Jesus, Mary and Joseph: a philanderer, a fruit, and woman-beater. I have to tell you right here and now, that that last bastard nearly killed my wife. She is hyper-vigilant now when it comes to Katie."

"The first two that she was engaged to was one thing, but what happened to the last one that beat her?"

"Katie was in the hospital; her face was so bruised she couldn't keep her eyes open. Her lips were so split that we couldn't understand her when she tried to talk. I cried like a baby for an hour, and then I went looking for that bastard. I found him at the Harvard Club and I confronted him. The little weasel denied it, and then he told me I should have taught my daughter better manners and maybe her mouth wouldn't have gotten her into that kind of trouble. Then he told me that the bitch got what she deserved. It took nine men to keep me from getting to him. He just sat there and laughed at me with a smug look on his face."

Shamus wiped his eyes with a handkerchief and tried to regain his composure.

"I can see why you hired the Pinkertons. I'll make a guess: I was not the first guy you had checked out?"

"True, I'm sorry about that, but I had to know who my little girl was seeing. They wrote a glowing report about my boy. I did have a question; you hit .340 and no errors at first base in your senior year and were offered a contract by the Seals?"

"I couldn't accept it; I was committed to the Navy after college.

Besides, I was married and a baby on the way, and baseball wasn't that solid of a career. What became of the last guy that hit Kaitlin?"

"He got his comeuppance. Three weeks later he was robbed in an alley three blocks from the club. They beat him with a shillelagh and broke his arm in two places, and his left knee was shattered. Before you even ask, I was home with Catherine and Katie."

"How much did it cost you?" I asked.

Shamus didn't hesitate.

"One hundred bucks for the two of them. Best money I ever spent." He spoke with a great deal of satisfaction.

The bartender, Patrick, brought another round.

"A month after he was taken care of, he came limping into the club. This time he didn't have the smug look on his face. I looked right at him, and he knew I had it done. The lad didn't understand the concept of the eleventh commandment."

"The eleventh commandment?" I asked.

"Thou shall not get away with it. Little bastard laid hands on my little girl. He's lucky to be alive."

We were quiet for a moment.

"She is scared to death, Sean; her mother is even more frightened. I'll be perfectly honest with you; her mother is going to be a real problem for you. You need to hear this from me; I'm in your corner. I know you just met her a few days ago, but I have a strong feeling about you. I haven't seen my little girl smile like the way she smiles at the mention of your name since we left Boston four years ago. I like to think that I am a good judge of character, Katie can be a real handful, but I think you are up to the task. If you want to pursue her, I'm all for it. I'll help you with her mother. As far as Katie goes, you are on you own with that chore, lad. I only ask one thing."

"I can guess: don't ever hurt her."

"Right you are. I won't have to pay a hundred bucks to have it take care of you. I'll have the lads here eat your balls for breakfast."

A low-level growl in unison came from under the table.

"Okey dokey. Point well taken."

CHAPTER TWENTY-THREE

I took the elevator down from the Mark with Shamus. We shook hands and I saw him walk off with the lads in tow. I liked him. He was a straight shooter and that's a rare item in this world. Kaitlin's mother and father were strong-willed people; I could see where she gets her independent streak.

I climbed into the Ford and headed home. I had spent a great deal of time with Kaitlin and her family this weekend. Tomorrow was Monday, and I had a load of work to accomplish during the day. I had to arrange the meeting with the Wang's and the Broadcreek's, as well as their entourages. I was taking the Delta Queen to Sacramento to follow Morehouse for perhaps the last time. This time I needed to visit his bookie.

I got home and went right to bed. It had been a great weekend, but it was over, and I needed to get serious and get my head back in the game. I needed to rest, and most of all I needed to get Kaitlin O'Doherty out of my head. That would be hard to do. It took me over an hour to fall asleep even though I was exhausted.

In the morning I packed an overnight bag, put on the double-holster rig, and drove to the office.

Marty waved a Boston cream donut under my nose as soon as I walked in. I reminded him about the summit at the St. Francis, set for Wednesday evening at six. I got up the office and started making phone calls.

Special Agent Ashwythe at the Special Task Force Office said that he and Dunderbeck would be available. I told them that I expected the Broadcreek's to come to this meeting on their own. They just needed to show up at the St. Francis. I gave him Jerry Ronkowski's name and phone number. I told him which room the meeting was going to be in. There was a long pause on the phone.

"Listen, O'Farrell, Dave and I were talking. We don't think you are going to be able to talk the old man into coming. He is one tough bird; he is so stubborn he may not come, just to be contrary."

"I kind of thought of that. That is why I am calling Mrs. Broadcreek for the appointment. She'll get her old man to play ball," I said.

"I got to hand it to you, O'Farrell, you have got some balls." Ashwythe was chuckling.

"I've got plenty of balls, no brains though."

Ashwythe was still laughing as he hung up.

I called the Social Club and asked for Jimmy Chin. I gave him the scoop. He agreed to get both Mr. and Mrs. Chin to the Borgia Room at the St. Francis Hotel on time.

My last call was going to be tricky.

"Good morning, Mrs. Broadcreek. My name is Sean O'Farrell. I am a private investigator in San Francisco and I am calling about your daughter, Dorothy."

I had her complete attention.

"Dorothy? Is something the matter?"

"She is fine, madam. I have been hired to do a background investigation on your daughter by the parents of a young man she is dating."

"My daughter is not dating anyone at all. What kind of trick is this?"

"Mrs. Broadcreek, this is not scam or a trick. I need to meet with both you and your husband to discuss this matter."

"Do you have any idea who my husband is, young man?"

"Yes, madam, I do. He is a Deputy Attorney General of the United States in charge of Organized Crime Task Force in San Francisco dealing with Chinatown."

That brought silence to the line.

"Mrs. Broadcreek?"

"Yes, I am not sure what to say or think. I don't even know who you are. Who is she supposedly dating?"

"That's what the meeting is about. There are complications for both families and these matters are better discussed in person. I have arranged a meeting room at the St. Francis Hotel, the Borgia Room for six p.m. this Wednesday. It will be private and agents of the FBI will be attendance to provide security for all those in attendance."

"I will call my husband and call you back."

I hung up, took a drink of coffee, and opened a fresh deck of Luckies. I lit a smoke and waited. It didn't take long.

The phone rang and the man on the other end was completely out of control.

"O'Farrell, you son of a bitch, who the hell do you think you are calling my home, talking to my wife, and discussing our daughter? I've got a good mind to come down there and kick your ass all over Union Square, you two-bit peeping bastard."

I was amused by the onslaught, but I'd be upset too, if it were my daughter.

"Easy, Mr. Broadcreek, you are running your mouth pretty carelessly to a fellow member of the bar."

He calmed down a little bit. "You are an attorney at law."

"Yes, sir, a member in good standing with the California Bar."

"Still, you have been poking around in my daughter's business. You have no right."

I explained. "I am not blowing smoke, wasting time, or looking to make a buck here. There is very sensitive information you both need to hear in person. You are a Deputy Attorney General of the United States; you have a reputation and family to protect here. I need you to be at this meeting. Special Agents Ashwythe and Dunderbeck will be present to ensure you and your wife's safety. You really need to be at this meeting, sir. You will regret it if you pass on this." I was doing my best sales job.

"Forget it, O'Farrell. I smell a rat." He was starting to heat up again. "You are just some shakedown artist with a law license. All you are is a thug with a smart suit. You call me or my wife again and I'll—"

I cut him off. "Look, Mr. Broadcreek, I am going to contact someone that I know who may know you and I think he would be willing to vouch for me. If he contacts you, please listen to him, then call me back at this number."

He chewed the idea over for a minute.

"All right, but I am not going to wait here all day. I'm a busy man." He slammed the phone down.

I hated to do it, but I had a suspicion that I knew someone who knew Broadcreek, and I didn't mean Danny O'Day.

I dialed the phone and waited for an answer. "Good morning, Standard Oil of California."

"Good morning. Shamus O'Doherty, please."

"May I say who is calling, sir?"

"Sean O'Farrell."

It took ten minutes for the big cheese to come to the phone. "Sorry, Sean I was in a meeting. What can I do for you?"

"This is a business call, Shamus. I am working on a very sensitive case with two of the biggest wheels in San Francisco. I am trying to get them to come to a meeting. The first party is all set; the second is a real hothead. I think you might know him."

"Who is he then, lad?"

"His name is William Broadcreek."

"Oh, yeah, I know Bill. He is a member of the University Club. We have played cards a couple of times. He is a senior guy with the Attorney General's office, I think. A real good Joe."

"He's not real fond of me. I need him to come to a meeting about his daughter; he thinks I'm shady or trying to pull a fast one. This is pretty serious. I really need him and his wife to come."

"His daughter, aye?" Shamus mused.

"I can't give you any details, Shamus. But his family is in a real fix, personally and professionally."

"I got a feeling you wouldn't have called me unless it was important. I'll give Bill a call. As a matter of fact, I'll call him now." The line clicked off.

I started handwriting a report for Connie Morehouse. I gave her a call and set up a meeting for Wednesday afternoon next week. I gave her an overview of what I was up to, and told her that we would meet and decide where to go from there. She agreed; I hope this was going to be a business meeting only this time.

The phone rang and it was William Broadcreek.

"Mr. O'Farrell, William Broadcreek here. I don't know what is going on; my wife tells me my daughter isn't dating anyone. But Shamus O'Doherty tells me you are a straight shooter and a man that can be trusted. If you don't mind me asking you, how did you come to know Shamus?"

"I don't know him well, but I have gone out with his daughter Kaitlin."

There was a long pause.

"My wife and I will be there. I'll take Shamus's word that you are on the up and up. But I'll tell you right now this had better be legitimate." The line quietly went dead.

I called Shamus back and thanked him for vouching for me.

"Watch yourself, boyo. Bill Broadcreek is a boiling pot that is ready to overflow, if you know what I mean. It's his only daughter."

"It must be a club with you guys, fathers of only daughters." I was being serious.

"Don't worry, Sean. Bill doesn't have dogs. His wife is allergic. He'll just rip your balls off with his own two hands." He laughed like a leprechaun. I thanked him again and hung up. Great another psychotic father out for my testicles. Wonderful.

CHAPTER TWENTY-FOUR

My next call was to Kaitlin.

"Hey there, good-looking. When are you working today?"

"Boy, just because you schmoozed my parents, that doesn't mean you cut ice with me, buster." She laughed.

"Schmoozed? I am deeply insulted." I changed my tone to a serious one. "Thanks for the wonderful evening last night."

"Any time, sailor." She giggled again.

"Listen, I am going out of town tonight to Sacramento. What time do you work today?"

"I work three to close tonight."

"Can I buy you lunch? Don't worry, I'll take you somewhere where you don't have to stand to eat."

"And I thought you would try to impress me with the hot-dog stand at Union Square."

"How about Sears again? It's close."

"I'll grab a cable car and be there in half an hour."

I locked up the office and stopped by and talked to Marty. He was his usual friendly self.

"You're just as ugly as ever, O'Farrell." Then he leaned over the glass counter. "That architect rolled in here ten minutes ago looking like he slept in the gutter. He had a couple of gees helping stay upright. You got a guess when he is going to take a powder to later?"

"My guess is he'll go to Sacramento and gamble all night on the boat. This gee is to a point where he can't help himself anymore."

"For what it's worth, there have been two thugs hanging around out in front of the building. They are definitely somebody's apes. They seem to disappear when you are around, and they didn't look too sharp to me. But watch your back. It don't take brains to pull a trigger."

I thanked Marty and walked over to Sears. I stopped and tied my shoes, and as I did so, I looked in a store window. Wherever the muscle guys were, they were not around.

The cable car stopped at the intersection and Kaitlin hopped off.

"How come you were standing at the front of the car? It was empty," I said as we embraced.

"I love the rush of the wind coming down the hill." She waved her hand in the air.

We got a table and looked over the menu. Then Kaitlin surprised me.

"So how was the Top of the Mark with my Dad?"

"You knew?"

"Oh course. He walks the dogs every night, and he ends up there. It's his little private getaway for him and the lads. And by the way, don't swallow that nonsense that those dogs are his. I let him think that, but they report back to me."

"Some well-kept, well-guarded secret," I said.

"He goes there a lot. But it is the first time he has every invited anyone to go with him. It's also the first time he has ever had a drink with anyone I had been out on a date with. He likes you, and you made some progress with my mother. But she doesn't like the private-eye thing, now that worries her."

"Does it worry you?"

"It doesn't worry me. But the fact that it worries my mother so much … that concerns me."

I ordered a bowl of soup and a Coke. Kaitlin ordered a half sandwich and salad special.

She looked at me with a smile. "So how long are you going to be gone?"

"I should be back on Wednesday. But I am booked through until Thursday evening."

"Well, I might drop by after work and visit."

"It is always a pleasure to see you, anytime, anywhere."

That got a got smile out of her. "Mabel will want a blow-by-blow on the date, what should I tell her?" She giggled.

"Tell her your parents turned the dogs loose on me. She'll like that a lot."

I looked out the window and glanced into Union Square. There they were. It was the two apes from the bar in Sacramento. They worked for Little Joey Patrone, the runt who owned that rat hole bar. Little Joey may have been tough, but he wasn't the sharpest knife in the drawer, and these two clowns didn't add up to college material either. I decided I could take care of them on the Delta Queen, or at the very least, I could have a little fun.

I excused myself and went to the phone booth in the rear of the restaurant. I called police headquarters and told the desk sergeant that there were two thugs in Union Square with guns. I gave their description. I went back to the table and joined Kaitlin.

"Who did you call?" she asked.

"Hold on, you'll get a front row seat to the event."

She gave me a puzzled look. It took only a minute for the prowl cars to show up. There were two of them. The flatfoots got out and started roaming around. Those two dummies scattered like cockroaches when the light goes on. The cops didn't see them before they faded.

Kaitlin observed the show. "You did that, didn't you?"

"I sure did, but don't worry. I'll see them tonight on the boat for Sacramento."

"How do you know?"

"They are dumb, that's why. They can't help being stupid. They will be in a time and a place that I will control, then I will find out why they are following me."

"You are pretty good at setting them up, aren't you?"

"It's not something I do every day, but I know how to."

"That you do, and pretty well, I might add."

We both smiled.

I accompanied her on the short stroll to the library. There was a line a mile long at the desk, and Kaitlin went right to work, I waved to her as I checked in the corner at the lovebirds' table. Sure as rain, there they were. I worked hard in school, college, and law school, and I busted my hump studying for the bar exam. But nothing like these two. I went outside for a butt and was enjoying the sun when the lovebirds came out holding hands. She had her head on his shoulder. They looked happy, which is something everyone one of us wanted in this world. They talked for a while and went back in to work some more. I could follow these two kids for a year, and they wouldn't alter their schedule by a minute. I wondered how the meeting with their parents would go. I had a suspicion that it would not go well. The Wang's and the Broadcreek's, they might as well be the Hatfield's and the McCoy's.

I walked back to the office, grabbed my bag, and returned to the lobby. I told Marty where I was off to and told him about the incident with the cops.

"Meatheads," he said, chuckling. "At least they didn't get picked up by the cops for carrying a roscoe, dumb as a bagful of hammers."

We looked across the street. There they were, holding up a building and reading a newspaper. I told Marty that both of these gees were too dumb to read.

I crossed the street and walked right in front of Mutt and Jeff, then got into the Ford and headed to the Embarcadero. It was four thirty, too early, but I parked in my usual place and walked to the waiting room for the Delta Queen. I pulled out a magazine and tried to look enthralled. After a while I purchased my ticket, then I lit a butt. At ten minutes to five, Morehouse arrived. He was all cleaned up and sober. I couldn't believe that I didn't have to follow this gee around, that he came right to where I knew he would be. He lit a smoke in his cigarette holder while waiting to purchase a ticket. At five we started boarding. I went up to the deck that was open and above the bow. Just as the whistle blew and the workers were ready to remove the brow, here came Mutt and Jeff. I was going to make them wish they missed the boat.

I ran up to the pilot house. Charlie was at the wheel.

"Hey, Sean, how's it going?"

"Great, Charlie, I'm working a case. I need your help."

"Anything you need."

"Is there a dock you can pull into between here at Sacramento that is in the middle of nowhere?"

"Once we leave Suisun Bay, there are a million docks up the river."

"I've got a pair of tails. I am going to eat dinner, come up here, and put the drop on them when it gets dark. "

"I'll let the first mate know what's going on. If you could keep it quiet, I don't want to upset any of the passengers. I know a place in the bend of the river near Antioch where we can dump them off. I'll be going real slow and close to the pier, you just throw them off."

I nodded. "I have to check on the poker player. I'll be back later with coffee."

"Hey, Sean, if you shoot 'em on board, I don't want any blood on the deck, please." Charlie laughed.

"Don't worry, I won't shoot 'em. It will be too much fun dumping them off on a dark pier in the middle of Nowheresville."

CHAPTER TWENTY-FIVE

I slipped out of the pilothouse and made my way down to the dining room for supper. I went by the stateroom where the poker game was going on. The evening was warm and the windows were open and the wooden shutters were angled so I could see in a little. Morehouse was in the game. Smoke billowed out of the windows.

I dashed below. Tonight's special was beef stew and biscuits. I got a table and ordered a cup of coffee with fresh cream. I was looking over the sports section in the newspaper when Mutt and Jeff came in and got a table ten feet behind me. You could tell these two dopes were small-time; they both looked directly at me when they walked in. I was looking too, but I never raised my eyes up from the paper. When you are shadowing someone, you never make eye contact, period. You can walk by someone you are following twenty times in one day; they will only notice you when your eyes cross. These two clowns did everything but stop at the table and inform me that they were following me.

The waiter stopped by and refilled my coffee.

"What can I get for you, sir?"

"I'll have the stew special and an order of peach cobbler with vanilla ice cream. Hey, buddy, are you waiting on the table with those two gees behind me?"

"Yes, sir."

"Have you taken their order yet?"

"No, sir, I was on the way."

I slipped a five-dollar bill on the table. "You take their order, then you make sure you are real slow delivering their dinner. As a matter of fact, don't deliver their order until I am about finished with my dessert.

Okay?"

The waiter was perplexed, but he kept looking at the fiver.

"Is there going to be some kind of trouble, sir?"

"No trouble, just a little joke."

He looked over at the five again.

"What the hell, why not."

He took my order to the kitchen, then in about ten minutes he took Mutt and Jeff's orders. I could hear one of them complaining about the wait.

The waiter delivered my dinner and he asked if I wanted my dessert soon. I told him to go ahead and bring it now. I plowed through dinner and took my time with dessert. Mutt and Jeff were getting antsy; I could hear them calling the waiter. I finished my dessert, swallowed the rest of my coffee, and dropped three dollars on the table as I got up to leave.

The waiter was perfect with his timing. He delivered their dinner as I got up. I started strolling out of the dining room and Mutt and Jeff got up to make chase. I heard the pair complaining that they had to pay even though they were leaving. The waiter was great.

"I'm sorry, gentlemen, but we are in the middle of Suisun Bay and we don't pull in until morning. What's the rush?"

I ran as fast as I could to the pilothouse. Charlie was ready.

"We are ten minutes from Antioch. You got your pidgins ready to go?" Charlie asked.

"The two idiots ought to be up here looking for me in about a minute."

It was funnier than a sideshow with two geeks. Mutt and Jeff were right behind me, they knew I came to this deck. There was a chain across the access to the stairs to the pilothouse. It said CREW ONLY. They went around the upper deck, clockwise, and looked around every corner. When they started to round the corner to go to the starboard side, I moved to the port side of the pilothouse. I timed the two idiots, who were very helpful. When they came around for the third time I went to the bottom of the stairs from the pilothouse, where there was a little alcove that went out on to the deck. Mutt and Jeff walked right by me, I came in right behind them with a .45.

"Evening, boys. Bring those hands out of the pockets real slow and turn around." They did so in complete shock.

"Where did you come from?" Mutt said.

"I was behind you two the whole time."

They looked at each other in amazement. I waved the gun to my left and motioned them to a bench right behind me.

"Put your hands on the wall, bring your feet way back and get on your toes," I said. "Come on, lean into it. You two mugs know the drill."

I patted them down. They each had a roscoe, wallet, deck of smokes, and a bad attitude. I told them to stand up, put their hands in their coat pockets, and lean against the rail. They did as they were told, and started sniping at each other.

The tall one started barking at the short fat guy. "Nice going, Frank. You really knew where this guy was all right."

"Shut up, Karl, you moron. We screwed up. Leave it at that."

I looked over the wallets. There was fifty bucks in each wallet: four tens and two fives apiece. I pulled the bills out and laid them on the bench. I looked over the IDs.

"Francis Flegger?" I gave him a puzzled look. "I got a sister named Francis." It was a hot button, you could tell.

"It's Frank, gumshoe."

"Hey, if my name was Francis, I would go by Frank too. Francis is kind of feminine sounding, you know."

"Keep riding me, flatfoot, and I'll strangle you with your own necktie." Francis was red and boiling now.

"Just to fill you in, Francis, I'm the one holding the gun. Shut your cake hole."

"You are going to pay for this, peeper. I guarantee it."

"Talk's cheap, just like your mother, Francis."

I looked over the second wallet, property of Karl Krieger. "Nice Kraut name."

They were steaming, but they kept it shut. "By the way, how was dinner, boys?"

They both got a look on their face like the light just went on. I looked over the rods.

"Wow, a 1908 Parabellum Luger. I'm impressed, you don't see many of these around. Over here, over there, that the Yanks are coming." I threw it over their heads and into the river. It made a loud splash.

The tall guy was not happy. "I paid fifty bucks for that rod, pal."

"Don't worry. You have fifty bucks here to buy a new one, yegg. Well, you had fifty bucks." I took the bills off the bench and folded them in half and put them in my left side suit pocket. "Dinner bucks for dates with the girlfriend. Thanks, boys."

They were growing even more agitated. The tall one was starting to come unglued.

"You are a real coldhearted bastard, pal."

"That's what everybody keeps on telling me, pal. Wow, a Webley-Fosbery. Even rarer yet." I threw the other gun over their heads again, and it made an even louder splash then the last one. That brought a response from the little guy.

"My mother gave me that roscoe."

"My heart bleeds for you, Francis. All right, let's get to brass tacks, boys. I don't have all night. Who sent you to follow me?"

"Screw you. Figure it out for yourself, asshole." Karl said.

"I know you boys work for Little Joey Patrone. Why does little Joey care about me?"

"You are such a know-it-all wise guy. Ask your slut girlfriend, maybe she knows." He got a broad smile on his face.

I never took my eyes off the pair. I called up to Charlie and asked him to blow the whistle for ten seconds. He did.

I fired a round, right between the two of them while the whistle screamed into the pitch-black night. They jumped three feet in the air.

"Jesus Christ, you could have killed us."

"If I wanted to put a round in you two, you'd be floating face down in the river. Last time I'll ask: Why is Little Joey having you two follow me around?" I aimed the gun right at Karl.

"You are poking around some architect guy that owes him a lot of money. He thought you were muscle from somebody else. He wants to make sure he gets his dough first. We were supposed to scare you off."

"Tell Little Joey that I was shaking in my shoes. All right, clowns, we are going down to the main deck, no trouble, don't bother the passengers. You two are getting off the boat." I called up to the pilothouse above.

"Hey, Charlie, how much time do I have?"

"I'm slowing down now, Sean. About three minutes."

"All right, boys, let's go, down the stairs, nice and quiet. You make any false moves and I'll throw your bodies in the river just like the rods. Trust me, it's better to walk off than swim off." They went where they were told. We walked all the way up to the bow. The first mate was there and opened a gate that led to the bow and the capstan area.

The Delta Queen snugged right up to the pier. It appeared out of the darkness; there were no lights at all. The boat suddenly was suspended in its spot.

"Get off both, of you." They did as they were told.

I threw them their wallets and smokes, with ten bucks each folded inside the cellophane cover. After all, they were in the middle of nowhere.

"I see you two mugs again, anywhere, anytime, and I'll kill you right on the spot." They said absolutely nothing.

Charlie was like a magician with the Delta Queen. All of a sudden, the paddlewheel went into reverse and we stated going sideways away from the pier. As we backed away, Charlie laid on the whistle for three short blasts. He spun the boat around on a dime and we returned to our intended course. It was ten o'clock by my watch. I felt a little sorry for

Mutt and Jeff. OK, not really.

I ran to the bar and got two fresh cups of coffee and went to the pilothouse. Charlie was laughing.

"That was great, Sean. That whole thing couldn't have been better timed."

"Hey, Charlie, where did we dump them off at?"

"You'll love this: a sewage treatment plant, ten miles from anything."

The first mate, name of Logan, came in. "That was perfect boss, you timed it like a Swiss watch. Then he addressed me. "Hey pal, why did you give them their smokes and money back?"

"I gave them ten bucks each to get home on. I gave them their butts, but I kept a little something they might need right about now."

I opened my mitt and showed them Mutt and Jeff's matches. They were rolling in the pilothouse. Yep, I said to myself as I lit a butt, I am a real coldhearted bastard. The coffee and smoke tasted extra good tonight.

CHAPTER TWENTY-SIX

Charlie was relieved of his watch at midnight. Since he was off, and I was all keyed up, we went down to the bar for a nightcap.

"Thanks, Charlie, that worked out great." I said.

"No problem, Sean. You have to do this kind of thing very often?"

"Most of the time I am sitting in a car, standing on some street corner, or standing in the freezing rain. It usually isn't this much fun."

We talked about life in the Navy, law school, women, the freedom of being in command in the pilothouse, baseball, and more about women. It was all laughs, most of it.

Charlie got quiet for a second. "They spent a fortune on these boats and now they're building bridges all over the delta. A lot of people think these boats will be obsolete in a year or two. Then I guess it's back to tug boat work for me." He waved at the bartender for another. I asked for one too.

"What else could you do if this line of work went away?"

"I could do a lot of things for money, but I love doing this. I love working the river. I'll tell you, Sean, it kind of scares me, all this bridge talk shutting the business down."

We finished our drinks and went out on deck for fresh air.

"Charlie, give me a call if you ever need a reference or to point you in the direction of a job." I handed him a card. "I know we are going to run into each other again, pal."

Charlie shook my hand with great warmth. "Back at you, pal." Away he went to catch a few winks. I did the same thing.

I woke up just as we were pulling in at five thirty. I got a shower, cleaned up and went below for eggs, sausage, and biscuits and gravy.

Man, do I love biscuits and gravy, especially when the biscuits are light and fluffy, and these were. I had a couple of mugs of fresh coffee with that farm-fresh cream.

At six forty-five, I went to the purser's office and asked if I could stay onboard for a few hours. I told them I had an appointment in town at eleven. He told me I could wait as long as I liked since I had a return ticket to San Francisco. I was in the forward lounge. I took a pair of stairs up one deck to the Texas deck, located right above the purser's office. The bar there had a wraparound view of the city. Since we were docked bow in, I was in a position to see everything, including that sleazy little hotel and bar where I would find Little Joey Patrone.

The bar was closed, but coffee service was available and I took full advantage of that. I wasn't here to follow Morehouse, as I knew he was sleeping it off at the fleabag. I was here to meet Little Joey, but I wanted Mutt and Jeff to come home before the visit.

I thought it would be a couple of hours, but I was wrong. I had read the entire Sacramento Bee and San Francisco Chronicle, even the obituaries. Several crew members asked if they could get anything for me. At noon, I asked a housekeeper to send up a waiter so I could order lunch. She told me they were closed, but they could rustle up a sandwich. At twelve thirty she brought me a great roast-beef sandwich on sourdough, macaroni salad and a pickle. She even brought me a cold bottle of Coke and a glass with ice. I was in heaven. She gave me a bill for sixty cents. I gave her three dollars and thanked her.

At one thirty, the purser came by to check on me. He asked if he could get me anything. I told him my appointment was a no-show so far and that I had run out of things to read. He said there were a couple of books left on board he would bring a few by. Ten minutes later he came with three books. One of them was an Ernest Hemingway book, The Fifth Column and 49 Short Stories. I grabbed that one and thanked him profusely. It was a San Francisco Library book. I guess I was going to have to read it, then return it to a certain librarian I know.

I skipped the play and went to the short stories. I was reading one called My Old Man, about a grumpy old man who was a horse trainer and his estranged jockey daughter. It was a pretty good read. That carried me to four thirty. I went to the head again and I was ready to sit down when an old battered truck stopped in front of Little Joey's place. Out of the back of the bed crawled Mutt and Jeff. They looked like they were dragged all the way there. They dusted themselves off, put their hats on, and marched into the bar heads down. It was time for a short visit.

I left the Delta Queen and walked across the street and into the bar. I stood in the corner closest to the door, wanting to scan the place before I barged in. I ordered a beer. The bartender that was here the last time I was here was working. I asked him if Little Joey was in. He was indignant. "Who wants to know?"

"A guy that needs to see him about some business," I said.

"Buzz off, copper." He wiped the bar with a towel and walked away.

I threw a buck on the bar and walked toward the office door in the back. The bartender called me back.

"Hey, buddy. Why didn't you tell me you were a private eye and not a cop?"

"How did you know I was private?" I asked.

"You paid for your beer. A cop would have walked without paying. Little Joey is in there, but be careful. He keeps a short-handled shotgun in a leather holster under the desk."

"Does he have any other apes besides the two garbage men in there now?"

"One other, but he is out. If he comes, I'll throw a glass against the wall to warn you."

"Why would you do that?" I asked.

"Little Joey just beat that old woman Alice for no good reason. He did it for kicks, so I figure he is due a little payback."

I thanked the guy and made my way to the office door. When I got there I drew both .45s and kicked the door in. The office was long and narrow, with thin windows at the top of the ceiling and a large desk at an angle in the right corner. Mutt and Jeff were in chairs to the left side of the desk. Little Joey Patrone was sitting behind the desk like a king. They froze when I blew the door open, and kicked it closed for privacy. With one .45 aimed at Mutt and Jeff, the other at Little Joey, I bull rushed in and butted the desk as hard as I could into the corner and against the wall. Little Joey squealed, squirming to get his pinned arms free.

"Anybody moves and I'll paint your brains on the walls," I said. "Not that there would be that much to get on the walls."

They all sat there with not a whole lot to say.

"Hi, boys. How was the ride home?" I smiled broadly.

"Asshole," was all Mutt said.

"All right, Little Joey, with your left hand bring that little shotgun out by the handle and drop it on the desk." I pushed on the desk again and he squealed even louder.

"You only get one chance to get this right, fat boy."

I let off on the desk and Little Joey slowly brought out the shotgun. He tossed onto the oak desktop and it bounced a couple of times. I picked it up and threw it through the open window; it made a loud splash when it hit the water.

"All right, boys. On your feet and up against this wall. You two should be experts at this by now."

They did as they were told. It was a good thing I checked; they weren't back for long, but they both had roscoes again.

"Well, Francis, it looks like Mommy went out this morning and bought you a new rod, how thoughtful." Out the window the rods went.

"Put your hands in your suit pockets and sit down and shut up." They obeyed like a pair of trained seals at the circus.

I heard a glass hit the wall and the door creak behind me. I put a .45 against Little Joey's forehead. "He comes in, you all die."

They all screamed in unison. "Bobby, get out and stay out, you are going to get us all killed."

The door slammed shut. I took the .45 away from Little Joey's head and sat down in front of the desk. "Why are these two hatchet men following me around, Little Joey?"

He was covered in sweat; his eyes were darting back and forth between me and the .45.

"Morehouse owes me a bundle of greenbacks. I thought you were horning in." His upper lip was quivering.

"How much does he owe you?" I said.

"What are you, his accountant?" Little Joey summoned a little indignant smile. I got up and hit him on the side of the head with the .45. He started bleeding.

"Jesus, O'Farrell, take it easy," he screamed.

"How much, Little Joey?" I pressed the .45 harder into his forehead.

"Fifty-seven grand." He turned and closed his eyes.

"FIFTY-SEVEN GRAND? How come you let him get that deep in the hole? No bookie would ever let a loser like Morehouse keep on gambling. Has he ever paid you?" I said.

Little Joey was looking at the gun.

"No, he has never paid me a thing. His partner Wheeler has been giving me a taste every week or so to keep the train rolling, so to speak." He raised his eyebrows in a knowing way.

"And why would Wheeler do that?"

"Hey, O'Farrell, you're the private detective. DETECT."

I fired a round over Little Joey's head. Mutt and Jeff jumped so high they nearly hit their heads.

"I kill you three and they will give me a public-service award for helping keep Sacramento clean of garbage. This is the last time I ask: Why would Wheeler do that?" I brought the .45 right under Little Joey's nose.

"Wheeler is connected, for Christ sakes. He's part of the mob in

Chicago." I moved the end of the barrel back and forth over his lip.

"Holy shit, watch it with the gun, O'Farrell. Wheeler has Morehouse by the short ones."

"What does he want?" I screamed.

"I swear to God, I don't know. But whatever it is, it worth a hell of a lot more than fifty large to these guys. They pay me five hundred a week to keep Morehouse drunk and losing."

A thought came to mind. "How does the wife fit into this?"

"The good-looking doctor? Hell if I know where she fits in. She's a cockhound, that's for sure, and Wheeler is banging her every chance he gets."

"Shit" was all I could say.

CHAPTER TWENTY-SEVEN

I stood there staring at Little Joey. What was there to say? I blasted more questions at him, but he was spent. It seemed that Wheeler ran the game at the St. Francis, the game on the Delta Queen, the backroom game at Little Joey's, and he even had guys at Bay Meadows race track with markers on Morehouse. Morehouse was so deep in a hole he was never going to crawl out. The big question was: Where did Connie fit it with all this? Where did I?

As I backed out of the office. I threw two books of matches to Mutt and Jeff. "I forgot to give you two these last night, boys."

That brought a hearty "Screw you, O'Farrell."

I kicked the door open and the third guy, Bobby, was leaning against the bar, both hands on the morning paper. He was smoking and his gun was lying on the bar. I put the .45 on the top of the paper and pushed it down. The gunny was surprised.

"Nice cover work on the door, junior," I said.

With my left hand, I grabbed his revolver and slid it into my coat pocket. I nodded to the bartender and left a five on the bar. He returned the nod. It was the best money I spent on this trip.

I slowly walked across the street to the Delta Queen, and made it just before the whistle blew. I was at Little Joey's just less than fifteen minutes, but I had lost complete track of time. I was lucky to make the boat. I checked in with the purser, got my room key, and learned that Charlie was off this run. That was okay with me, I wasn't in the mood for talk. I had a quick dinner and went back to my room to read and get a good night's sleep. But first I had a smoke at the rail and tossed the gunny's rod in the river. I was beginning to fill the Sacramento River with armament.

The next morning, I was waiting in the front lounge when Morehouse came in and sat two chairs over from me. He was crying and couldn't control himself. He looked the worst I had ever seen him. Some guy walked by and laughed at Morehouse, and that made me sick to my stomach. To see any man suffer like this was more than I could take. The thought that his wife was giving up on him was unforgivable. The fact was that Randall Morehouse had given up on himself too.

We docked at the Embarcadero and Morehouse pulled himself together and staggered off the boat. Two gees from his office were there. The two suits each grabbed an arm and helped him walk along. It was pathetic to watch. I hung back for a couple of minutes, then I walked over to the Ford and drove to the office.

I called Connie Morehouse's home. It was Wednesday and she was scheduled to be off. The maid answered the phone and she told me Connie was out, and didn't know when she would return.

I had a hunch, I called Morehouse and Wheeler, and asked for Wheeler. Surprise, surprise, Wheeler was out for the day and they didn't know when he would return. I played another hunch, and played the secretary.

"Hey, this is Bennie from Thompson Motors. We were expecting Mr. Wheeler to pick up his Chevy convertible, and it's been ready for a few hours."

"Well, I'm sorry," she stammered. "Hold on one minute." She came back a few seconds later. "Mr. Wheeler drives a red Ford convertible. Do you have the right Mr. Wheeler?"

"Oh, I'm sorry. I pulled the wrong index card and the wrong Mr. Wheeler. Sorry for the trouble."

I drove over to Connie Morehouse's. Sure enough, there was Wheeler's red Ford Deluxe convertible parked right behind her yellow Cadillac LaSalle. I parked right in behind them, I didn't bother to knock on the front door. It was three in the afternoon and the last time I was here the staff left at noon on Wednesday.

I walked around and looked over the fence into the back yard. It was just as Little Joey described it. They were on a chaise lounge. He was letting her have it, and they were definitely enjoying themselves. The all-white outfit that she wore to seduce me was on the deck. There was nothing seductive or sexy about it; she was working the guy like a pro skirt. It was almost violent; he was behind her, pulling her hair like it was a horse's mane. He finished, got off her, and they jumped into the pool, where they started up again. How romantic. I breezed before I puked.

I got back in my car and drove off. It was at moments like that, that I hated being a private detective. I drove back to the office, head spinning the whole way. Was Wheeler using Connie the same way he was using her husband? Was she in on it, or was she just another stupid twist?

I parked in front of the office. Morehouse, looking all cleaned up, was coming out with the two assistants that had gotten him at the boat. They got in a car and drove off. I passed a brunette in a blue dress on her way out and asked Marty if Morehouse had a secretary. He said, "Yes, that was her you just passed."

I took the stairs up to Morehouse and Wheeler. The lights were out; everyone had bugged out early. It took ten seconds to pick the lock and gain entrance.

I flipped the lights on, so if someone saw me they wouldn't be suspicious of a guy in a dark office. I went through Wheeler's office first. There was not much there, but I found a personal letter addressed to Tony Giovanni. It was from his mother. I made note of the name. There were some files without labels or headings. Definitely balance sheets. On one it was marked in pencil on the upper right hand corner as DQ. It had a long list of dates with amounts lost. Another was HOTEL, STF, and another BAR. All had dates and amounts. I ran a quick total; it was over one hundred grand. Morehouse was up to his neck in debt to these guys. As I was rifling the top desk drawer I found a bunch of matches, which is not uncommon. But there was a box of matches from the Chinese Social Club of San Francisco. It's not the kind of night spot a white guy drops into. There is gambling going on there, though, and maybe it was Giovanni's kind of place.

I moved to the next office, that of the little guy, Brian Child. There was nothing there as well. It didn't even look like these guys did anything at all. He had an engineering certificate on the wall from Stanford University that looked phony to me. The left-side middle drawer had a .38, with a filed-off serial number. In his credenza, I found an Illinois driver's license for Paul Petri. Again, I made note of the name.

In the next office, Michaels and Linderman shared the space. They also had phony-looking degrees. But they were pretty good fakes. Someone spent some big bucks. Michael's desk had .38 ammo and Linderman had a blackjack. Not the usual tools for young architects. They too had Illinois drivers' licenses. Linderman's real name was Walter Rossi and Michael's was James Rizzo. Both were from the near west side of Chicago.

I made a couple of notes and faded. As I closed the door, I heard the elevator ding. I slipped into the head and waited. It was Wheeler, who went into his office and closed the door. I quietly slipped up the stairs to my office.

I called Vinnie Castellano and asked him to contact Chicago and run the names Tony Giovanni, Paul Petri, Walter Rossi, and James Rizzo. I told Vinnie it was important. He said he would call as soon as possible.

I called Righty and Lefty at the club. I made a request and they agreed. A little slow to say yes, but they knew the score.

I then called Ashwythe and Dunderbeck and made the same request. Dunderbeck whistled. "Are you off your nut, O'Farrell?" I didn't answer. He agreed and I hung up.

I called Kaitlin at the library. Just my luck, Mabel answered.

"Oh, it's you, handsome. You calling for Katie? Hold the line while I look for her." She slammed the phone hard in my ear. I was out of gas and didn't have time to play with Mabel. I put on my hat and coat and turned off the light.

As I was closing the door, the phone rang.

"Hi, Sean, it's Kaitlin. Sorry about the phone. Mabel slammed the phone down on you, but at least this time she told me you called. I think she is warming up to you, big guy. What's up?"

"I've had a bad day, Kaitlin, and it's not over. I just wanted to hear your voice, okay?"

"That's really nice to hear Sean, really nice."

"I have to run but I'll call you for a date, if you are available?"

"For you, anytime." My heart skipped a beat. I hung up the phone and checked my watch: 6:30 p.m. I grabbed Marty from the newsstand and we walked across Union Square and checked in at the front desk of the St. Francis, where I asked for Jerry Ronkowski. He took us up to the Borgia Room.

All I had to do was wait. The fireworks were about to begin and there was no way to stop it.

CHAPTER TWENTY-EIGHT

The Borgia room at the St. Francis Hotel was very elegant. A little on the small size, but perfect for our purposes. It was generally used for weddings of one hundred or fewer. There was a divider in the middle of the room, and I decided to put one couple behind it.

There was a small conference table set up with eight chairs and a tablecloth. There were pitchers of water and glasses.

The Broadcreek's were the first to arrive, at 6:55. Charlie was outside; I told him to keep everyone out except the principals. I shook hands with both of them and thanked them for coming. Broadcreek didn't seem to be in a fighting mood. I shook hands with Ashwythe and thanked him too. I escorted them to some chairs behind the divider.

The Wang's arrived with Loc, or Lefty as I called him, and Jimmy Chin. Jimmy held a chair for Mrs. Wang and they sat at the conference table on one side. Lefty took up a spot behind them, and Jimmy found a quiet corner.

Heart racing, I brought the Broadcreek's to the table. Ashwythe got the chair for Mrs. Broadcreek. The two sides were staring hard at each other. No one knew what to make of this, or why they were here.

I started the ball rolling.

"Before I make introductions, I have to request one thing from all parties. When children's welfare and best interests are in jeopardy, parents will do anything to protect them. I know that all the parents in this room have the best interests of their children in mind. I request that everyone remain seated and please be civil."

I took a drink of water. I pointed to the Broadcreek's. "May I present Mr. and Mrs. William Broadcreek. Mr. Broadcreek is the Deputy

Attorney General of the United States of America in charge of a special task force investigating crime and corruption in Chinatown here in San Francisco."

The Wang's turned bright red, but did not move.

"Mr. and Mrs. Broadcreek, may I present Mr. and Mrs. Chin Wang, owner of multiple business enterprises in Chinatown and the President of the Chinese American Benevolence Society."

It was the Broadcreek's' turn to go red. Broadcreek was the first to blow. "O'Farrell, what the hell kind of trick is this? Why the hell are we here?"

He started to get up, but Mrs. Broadcreek and Ashwythe helped him back into his chair.

"Mr. and Mrs. Wang have a son named Kuai. He is an engineering and architecture student at the University of San Francisco. His parents hired me to gather information about the young woman he is dating. They wanted to ensure that their son was safe."

I let the words hang there for a minute. "Mr. and Mrs. Broadcreek, your daughter Dorothy is that young lady."

All four parents went numb. They just sat there with blank looks. A couple of minutes passed before Mr. Wang removed his glasses and wiped them with a hanky. He was more shaken than his wife. But she was pretty shaken too.

Mrs. Broadcreek was tearing up. But Mr. Broadcreek was getting angry.

"My beautiful daughter is dating a murderer. How low can she possibly go? I never dreamed she would crawl in the gutter with a lowlife like you, Wang."

Wang was starting to get up, but Mrs. Wang and Lefty helped him back into the chair. He composed himself.

"I know it is your duty to destroy my business interests and me personally, Mr. Broadcreek. This is entirely acceptable, for that is your duty and your job. When I arrived in San Francisco there were three to five murders a day in Chinatown, we were killing each other like dogs in the street. Children were sold like cattle and drugs were everywhere. I have fought off many enemies for many years and now I control Chinatown. There has not been a murder in three years, and before that it was seven years. I know that I am not a saint, that I am what I am. I have several children, but none of them are involved in my business.

"The youngest is my son Kuai. He plans to do good works, build public housing and assist the poor. He is honest, hardworking, and he rejects my ways and we are at odds at most times. I am many bad things, but I am a good father, and my son's greatest sin is that he has me for a father. He does not deserve to be called a murderer, by you or anyone for that matter." Wang was shaking; his wife put her hand on his arm to calm him.

The Broadcreek's were taken aback. But Mrs. Broadcreek spoke. "Our daughter is the exact same way; she talks about public housing, designing city parks, beautifying the city. If I may ask a question, Mrs. Wang, please do not be offended? How do you feel about your Chinese son dating a Caucasian girl?"

Mrs. Wang met her eyes. "There is much hate and distrust in the Chinese community towards whites. All I ever told my son was to marry someone who was true, honest and loyal to him. I never mentioned what her color should be."

Both mothers were in tears.

I stuck my nose in. "Ladies and gentlemen, I started this assignment expecting one thing and I got another. Both of your families are in a very precarious situation. How you approach and handle this situation could greatly affect your future relationships with your children."

All the parents' eyes were locked in on me.

"I'm a Catholic. A high school buddy of mine went to UCLA and fell in love with a beautiful young girl. They got married; the problem was she was a Presbyterian. Both sets of parents boycotted the wedding and broke off all contact. My buddy and his wife had two of the cutest twin girls ever to step foot on the face of the earth, and the grandparents have no idea. I am a private detective, not a family counselor. I don't know what your children's intentions are. All I know is that both sets of parents here can do a great deal of damage."

As I was finishing this statement, Dunderbeck and Righty came in with the kids. The lovebirds were holding hands. Dunderbeck and Righty got them chairs at the head of the table. All was quiet.

From out in the hall there was a scuffle. I checked and Marty had given a reporter a wooden shampoo with his old billy club. He and Jerry were dragging the reporter's unconscious body to the elevator. Marty shrugged.

"I told the newshawk the mayor wasn't in here holding a secret meeting, and the dumb bunny wouldn't listen."

I went back in. It was quiet for several minutes; I don't know what I was expecting. I don't think anyone else did either. Finally Dorothy Broadcreek broke the silence.

"Mom, Daddy, I am engaged, and I have been engaged for almost a year. Kuai and I have been discussing the entire year how to tell you. I know what Mr. Wang does, and I know what you do. Kuai and I have never had an argument over anything at all, with one exception. When, and how we should tell our parents about our relationship. This thing is tearing both of us up. We just simply want to get married and be happy. We don't know what to do."

Broadcreek was composed.

"Dorothy, what would you expect me to do? Go to the wedding, sit at a table with the Wang's, then go back to work and do my best to put him on Alcatraz for the rest of his life? Jesus Christ, Dorothy, he isn't just an incorrigible street thug in Chinatown. He is the Lord of Chinatown. Do you have a plan for holidays, christenings? Do these savages believe in baptism?"

Wang responded. "Mr. Broadcreek, does the name Chin Fong mean anything to you?"

"No, why should it?"

"Your special task force took Mr. Fong into custody for questioning. You believed him to be involved in a smuggling operation. He was not. He owns a grocery store. I control all the smuggling in this town, I would know. Your men broke every bone in his hands with a ball peen hammer, then you released him when you discovered he had no useful information. He was an innocent man. But then again, the ends always justifies the means with your FBI, and you dare to call me a savage."

Dunderbeck, Ashwythe and especially Broadcreek squirmed on that one. Mrs. Broadcreek was looking real hard at him. She now knew the score.

Broadcreek got to his feet.

"I've had enough of this. Dorothy, if you want to lie in the gutter with this trash, you go ahead. But if you do marry this chink, you will be cut off. Home, school; your entire family will disown you."

Dorothy was crying, as was her mother and, believe it or not, Mrs. Wang. Mr. Broadcreek walked to the door, and without turning around, he called his wife. She didn't move.

"I said, we are leaving." There was still no movement.

The atmosphere was so thick you could cut it with a knife. The silence was deafening. Mr. Wang broke the silence.

"Jimmy."

"Yes sir, Mr. Wang."

"Put on your list of things to do tomorrow to call the University of San Francisco and ensure the registrar receives sufficient funds for Miss Broadcreek's tuition. I am sure the university will accept money from a murdering chink."

That got Broadcreek turned around, all right.

"Mind your own business, Wang. You stay out of my family business."

"If I am not mistaken you have disowned your daughter, therefore you are no longer concerned."

Wang was sure smooth, all right. He was pressing the right buttons.

Broadcreek started walking around the room, huffing, puffing, stomping his feet, mumbling, muttering, and throwing a good old-fashioned tantrum. Ashwythe and Dunderbeck had seen this act before, and were doing a good job of staying composed. But you could tell that they were starting to grin, that they were greatly amused. Finally Broadcreek composed himself.

"Dorothy, I love you, and will always love you. You are my daughter and that will never change. I am sorry for the things that I said. Young Mr. Wang, I am sorry, I am not a prejudiced man, but my zeal in the performance of my duties has clouded my judgment. Mrs. Wang, I apologize if I have insulted you in any way. Dorothy, please forgive me, my temper has gotten the best of me again. I don't know what to do, so I will sleep on it.

"Special Agents Ashwythe and Dunderbeck, will you please take our daughter home, then take Mrs. Broadcreek home. Mr. Wang, would you have your men take Mrs. Wang and your son home?"

Wang nodded.

"Mr. Wang, would please join me in the bar for a drink. O'Farrell, you organized this mess, you're coming too. And while I'm thinking about it, you can pay."

CHAPTER TWENTY-NINE

Wang ordered a Johnnie Walker Black, neat. Broadcreek ordered a Glenlivet. I ordered whatever was the cheapest they had. It was the most I could afford. I don't make the kind of lettuce these high rollers make.

After the drinks arrived, the staring, glaring, and evil-eyeing began. They appraised each other like prizefighters.

Finally I had had enough and called for the bartender and asked for a bowl of nuts. I started barbering about absolutely nothing: Which nuts go better with Scotch; which was better, Johnnie Walker or Glenlivet.

Finally, in unison, they said, "SHUT UP."

I went to the other end of the bar and left them alone. Jerry Ronkowski and Marty pulled up a stool next to me.

"Are they talking at all?" Jerry asked.

"No, they are sitting down there, not a word."

After about an hour, they got up simultaneously and shook hands. Jimmy appeared in the doorway and handed Mr. Wang his hat, and they quietly slipped out. On his way out, Jimmy turned around and gave me the sign that he would call, and nodded.

Broadcreek was alone. I approached him and asked him if I could give him a ride. He asked for a ride to the ferry; there was one in twenty minutes. We piled into the Ford and drove without a word to the Embarcadero. As he got out, he put both hands on the door and looked in to me.

"You handled this whole thing like a pro, O'Farrell. I am at a loss for words, but thanks for your efforts."

He buried his hands deep into his trench coat pockets, lifted his collar, adjusted his Hamburg and walked to the ferry entrance. Within seconds he disappeared into the fog.

I went home and hit the rack, exhausted. However, there was no closure, no peace for anyone. I felt sorry for the kids and the parents. There would be no easy answers for anyone.

I got to the office at eight. I grabbed a paper from Marty and thanked him for his help.

"You missed the fun. The reporter got tough with Jerry; he wanted to call the cops for slugging him. Jerry told the guy to go ahead and call the cops; he would have him arrested for trespassing on private property. That shut that dummy right up."

I thanked Marty again, went to my office, and called Jimmy Chin. I asked how the Wang's were doing.

"They are okay, Sean. They were a little put out about the way you set the meeting up. But after I talked to them they realized you were in a no-win situation and you did what was best for all parties. I explained you were thinking about the kids and how to best control the meeting. It was a smart play. At the very least, Sean, Kuai is relieved that he doesn't have to sneak around anymore, and to be honest with you, I think Mrs. Wang knew something was up. She was not caught as flatfooted as Mr. Wang."

"Okay, Jimmy. Where do we go from here?"

"Obviously, there is no need to follow the kids. But be around; the Wang's may want to talk to you. I'll let things ride for a day or two, then I'll close out your bill, buddy. The Wang's really appreciate what you have done for them."

"Thanks, Jimmy. Keep me in the loop." I hung up.

I then called Kaitlin at home and got no answer. I looked at my watch: 9:15. I opened my bag and got out my two library books and decided to walk to the library and visit Kaitlin, a sort of kill-two-birds-with-one-stone type of visit. The elevator stopped on three, and Morehouse and Wheeler got on. Morehouse looked fit as a fiddle. I let them get out and head to the door. I handed Marty my library books and asked him to hold them.

Morehouse and Wheeler got into a large black 1936 Packard 120 closed coupe sedan. I was lucky that my Ford was handy, and I was behind them in seconds. They headed out of town going east. We were on the road for forty-five minutes.

When we arrived at Bay Meadows Racetrack, why should I have been surprised? Morehouse was a gambler; it would seem only natural that he would bet on bangtails.

The first time I laid eyes on Morehouse, he was reading a paper in the Delta Queen waiting room. I sensed he was hiding something behind it. It must have been a racing form. Morehouse was betting the ponies the same time he was in a card game.

All I know about horses is which end the feedbag goes on and which end the political promises come out, and that end requires a shovel. Morehouse and Wheeler wandered around the paddock and examined the horse flesh like experts. They made the occasional note on their racing forms with a pencil.

When it came time to place a bet, Morehouse went right to the twenty-dollar window and walked away with a fistful of betting slips. They went to the club stands and waited for the first race. It was ten thirty in the morning, but they were already taking a sniff from the barrel. Not my way of getting the day started.

The first race was called and the gamblers crowded to the rail. Morehouse was yelling for some nag named British Bobby to make the move.

"Come on, British Bobby. Here is the turn. Pour it on, kid," Morehouse cheered.

I checked the tote board. British Bobby was twenty-to-one. He finished last. Morehouse spent five minutes tearing up the betting slips. When it came to the second race, he dropped another bundle on another surefire winner named Bug Juice. At six-to-two odds, Bug Juice fared a little better, coming in fourth.

The same held true for the next four races. He went with long odds and lost. By four in the afternoon, Morehouse was tanked. There was one race left. He raided his wallet and all that was left was a dollar. He went to the one-dollar window and bet it on a horse called Lucky Lady, two to one.

The race was very close; all the horses were in a tight bundle at the rail around the clubhouse turn. There was some pushing and shoving going on, but Lucky Lady broke to the outside and won by a nose.

Morehouse was beside himself with joy. He must have lost a couple of thousand, but he waited in line to collect two bucks on a one-dollar bet. The line was so long, Wheeler convinced Morehouse that they had to leave. He looked at the betting slip with pride and put in his suit pocket for safekeeping. It was his greatest accomplishment of the day, maybe the week. He staggered back to his car.

I made up my mind that this was the end of the line for me on this case. I couldn't watch this guy destroy himself every day.

I followed them back to the Morehouse place; Wheeler helped him into the house. A few minutes later he came out with Connie in tow. She was dressed rather conservatively; she apparently had just got home from the hospital. She closed the front door and he was all over her, right in front of all the neighbors, dry humping her on the door and pawing her tits.

I wasn't trying to figure out what Randall Morehouse was doing anymore. I was trying to figure out what Wheeler was up to and whether Connie involved with him on a criminal level. It was time to talk to Connie Morehouse.

When Wheeler was done with Connie, he jumped back in the Packard and bolted. I stayed where I was for a few minutes, then faded.

I went back to the office and called the Morehouse place. Connie answered. "What can I do for you, Mr. O'Farrell?" She seemed a little miffed with the interruption.

"I have the complete picture on your husband. It's time for us to meet. When are you available?" I said.

"I'll clear my schedule, let's meet at the Cliff House tomorrow at noon. I'll make a reservation."

"I'll be there, and Doctor, please be prepared for a complete report."

"What does that mean?" she stammered.

"I have some information that could be unsettling; I just want you to be ready."

"All right, I'll see you at noon."

I hung up. I wanted her to be edgy. What she would tell me tomorrow will help me to determine her level of involvement. Whatever my suspicions were about Connie Morehouse, I still didn't think she knew that Wheeler was up to no good.

I called Kaitlin at home. I asked her to breakfast in the morning. She said she was working at nine and was getting a ride from her father. I told her to be at my place at seven thirty, and to tell her father that I was feeding him too. She giggled and said they would be there. I loved that giggle of hers.

As I was getting up to leave, Vinnie Castellano called.

"Boy, Sean, you can sure pick 'em. All four of those guys you asked me to check out are Chicago boys, all right. They are part of the Frank Nitti mob. He is the gee running the store while Big Al Capone is cooling his heels at Alcatraz."

I could hear Vinnie flipping through his notebook. "All of these guys have got sheets, but this guy you call Wheeler—his real name is Tony Giovanni—he is a real sweetheart. A Chicago cop told me that he killed a twelve-year-old kid with a knife because he was shaving a few pennies off the numbers rackets he was running. They couldn't make the charge stick. He knifed a cop when he was eight, for Christ sakes. He is ruthless as hell, Sean."

"Charming. Why can't I get an easy case for once?" I groused.

"Knights of Columbus meeting tonight, pal. See you there."

As I hung up the phone I began to wonder if maybe I should go back to practicing the law. It was safer.

CHAPTER THIRTY

I got up at five thirty and got cleaned up for the day, then got fresh bread from Petey at the bakery.

I returned home and went to work. I made coffee and starting browning my corned beef. I peeled and diced potatoes, onions, and beets, then mixed them and ladled them into some individual cassoulet pans. I set the egg timer and set the table.

I was making toast when Kaitlin and Shamus arrived. I gave Kaitlin a kiss and shook Shamus's hand.

I brought the dishes out and placed them on a plate and served. I thought Shamus was going to pass out.

"Red flannel hash. You are playing dirty, trying to win me over."

I reached for the plate. "Well, if you feel I am attempting to unduly influence you, I'll understand if you don't eat."

Shamus protected the plate. "I'd pull those fingers back, boyo, if you want to keep 'em."

I took a seat and asked Shamus to do the blessing.

"Oh Father in heaven. Please bless us and protect us, and we thank you for the food you gave us to nourish our bodies. In your name we pray; in the name of the Father, the Son and the Holy Ghost. For you, Sean, may you be in heaven for an hour before the devil knows you're dead." Shamus winked at me and smiled.

"So what's on your agenda, Sean?" Kaitlin asked.

"I am finishing two cases at once, and once I am done with that I am free till the next case."

"Well, good. You are free Saturday night."

I didn't like the sound of this. Shamus lowered his head and carefully examined his hash.

"Okay, what gives?"

Kaitlin buttered her toast and kept the suspense up.

"Saturday night is a fundraiser for Catholic charities, at the Fairmont. It's a formal dance. Do you dance, by the way?"

"I went to Catholic schools with nuns, Kaitlin. It was Dance or Die. By the way, I am aware of this event; the Knights of Columbus are the sponsor. Let me head off your next series of questions: Yes, I own a tuxedo; yes, I have a ticket; yes, I was going; and yes, I was going to ask you to come as my date."

Kaitlin spent a couple of moments formulating an answer. She was really milking it. Finally Shamus could stand no more.

"For goodness sakes, Katie, answer the man. Paint dries faster than you sometimes."

She was perturbed. "All right yes I'd love to go, and you"—she pointed to her father—"you mind your breakfast."

Shamus ate a spoonful of hash. "I kid you not, Sean. It's like her mother is sitting right here."

That brought a great laugh from everyone.

Shamus ate his toast. "Sean, this raspberry jam is wonderful. Where did you get it?"

"I made it. My mom and I use to make jam and jelly every summer when I was a kid. We kept on doing it together until I went to college. Now it's sort of a hobby. My cousin Petey and I go over to Marin County in the summer and pick raspberries, then we make the jam."

Time flew and they both had to get to work. I gave Kaitlin a kiss and shook hands with Shamus.

"My boy, it was like a little piece of Boston. I have missed red flannel hash so much, thank you." Shamus said.

I watched them drive away and they both waved. I cleaned dishes and straightened the living room a little, running the vacuum around for a few minutes. As I was doing this, I reviewed in my head the questions I would ask Connie. I knew the answers; I just didn't like any of the questions. I had a low sinking feeling about Doctor Constance Morehouse.

I did housework until eleven forty-five, then I hopped in the Ford and drove to the Cliff House. The Cliff House is located on top of a hill overlooking the Pacific Ocean. It was built as a private home, then converted to a restaurant, but it folded in 1925 due to Prohibition. It reopened this year after being extensively remodeled. This was my first look at the place.

I pulled up to the valet and the kid came running. He hopped in and gave me a kind of disappointed look.

"Is there a problem, kid?" I said.

"No, no problem, sir, other than the car."

"What does that mean?"

"It's a shame you couldn't get a good car." He smiled.

"Oh, you mean like a Chevy," I said.

"Now you are talking, pal." He pointed his index finger at me to punctuate that I was correct.

"Do you know how to double the value of a Chevy?" I asked.

The kid's face went blank. "No."

"Put half a tank of gas in it." I strolled for the door.

The kid rolled over laughing. "Okay, mister, you won that one all right. Have a great lunch."

The restaurant lobby was lovely. The view in the restaurant was million-dollar, one of a kind. You could see for miles in any direction. Directly below the windows were rocks on the beach with waves crashing into them, sending spray hundreds of feet in the air. You could hear the dull roar from below. The sun was bright and the fog was almost completely burned off.

It was high noon, and sitting all the way in the corner was Connie Morehouse, drinking a martini.

"Good afternoon, Doctor Morehouse," I said.

"Good afternoon, Mr. O'Farrell. I have been waiting all morning for your report." She smiled pleasantly.

I sat down and adjusted my chair. I put my hat in another chair. A waiter came hustling over and asked if I wanted a cocktail. I ordered black coffee instead. He returned to fill my cup with the steaming hot liquid. How appropriate, because the conversation was about to get hot as well.

"Dr. Morehouse, I have a lot to tell, but I have a great many questions for you," I said. "I have a feeling you aren't going to like them or me very much."

"Please, Mr. O'Farrell, I hired you to do a nasty job. I am expecting it." She took another sip of her martini.

"Yes, it was a nasty job." I said.

I lite a smoke and added cream and sugar to my coffee. I stirred with the silver spoon. I was stalling, so I just got to it.

"Your husband, Doctor Morehouse, is a degenerate gambler. He owes almost one hundred thousand dollars to bookies." I said bluntly.

That got her attention. She downed her martini and held up the empty glass and waved it at the waiter, who waved back.

"You must be exaggerating, Mr. O'Farrell?" There was a crack in that steely demeanor of hers.

"No, Doctor, I'm sure. He plays cards on the Delta Queen, he plays cards at the St. Francis Hotel, he's a regular at Bay Meadows Racetrack, he plays cards at a sleazy little fleabag hotel in Sacramento. He bets every nickel he has, and he always loses. He drinks while he losing and then he drinks after he loses. He sleeps in hotels that you wouldn't walk in, let alone sleep in."

She did not lower her eyes or break the gaze. Instead, she took a pull on the new martini, and without thinking she ate the olive and pearl onion.

"Is there another woman?" she demanded.

"No chance on that, Doctor. He just gambles. Now here comes

the really hard questions for you, Doctor. Are you faithful to your husband?" I delivered that question without fear.

She exploded.

"That is none of your fucking business, mister. I hired you to snoop into my husband's business, not mine." She spit out the words with the greatest amount of indignation she could muster.

"What do you know about your husband's business partner, Jonathan Wheeler, Dr. Morehouse?"

A shrug was all she gave me.

"Here comes the really bad news, Doctor Morehouse. Jonathan Wheeler is the man who owns all the paper for your husband's gambling debts," I said.

"Well, what about this Joey person in Sacramento?" She was starting to lose control; she was fidgeting in her seat.

"He works for Wheeler. Since we are getting everything straight, Doctor, you need to know that Jonathan Wheeler is not his real name. His real name is Anthony Giovanni, he is from Chicago, and he works for the mob. Organized crime." I let that sink in for a minute.

"Al Capone's mob, to be exact. His organization is being run by a guy named Frank Nitti. These guys kill people the same as barbers cut hair; it's just part of the business. Wheeler is a convicted, hardened criminal, and the son of a bitch has got his hooks into your husband, and he has got you in his bed." I glared at her without mercy.

I guess I should have left off that last part. It wasn't appreciated. She did her best to compose herself. She carefully dabbed her lips with a napkin and stood up. I kept my chair.

"We are done here, Mr. O'Farrell. Jonathan Wheeler is a decent man, a respected member of the community, and frankly, a better man than you are. You are fired. Send your final bill, you two-bit peeper. One of these days you will end up dead in the gutter or show up in my hospital with a bullet in you. You pathetic loser," she hissed. She allowed herself the satisfaction of a superior smile. She was feeling the full effect of the martinis and starting to slur her words.

"As you wish, Doctor. But one final piece of advice: Get a new fence in your back yard. I would recommend one that is a little higher, a tall guy like me can see over the top while you and Wheeler are doing the horizontal mambo."

She went to throw her drink in my face, but her glass was empty. Just like she was. She didn't know what to do, so she stormed off. As she was scurrying out, I called to her.

"Hey, Doc, you forgot to pick up the tab, don't worry, I'll put it in the final bill." I laughed as she stormed to the lobby. She heard me all right, as she hesitated for a second. Then she just kept going. She wouldn't give me the satisfaction.

I paid and went to the front. The parking attendant was there. "Hey, did you almost get run over by a yellow Caddie LaSalle?" I said.

"Gees, that twist is nuts. She almost closed the door on my hand too, plus she almost hit two people in the parking lot. And, if that isn't enough, she stiffed me. What's eating her?"

I handed the kid a buck. "Probably upset that she doesn't drive a Chevy," I said with a twisted smile as I lit a smoke.

CHAPTER THIRTY-ONE

In my office, I prepared the bill for Connie Morehouse. I was struggling with the idea of what not to include. Screw it; she was going to pay for my drinks with Charlie on the Delta Queen, as well as the drinks at the Cliff House. This was business, after all. Just because she wasn't happy with the facts, that was no reason for her to skip on the bill. I folded the bill and placed it in an envelope, I licked a stamp, and we were ready to go. It was hot this afternoon; I had the fan going in the office and it was still warm.

The phone rang. It was Marty from downstairs.

"Hey, Sean, Vinnie Castellano is a friend of yours, isn't he?"

"Yes, Vinnie and I are buds. Why?"

"His wife and little girl are down here in the lobby. The mom is taking the kid to see Dr. Grayson the dentist; the kid doesn't want to go and is throwing a first-class fit. The mom is beside herself. I called Vinnie and he is on the way, but she could sure use some help down here."

I grabbed my envelope and headed for the elevator. I didn't have my suit coat on because it was so warm. My guns were in the desk drawer. I left them there because I didn't want to scare little Mimi. She may be used to seeing her dad with a gun; I don't know how she would take seeing me with one.

When the elevator doors opened, Gina and Mimi Castellano were sitting on a bench next to Marty's newsstand. Mimi was pitching a fit all right: screaming, kicking, yelling, and crying, the full crop. I sat next to Mimi and didn't say a word. After a couple of minutes she stopped and said, "Hello, Mr. O'Farrell."

"Hi, Mimi. It's been a while since I saw you last. What are you, twelve years old now?" I said.

She smiled, "No, I'm nine."

"No, you can't be nine. Are you sure you aren't ten or eleven? You look a lot older than nine?" I smiled broadly at her.

"No, I'm nine." She lowered her head because she was ashamed of her tantrum.

"What are you doing today?"

She was kicking the heels of her shoes against the leg of the bench. Gina's eyes were moist; she was exhausted from dealing with Mimi. She gave me a warm smile.

Mimi was trying to explain herself. She had a tissue in her hand and was tearing at it nervously. I was about to say something to her when I saw it.

There are moments in your life when time stands still, when everything comes to a grinding halt. I looked out the front toward the large windows and the glass revolving door. There were three of them. All wearing long black coats and fedoras. It was too warm for outer coats. It came from underneath the first one in the revolving door: a Thompson submachine gun with a large barrel magazine. All three had matching Tommy guns, and now they were shoulder to shoulder.

"MARTY, GET DOWN! IT'S A CHOPPER SQUAD!" I yelled.

I grabbed Gina and Mimi and got behind a large pillar in the lobby, and heard the bolt actions go back on three Thompsons. One of the guys said:

"That's O'Farrell. The guy with the red tie."

I squeezed Gina and Mimi as hard as I could. They all opened fire at once. Bullets were flying everywhere. Their intent was to shower the lobby in bullets and let them bounce off the marble floor and walls, and find their way to me. For the moment I was safe; a design flaw in the lobby was saving our lives. When the building received its final engineering inspection in 1915, the city engineers determined that the lobby did not have sufficient bracing to be earthquake-proof. As a result, all the marble was destroyed, and additional steel structure and framing was installed in the lobby. The owner could not afford to replace the marble a second time. So he had the columns and walls made out of plaster, painted to look like marble, and varnished to shine like marble.

The bullets, instead of bouncing, went into the walls and columns and stopped there. The mechanics were out of bullets and stopped to reload. It was my chance. My only chance. My last chance.

I called out to Marty.

"Marty, I need my backup rod." I looked over at the counter; Marty's arm came out in a single move. The .45 skidded, skipped and danced across the floor. It stopped two feet from me. I told Gina to hold on tight to Mimi. I laid flat on my back and rolled into the open, and grabbed the .45. Two of the torpedoes lowered their Thompsons, set to finish me off; the third guy had a gun jam and was violently trying to clear it. I came out of the roll and put four slugs into the first guy. He dropped the Thompson; his arms went high in the air as he jolted backward. Then he was still.

But I was out of position to fire on the second guy, and he knew it. He smiled as he took aim and pulled the trigger.

Then God answered my prayers. From behind the counter, Marty stood tall with the Greener on his shoulder and let a barrel go. It lifted the guy two feet into the air. He landed against a pillar and froze there for a second before sliding down, leaving a trail of blood as wide as his shoulders. The gee had an astonished look on his face as hit the floor, deader than Kelsey's nuts.

Marty came from behind the counter and stuck the Greener in the third shooter's eye.

"What's it going to be, bucko: six years in the can for attempted murder, or six prisoners carrying your casket to an unmarked grave?"

The shooter tossed the Thompson and never took his eyes off Marty or the Greener.

"Okay, okay, I give up."

"Good move, kid," Marty said.

He took the butt of the Greener and coldcocked the guy, right on the forehead. The guy dropped to the floor. Marty ran to the cash register and tossed me a pair of handcuffs.

"Sean, put the nippers on this clown."

I put the cuffs on the guy, and ran over to Gina and Mimi. Gina was all right, but Mimi had been grazed on her leg by a bullet. She was white and in shock. I ran over to Marty's closet, took out a heavy coat hanging in there, and covered Mimi up.

I heard the sirens coming from every direction. Vinnie Castellano was the first through the door. Cops were everywhere, it was like a convention. The Chief of Police was there, along with ten to fifteen inspectors, a dozen uniformed cops, and finally an ambulance. The seas parted and the two attendants came through with a gurney. They carefully placed Mimi's limp little body on the gurney and secured her, and invited Vinnie and Gina to come to the hospital. Cops were yelling clear the way as they left the building. Gina and Vinnie looked scared to death.

The Chief Inspector, a guy named O'Malley, and Chief of Police Roger Gallatin came over to me. O'Malley did the talking.

"Marty tells me this ambush was aimed at you, O'Farrell. Is that true?"

"I heard them say my name and point at me before they opened fire. These guys worked the room like pros; I've never seen them before, though." My voice was a little shaky.

Gallatin looked around the lobby and shook his head.

"We had a quick look at the two dead guys. One of them was wearing a suit from Carson Pirie Scott and Company, and the other a suit from Marshall Field. Those are both Chicago outfits. All three had no ID. The Tommys had the serial numbers filed off. These guys were mechanics, all right. You are lucky to be alive, son." Gallatin put his hand on my shoulder.

"If Marty hadn't been here, we all would have been killed. I didn't have a roscoe on me. Marty keeps an extra .45 of mine down here for emergencies. Plus he has that street-legal cannon of his. He really came through."

"You saved the wife and daughter of one of ours, O'Farrell. We owe you." O'Malley said, trying to control himself.

"Vinnie Castellano is a lifelong buddy. I'd do anything for him."

Just as we were finishing up, Vinnie's loudmouth partner Jerry "Swede" Amundson showed up. He never wasted an opportunity to get under my skin. We are both members of the I Hate Your Guts Association.

Swede had a wide grin on his face.

"O'Farrell, I heard the good news you were in a shootout, too bad they missed."

I wasn't in the mood and stepped up to take a swing at the dumb ape, but Gallatin and O'Malley held me back.

O'Malley was honked off.

"Get back to headquarters, Swede, there's work for you to do there." The Swede faded.

"We are taking that Chi-town piece of shit down to the station; we are going to squeeze him for what he knows," the Chief said. "Why don't you come along with us, O'Farrell? You can be a big help."

"Let me go get a coat, hat and roscoe. I'll be there in a few." I shook hands with both men. They went to work cleaning up the crime scene. Police photographers were all over the lobby. One of the inspectors called out to anyone in general. "Hey we only got two Tommy guns. Where is the third?"

The Chief went to Marty, who was sitting on his stool, drinking coffee.

"There's a fresh pot, Chief. Want some?" Marty smiled.

"Martin Durrant, you slippery-fingered turd. We were partners for four years. You think I don't have you figured out?"

Gallatin went to the closet and took out the missing Tommy gun. "Marty, you'll never change."

"Gee, how did that thing get in there?" Marty took another drink of coffee, and everyone laughed.

I took the elevator up to my office and slumped down in my chair for minute. I replayed everything over in my head. It lasted a few seconds, but it seemed like hours.

I replayed it in my mind slowly. I was sitting on the bench, talking to Mimi. I saw the three men coming through the revolving door. I called to Marty. I looked at the revolving door again.

As I was replaying the sequence, it hit me like a ton of bricks. As the men were coming into the lobby through the revolving door, something caught my eye. Across the street, a woman was watching. She had a full-length white fur coat. She was wearing a white turban-hat kind of thing, and large dark sunglasses. I couldn't swear to it in open court, but I would have sworn it was Connie Morehouse.

CHAPTER THIRTY-TWO

As I drove the Ford to police headquarters, the radio announcer cut off the Andrews Sisters song "Bei Mir Bistu Shein."

"We interrupt this this program to bring you a special bulletin. A machine gun shootout at the Russell building in Union Square, San Francisco. Two men are dead at the scene and a bystander is at the emergency room at this moment. We will have a reporter on site and will file a report within minutes. The headline again: two dead in a Union Square office building lobby shootout. More to come at the top-of-the-hour news. This is Mitchell Baumgarter reporting. Stay tuned to KGO Radio for the latest fast-breaking news bulletins. We now return you to our regular programming."

Great, it's all over the news. I hit the gas pedal hard to the floor and flew to police headquarters. Once there, I ran up the stairs and asked the old gray-haired desk sergeant if I could use the phone. He didn't look up and thumbed in the direction of the front door.

He never looked up from his log. A young beat cop was walking by.

"Jensen, run this private eye piece of shit out of here." He looked at me hard. "This is a cop house, O'Farrell, for cops, not for two-bit peepers like you, regardless of the fact that Castellano calls you a friend. That means fade, gumshoe. Pay phone is down the street, pal."

I was scared, tired, and running on empty. I grabbed him by the shirt and pulled him close. "Please, I was involved in the Russell Building shooting. I have to call my girl right away. She may think I am dead. It's all over the radio."

He dropped the hard-guy act and handed me the receiver, asked the number, and dialed.

Just was my luck, Mabel answered the phone.

"What the hell do you want, handsome," she barked.

"Stop it, Mabel. I was just involved in a shooting at my office. Two guys are dead. It's being blasted over the radio. I don't want Kaitlin to find out and worry. I want to tell her I'm okay. Where is she?" My heart was racing.

"Jesus, she's in the stacks, Sean. Hold on, I'll get her." The phone hit the counter; Mabel screamed for Kaitlin across the library. A minute later Kaitlin, out of breath, picked up the phone.

I told her the story. "I didn't want you to hear this and worry," I finished.

"I'm off at three, where should I go?"

"I don't know, go on home. I'm here at police headquarters. One of the gunmen was taken into custody, I need to be here. I just didn't want you hear about dead guys in my building and have you worry."

"I'm okay. You take care of yourself right now. We'll catch up later."

"Okay, I'll call."

"Sean."

"Yes, Kaitlin."

"I love you."

"I love you too."

I hung up. This had been the worst day of my life. Two men were dead, and one of them at my hand. Then it hit me. I hadn't said those words in five years. I had only known Kaitlin O'Doherty for a month, but it was true. I did love her.

I handed the phone to the desk sergeant.

"Are you okay, laddie?" he asked.

"Yes, sir, I'm okay. I was also very lucky today; I could be on a slab right now. It's sort of hitting me."

"When you get out of here, young man, you find that young lady of yours and spend time with her. That's what is important in this life." His smile was genuine.

I climbed the stairs to the Inspector Bureau and looked around for O'Malley. Vinnie Castellano came up to me and gave me a big hug. "My God, Sean, how can I ever thank you, you saved my family, my wife, my little girl. What can I say?"

"Hold it, Vinnie, not so fast. That chopper squad was coming for me. I was the reason your family was in danger. How can I ever make that up to you?"

Vinnie put a hand behind my neck.

"Forgive what? Come on, the show is about to start. We need a hand."

"Show, what show?"

There were cops everywhere. There must have been fifty guys in the squad room. The old gray-haired desk sergeant was standing on a chair.

"All right, lads, the Chief and the Chief Inspector have ordered a show. We haven't done this thing in five years, so pay attention. Brown, you are the bookie. Select twenty officers to be bettors. Who is that young rookie from Union Square?"

Someone yelled out, "That's Tommy D'Amato."

"Where is he, then?"

Tommy waved and spoke up.

"Thompson, young D'Amato here is the designated puker. Show him how this works and make sure he has the timing right. Inspector Castellano, how is your daughter doing?"

"She is fine, Sarge, it's a minor wound. But they are going to keep her overnight because of shock. My wife is with her."

"All right then. Inspector Castellano, you are the hot wire. Make it look good. Friendly and Malone, you two along with Mr. O'Farrell here, will be the removers. Remember now, make sure, Inspector, you really sell it. Where is Amundson?"

"The Swede is coming up the stairs, Sarge," someone yelled.

"Good, thanks for making it on time, Inspector Amundson. You are the designated bull."

Amundson was as big as a mountain. He was six-five and easily three hundred pounds. He gave me a dirty look and moved off.

The sergeant ran his fingers down his clipboard. "Where the hell are those FBI guys? We need them for this. Bobby, will you run and get me a secretary from the pool on the fourth floor? We are almost ready to begin."

Ashwythe and Dunderbeck arrived in the squad room. They came over and Ashwythe asked, "Hey, O'Farrell, are you okay? We heard it was like the OK Corral at your office?"

"I'm lucky to be alive, guys, real lucky."

"We heard you saved a cop's wife and daughter, plus you capped one of the bastards."

"I'm just lucky to be alive. Damn it, I need a drink." I tried to light a butt, but my hands were shaking. Dunderbeck lit a match and patted me on the shoulder.

The sergeant was still getting things set up. "Bobby, get a blank warrant cover and give it to these two FBI guys. Are you two up to speed what you are doing here? Bobby, you brief these two Special Agents, and Inspector Castellano, you brief Mr. O'Farrell. Who is the designated suit?"

A young cop named Peterson came out of the locker room in a sharp-looking suit, tying his four-in-hand. "Ready to go, Sarge."

"Jennings and Columbus, you two are the coolers. When you take the FBI guys out, make sure that your guns are unloaded, no mistakes, and make it look good now. Closterman, you go down to the basement and get the tool bag, take it to the room."

The room was in pandemonium, with people yelling and cops running all over the place.

"Doyle, get a mop and bucket up to the room. Hurry, lad."

"Brown, you are the bookie. Get the petty cash box and distribute the singles to your bettors. Throw a few fivers in there for effect. Hustle, boyo.

"Crenshaw, you and Lafferman are strapping the suspect in. Make sure you go and get the wide straps out of the locker in the basement. Hustle, we only have a minute or two."

The Sarge continued to look up and down the clipboard. "Johnson, you be the handyman and go get the chair. Antonio, you and Peterson go down to the cells and get ready to bring our man up. I'll call when you are to come up. Is Marty Durrant getting changed in there, Peterson?" Peterson waved that he was.

Vinnie Castellano came over with two inspectors, Friendly and Malone.

"Okay, Sean, I know this looks like a circus in here. Let me explain what we are doing. Ten years ago they developed this show that they put on for suspects they want to talk. It's only been done a few times, and the Chief has to authorize it. We only do it when we need to break a suspect and time is against us. The last time we did it was five years ago, it was the Harrrigan kidnapping."

"I remember that one, you caught the guys, they confessed and then you found the boy in a box in warehouse a couple of hours later," I said.

"Exactly. We are doing our little show before the Feds came along and take the case away. These are out-of-town shooters; the Chief and the Mayor want the complete story before this bum gets taken away. It's pretty elaborate, Sean. I'm the live wire. My job is to try to kill the suspect. You three, your job is to stop me with everything you have and take me out of the room. We will go next door and watch the rest of the show through the glass. Trust me, Sean, you will enjoy this. It's a thing of beauty.

The gray-haired sergeant was screaming.

"Let's get moving, people. They will be bringing our man up in a few minutes. I want to tell the Chief that we are on schedule."

The Chief and Chief Inspector came into the room.

"That's all right, Pattie, I know you are on top of things. Well done, you got this thing set up in the less than an hour." The Chief walked over to Vinnie.

"Your friend O'Farrell here and Marty Durrant both have some balls. They saved your little girl and wife. How are they doing, lad?"

"She's okay, her mother is with her at the hospital."

"Maybe you should go back," the Chief said.

"Chief, she's okay. I needed to be here to thank Sean and Marty. Where is Marty?" Vinnie asked.

"They were taking his statement downstairs. Don't worry, you'll see him. He is going to be the bucket man." The Chief put his arm around Vinnie. "Everything is going to be fine, son. When we finish up the show, you head back to the hospital."

The Chief yelled across the room to the Sarge. "All right, Pattie, let's get this damn show rolling. Bring that Chicago turd up here. It's time for him to sing."

The room exploded into action, then suddenly it fell silent.

CHAPTER THIRTY-THREE

It was the greatest show on earth. That's what P.T. Barnum called it. I always considered the circus to be a sideshow with animals. Right now, they were getting the cage ready, which was the interrogation room. And the animal to be tamed was this mug from Chicago. The Chief of Police was going to be Frank Buck; hell if I know if the Chief was going to bring 'em back alive.

I went the station's largest interrogation room, deep in the bowels of the station. There were cops everywhere.

They brought the suspect into the room and closed the door. He was wearing a black hood. The only people in the room were me; the two Inspectors, Friendly and Malloy; and the two cops that brought in the suspect. The hall was dead quiet; you would think we were the only people in the building. The room had a couple of wooden chairs and a long table.

They pulled the hood off the guy and the show was beginning. I was leaning in the corner, smoking a butt. The shooter said nothing. He was a tough guy; his expression was all arrogance. He wasn't going to tell anybody anything.

The door opened and a cop came in with a steel-welded chair. There were steel square holes in the cement floor. The cop slid the legs of the chair into these slots and secured them with steel pins the size of pencils. He sat in the chair and rocked it as hard as he could. He stood, looked at the chair, and nodded. The cops who brought in the shooter shoved him in the chair and cuffed each hand to a hole in the chair seat. They took heavy straps and wrapped his legs and torso to the back and the seat. He wasn't going anywhere. Still, he kept that tough-guy look on his face.

They left and the sergeant who was the designated bookie opened the show. The room suddenly filled with cops holding dollar bills.

"All right, boys, the odds are two to one that the Swede gets him to talk. The last time a daisy was broke it took him twelve minutes. Here are the odds, boy: under five minutes, two to one. Between five and ten minutes, three to one. Over ten minutes, four to one. Over fifteen minutes are ten to one. I'm sorry, boys, but if you bet that the Swede kills him, it's only even money."

All the cops were griping about the odds.

"Enough already. The Swede has killed two guys, so I'm not laying down any large bets on him killing this Chicago piece of shit." He pointed to the hood in the chair.

The tough guy had to prove he wasn't scared.

"Screw you, gees, you don't scare me. Not even a little." He spit out the words with indignation.

The bookie went over and backhanded the suspect.

"You talk again and I'll carve your tongue out."

He turned back to his bettors.

"All right, who is in?" There was pandemonium; the bookie was taking bills and writing down numbers. You would think we were at Bay Meadows. All of this was not lost on the tough guy. He didn't look scared, but he was watching all right.

A little cop came in with a tool bag, and spread out a towel. He opened the bag and took out pliers, wire cutters, and a ball peen hammer. He placed a bucket with water on the table. The tough guy was looking at everything, but kept the mean look on.

Another gee walked in with a large truck battery on a rolling cart. It had some heavy-duty jumper cables, and heavy-duty rubber gloves. He took the bucket of water, threw in three sponges, and wrung them out. He then opened the clamps on the jumper cable and closed it again on a wet sponge. The tough guy was really paying attention now.

The door opened and the Chief walked in with a secretary. The room went silent and most of the uniforms flew out of the room. The Chief looked stern, cold, and steely. He walked over to the tough guy and got within two inches of his face.

"I'm Gallatin, the Chief of Police here in San Francisco. I'm giving you just one chance to tell us everything, do you understand?" The Chief was almost whispering. The tough guy was looking right at the Chief, not breaking his stare.

"You killed a little girl. Not just any little girl. That little girl was the daughter of one of my Inspectors. You don't come into my town and kill little girls; you sure as hell don't kill little girls of one of my cops, NOT IN MY TOWN!" He hit the guy in the face.

"What you don't know, dummy, it that our local Federal Building is being upgraded, and a few agencies were relocated to the building you hit. That makes this a federal bounce, which means one of two things. Murder in a federal case either gets you the Nevada gas, or you get to sit in the lap of Old Sparky. Either way, you are a dead man. I suggest you started talking while you can. Maybe we can cut a deal to save your skin.""

The door blasted open and Vinnie Castellano came flying in. He had a blackjack in his right hand. "You bastard. You killed my little girl, get the hell out of the way."

He flew toward the suspect. The three designated stoppers, myself being one, stopped him just within arm's reach of the tough guy. Vinnie was putting on a show; he got two or three swings with the blackjack as we were trying to pull him away. It took all three of us plus the Chief to stop him. He took three more really hard swings and almost connected. We were wrestling Vinnie back, and it really was a chore.

The Chief was screaming,

"You three get him the hell out of here." We pulled Vinnie out and the door closed. Vinnie kept up the screaming until we were at the end of the hall. We let him down quietly and went to the room next to the interrogation room. It had two-way mirrored glass and we could see everything. The show continued.

The Chief was talking to the secretary.

"Miss Hunter, please take a memo. The suspect was interviewed at five fifteen p.m. He confessed to the crimes at five forty-five and was killed trying to escape while in Central Booking. Please include the names of the twenty police witnesses. Make sure you get the coroner to sign a death certificate. Take a bottle of the good twenty-year scotch out of my lower desk drawer and give it to Doc Smith and be sure to thank him."

The tough guy was starting to look like a lobster being suspended over a boiling pot of water. He wasn't so tough now; he was tenderizing nicely.

The secretary left and Ashwythe and Dunderbeck entered the room, along with the cop who was designated the suit.

The FBI guys flashed their badges and held up the blue summons folder. "Special Agents Ashwythe and Dunderbeck, FBI. This is Deputy Attorney General Cranston."

The suit did the talking. "We have a material protection and witness order signed by a federal judge. You are to turn this suspect over to federal custody immediately."

Dunderbeck held up the folder. The tough guy was all for that by the look on his face.

The Chief yanked the paper and looked it over.

"This doesn't mean shit to me. This asshole killed a little girl of a cop and he is going to talk to me before he walks out of this room, or before we carry his body out."

The suit was putting on a good show. "That's enough of your crap, Chief. Uncuff him now!"

Next I got to see what the coolers were for. The three cops pulled their guns and stuck them in the sides of the FBI guys and the suit.

They pulled Ashwythe's and Dunderdeck's guns.

The cop with the suit was great.

"You will all go to federal prison for this."

The Chief was unrepentant.

"Who cares, take a bounce, mouthpiece. Boys, lock these three gentlemen in a holding cell, we'll let them go later," the Chief snarled.

They escorted the three men out. "You won't get away with this, Gallatin," the suit yelled. "I promise you that you are headed to prison for this."

The door to our room opened quietly. We all shook hands. It was an amazing performance. The tough guy looked like a giant marlin: hooked, landed, and about to be served up.

Marty Durrant came in a pair of janitor overalls, with a mop and a bucket on wheels. He was wearing a goofy-looking knit hat and thick glasses, and had an unlit cigar in his mouth. It took me a moment to recognize him. He even talked differently. He had a green heavy-duty garden hose over his shoulder. He hooked up the hose to a faucet in the wall in the corner and shuffled his feet like an old man.

"Here you go, Chief. I'll clean up the mess when you are done. Sorry, but I couldn't find any thick plastic to wrap the body in. I'll keep looking around." He shuffled out of the room.

The door opened and Jerry "Swede" Amundson entered the room. Vinnie keeps asking me why I can't stand Amundson. For one, he is a complete cement head. For another, he has a reputation for shaking down hookers, pimps, and gamblers. It is not simply a case of not liking the guy; I don't trust the guy, and I doubt that he has Vinnie's back. Coupled with the fact that he gets his jollies inflicting pain, he is my least favorite cop. I have to tolerate him to a certain extent because he is Vinnie's partner.

"Did a toilet back up in this room or something?" He grinned. "Oh it's only you, O'Farrell."

I didn't give the bastard the satisfaction. "Sorry about the smell,

Swede. I had lunch with your wife."

The smile became broader. "At least I got a wife, peeper. Plus, I can protect my family, unlike you."

I came pretty close to bopping him on the beezer. But I did my best not to react.

"Isn't it about time you beat the crap out of some guy tied to a chair? A fair fight for you."

He came right up to my nose. "Listen, O'Farrell, I would love to knock your teeth down your mush. But you got one thing going for you today. You saved Gina and Mimi's lives, so I'll give you a one-day pass, gumshoe." He slammed his fist into his palm to intimidate me.

"Easy with those hands, Swede."

He gave me a bewildered look. "What?"

"You need those paws for counting the bribe money."

"I'm sorry the chopper squad missed you, O'Farrell. I wouldn't have lost any sleep over you getting blasted to hell. However, another time, another place, gumshoe.

"That's what your wife keeps telling me, tubby."

That got a reaction. He dove for me, but Vinnie cut him off.

"Get out of here, Swede, you got work to do."

After Swede left, Vinnie let me have it.

"You just always have to have the last word, don't you Sean? God damn it, when are you going to learn to keep your mouth shut?"

Tommy D'Amato and Amundson, came into the room on the other side of the glass. Swede took off his hat, coat, and shoulder holster and handed them to Tommy, who folded everything neatly and placed it on the table. The Swede lowered his suspenders and took off his dress shirt, folded it and handed it to Tommy. He pulled the suspenders back up. He started whirling his arms around like a pitcher warming up in the bullpen. He stretched, and Tommy held up his hands so the Swede could do his warmup punches. He turned his head around on his neck and got loose. Tommy handed him a pair of black leather gloves. He put them on and slapped his right into left palm. He was ready.

The Chief came over to him. "We want him to talk, Swede. Take your time, don't kill him quick. We need to know what he knows." The Chief and the Swede knowingly smiled in unison.

The Swede delivered the first punch. It was a beauty; the tough guy's head snapped back. He was almost knocked out. Amundson delivered ten speedy punches to the head and six fast ones to the ribs. This immediately made it hard for the tough guy to breathe. The tough guy looked like Jim Braddock taking a beating from Joe Lewis in '37.

The Swede was walking in a circle around the hood; he spoke for the first and only time.

"You better talk now, pal, or you are as good as dead."

The Swede delivered four savage blows to the ribs, both sides. The hood couldn't breathe. Or talk, for that matter.

After a few minutes, blood was flying off the Swede's gloves and going airborne. As Swede was circling the chair the Chief have him a nod. Swede looked mighty disappointed; he was enjoying the work, the sadistic son of a bitch.

After one more minute of working on the gee, the Swede reached into his pocket and took out a small black balloon-looking thing. Swede nodded to Tommy, who moved over by the door. There was no one standing against that wall; unlike all the other walls, this one was painted bright white. The stage was set.

The Swede walked around to the front to the tough guy and hit him hard with a right then a left, and I found out what the balloon was. It was a bladder of fake blood. The Swede squeezed as he hit him with a left and it covered the tough guy with fake blood. Better yet, it splattered all over Tommy and the bright white wall. It looked like a slaughterhouse. Everyone in the room gave a moaning gasp of disgust. Tommy looked at his hands, splattered with the fake blood, and vomited in the mop bucket.

"Get that rookie out of here if he can't stomach it," the Chief yelled.

One of the uniforms helped Tommy up and out of the room, and wheeled the bucket with them. The Swede picked up a ball peen hammer and knelt in front of the tough guy.

The show was now officially over. The tough guy started singing. He was like a damn information booth. He was barbering faster than the room full of inspectors could write down the dope.

His name was Mickey Pellegrini. He worked for Frank Nitti. The other two guys were Frankie Cantone and Bobby Caspian. They took a twelve-hour overnight flight from Chicago on United Airlines and arrived at eight this morning. They were ordered by Nitti to report to Tony Giovanni in San Francisco, then to kill a private dick named Sean O'Farrell. They were met at the airport by Giovanni, who drove them to the location where they would find O'Farrell. They were to wait an hour until Giovanni could get to a meeting somewhere so he could set up an alibi.

The Chief asked, "Why did they want O'Farrell dead?"

"He was poking into Tony's meal ticket, some architect. He thought O'Farrell was getting too close to their business, so Frank and Tony told us to plug him. Get rid of the problem, so to speak."

"What was the business with the architect?" Gallatin demanded.

"I don't know anything about that."

"How did you know who O'Farrell was?" the Chief asked with a puzzled look.

"Tony had a couple of pictures of the gee. Plus he had a broad waiting across the street. She fingered the guy for us. We were told to wipe out everybody in the lobby and make sure we give O'Farrell the Chicago overcoat." He smiled broadly.

"Who was the twist?" The Chief said.

"I don't know, some blonde looker. She was all excited about the prospect of watching us drill the gee. She was all hot and bothered. She kept asking us how many times we were going to shoot him. The sick twist was enjoying it." He shook his head.

"Could you identify her?" the Chief pressed.

"No, she had on sunglasses. I never got a good look at her." The tough guy's eyes darted back and forth in terror.

I opened the door to the interrogation room and walked in.

"I know who she is," I said.

CHAPTER THIRTY-FOUR

I walked over to the Chief.

"I have a list of people that you want to put an APB out for. You are looking for four other thugs from Chicago. First one is Anthony Giovanni, goes by the name Jonathan Wheeler. He has three thugs that work for him. Names are, Brian Child alias Paul Petri; next is David Michaels, whose real name is Walter Rossi; the last guy is Michael Linderman, and his real name is James Rizzo. All four of these mutts are from Chicago; specifically, parts of Capone's organization. Frank Nitti sent them here.

"Next, bring in a Randall Morehouse, he's an architect, for protective custody and questioning. He is the linchpin to this business. Finally bring in his wife, Dr. Constance Morehouse, for suspicion of attempted murder; she's hip deep in this crap."

"How do you know all that, O'Farrell?" Gallatin demanded.

"She was my client. I don't know if she is involved or not, but it looks that way. She may be a willing participant or a sap who was taken for a ride by Wheeler. Bottom line, she needs to come in for questioning. The most important move is protecting Randall Morehouse."

"All right, lad," Gallatin said. "We will round up the bunch. Why don't you go home and get some sleep? It's almost ten and you have been at this for a while."

"Thanks, Chief. Call me if anything breaks," I said.

I got into the Ford and drove home. Kaitlin was sitting on the bench swing on my front porch. She looked cold and worried. I got out and wrapped my arms around her; she was all that mattered to me. After a long embrace in which we said nothing, I opened the front door and asked her to come in.

She was upbeat. "I'm glad I came over after work. Someone had to convince this neighborhood that you were not killed. You have a lot of friends around here." She smiled.

"The only one that matters is the one in this room with me," I said.

I went over and gave her a good kiss. She was cold, but she felt great. I asked what she would like to drink. She didn't hesitate.

"Whiskey, please."

I poured two good glasses. I handed one to her and the phone rang. "Hello." I said.

"Sean, its Shamus. I know you have had a hell of day. Are you all right, laddie?"

"Yes sir, I was lucky," I said.

"I don't like to be nosy, son, but is Katie there with you?"

Kaitlin rolled her eyes and held up her empty glass. She knew what was up.

"Yes sir, she is here. She was waiting for me, I'm going to fix something to eat, and then I will bring her home. She's okay."

"Thank you, Sean, We'll see you later." He hung up.

"My mother and father worry like there is no tomorrow."

"Kaitlin, I'd worry if I were them. I am about to wrap up these two cases. I am thinking it's time for me to think about practicing law again. It's not exciting, but you would sleep a whole lot better."

She smiled. "You worry about my parents, fella? My mom and pop are wearing out the Persian carpet in the main hallway pacing back and forth."

I filled our glasses and handed Kaitlin hers.

"Drink up, young lady, I think I need to take you home."

I paused for a moment and started to choke.

"I killed a man today, Kaitlin, I had no choice. They came to kill me. Still, I took a life and I have to say I feel sick about it."

Kaitlin came over and gave me a hug. It seemed like it lasted minutes, but it was a few great seconds.

The phone rang again. It was Vinnie Castellano.

"The Chief called me and asked to give you an update. No sign of the Morehouse's or those Chicago thugs. Those four may have bailed out."

"Any cars at the Morehouse place?"

"No. I looked up the registrations. He drives a 1928 green Ford Model A Roadster, same year as your old man's rig. You still have that thing, Sean?"

"Yeah, I keep it in the garage with a cover on it. I can't let it go, it was Dad's. Besides, it runs great. One of these days I'm going to take Kaitlin for a ride with the top down."

Vinnie continued.

"Her car is a 1938 Cadillac LaSalle, a real boat. Neither car was home. Interesting side note, Morehouse lost his driver's license last year. He drank a little too much tiger milk and wrapped a brand-new Ford coupe around a tree."

"That's our boy. How is Gina doing, and Mimi?"

"I'm calling from the hospital, Sean. They both are sleeping. I'm going to sleep in the waiting room and take them home in the morning. Thanks, buddy. I owe you a million."

"You know, Vinnie, we might be looking for a new fish fry chairman, and..."

"That will be enough of that, Sean O'Farrell, My wife would kill me, and where would you be then?"

"God bless you and your family, Vinnie. Get some sleep."

I hung up and looked at Kaitlin. "God, I wish you could stay."

"I want nothing more than that. But every member of your family has been watching this place like a prison. I stay and the tongues will wag. Plus, you know my parents..."

I finished my whiskey, smiled, and put on my hat and coat. I opened the drawer in the dining room and took out a fresh .45.

"I know what you are thinking, Kaitlin. No, I don't expect trouble, but after today...."

I drove back to her place.

"What this I was hearing about your dad's car?"

"My dad saved for years to buy a new car. He kept an old Ford Model T going for years; that old car was held together by rust and bailing wire. All along he saved for his dream car. When I was in law school, he got it, a 1928 Ford Model A Roadster. Bright red with tan interior and matching top. Even the rumble seat matches. My mother complained about that car being impractical. Then they took the ferry one Sunday to Sausalito, and drove through the countryside and had a picnic, and she stopped complaining. My old man loved that car. When I bought this car, the dealer was trying to talk me into trading it. It just didn't seem right, so I keep it in the garage and bring it out on nice days. We'll do that soon; take it for a Sunday drive after church."

"You have got a date, Sean. Anytime, anywhere."

I pulled into the driveway and gave Kaitlin a good-night kiss. I walked her to the side door of her apartment and kissed her again. I could do this all night. She looked at me with those green eyes and smiled. She closed the door.

I walked back to the car and got in. Shamus O'Doherty was sitting in the passenger seat, with a bottle of whiskey and two glasses. I like the way the man thinks. He poured a generous glass for us both.

"Are you all right, Sean?" he said.

"Physically, I am okay, Shamus. But I killed a man today and I can't get that picture out of my head. It was the right thing to do, but it is going to haunt me."

"The Bible is pretty clear: thou shall not kill. Explain that to policemen, soldiers, U.S. marshals, and even private investigators. I fancy you wouldn't be feeling anything if those bastards got to you. Take yourself out of the equation. What about that little girl and her mother? Where would they be if you hadn't acted? You would all be dead, lad." Shamus winked knowingly and poured himself another.

"I quite admire Winston Churchill. Plus, like you, he is a wee bit of smartass, I like that in a man. He said, 'Nothing in life is so exhilarating as to be shot at without result.' Take your rest, lad. You deserve it."

Shamus put his hand on my shoulder and got out of the car. He came around to the driver's window. I finished my whiskey and handed him the glass.

"We are masters of our fate. We are captains of our soul." I said.

Shamus laughed. "Very good, Sean, quoting Winston Churchill. Nicely done."

I smiled at Shamus. "This is really a bad habit. You drink excellent whiskey, a lot better stuff than I can afford. I'll have to get you started on the cheaper stuff."

Shamus laughed.

"You best get used to the good stuff, laddie, Katie is like her mom; she won't drink anything younger than twenty-year-old Scotch. It's a matter of quality versus quantity." Shamus smiled and held out his paw for the crystal tumbler. Its sheer weight made a small slapping sound as it hit his hand.

"I don't need you starting a collection of my whiskey glasses at your house, boyo."

I had a good laugh as I waved and went home. I listened to the Glenn Miller Orchestra on the radio until I pulled into the driveway. I was a little paranoid and checked around the house before I went in. I opened the living room door slowly, and drew a .45 before flipping on the light. The place was clear.

I sat down on the sofa and poured another drink. It wasn't as good as Shamus's, but it was pretty good. I lit a butt and enjoyed my drink. What if Kaitlin had been there during the shooting? I closed my eyes. This day had been a nightmare, but Shamus was right. Gina and Mimi Castellano were alive, that would have to be enough for this night, and it was.

CHAPTER THIRTY-FIVE

I got maybe three or four hours of sleep. At five I got up; at six I drove over to the church. I knocked on the rectory door and Father Michael Eruziono answered the door. Father Mickey was my age, and was technically the assistant pastor, but the church's three ancient Italian priests were largely retired. Mickey did all the work.

He answered the door in his bathrobe with shaving cream on his face.

"Sean, is everything okay, pal?"

"I need you in the box, Mickey."

He didn't hesitate. He wiped away the cream, grabbed a key, and we hustled over to the sacristy. The door was already open. Some older ladies were saying a rosary and there were women from the altar society changing the linen.

Michael went right into the center door of the confessional and I went to the right. The little window slid open.

I went right to it.

"In the name of the Father, the Son and the Holy Ghost. Bless me Father, for I have sinned. It has been one week since my last confession. I have broken the Fifth Commandment, Father." I said the last with a heavy voice.

A whole lot of silence from Father Mickey. This just wasn't your garden-variety I-yelled-at-my-brother stuff; this was a heavy-duty commandment. Priests have this sort of script that they follow in the confessional. It usually ends with three Our Fathers and Three Hail Mary's and an Act of Contrition. Not this time.

"Sean, you killed that man to save multiple lives, including your own. Those men lived a life of sin and darkness. You are a good man. You are a Knight of Columbus: Your duty is to protect the Holy Mother Church, and protect women and children of the church from harm. You did what was required. While you may feel guilt, God knows and understands. Quite a few cops have ended up in this confessional with the same problem as you, Sean. The fact that you are here proves that you are righteous and pure. Say three Our Fathers, three Hail Mary's and make an Act of Contrition.

"And one last final act: You get this fish-fry chairman thing off my back. I'm tired of the Monsignor Dominic and Father Guido riding my ass about it. You and Danny O'Day solve this thing, will ya? Now go in peace, and get out here, you bum."

Father Mickey slid the little window confessional closed. I said my prayers and exited shortly after. Father Mickey was there and gave me a big hug.

"Thanks, Mickey. Do me a favor. Get a shave and comb your hair, will you? You look like crap."

"Sean O'Farrell, God love you. There are some things even I can't forgive you for you, smart aleck."

I hopped in the Ford and drove over to the bakery. Petey was there doing his magic.

"You okay, unc?" he asked.

"I'm good, Petey. You eat yet?"

"No, I got one rack of bread to put in then I was going to make some eggs. I'll tell you what: You make the espresso and I'll fry up the eggs. The morning paper is on the table." He returned to work with the bread racks.

I whipped up a couple of cappuccinos. Petey was slow so I started the eggs, too. I didn't really want to look at the paper; it would simply be a rehash of yesterday. I lived it; I didn't need to read about it. But I was curious to know how the Seals were doing. They were on a road trip up to Portland to play the Beavers. It was a tight season and we were in first by two games. Portland, however, was on the move; they had won six straight.

"You know, Uncle Sean, there were about twenty people waiting with Kaitlin on your front porch last night," Petey said. "Everybody bugged out as soon as we saw your lights turn the corner up the street. Everybody was worried."

I brushed the comment aside. "How are your folks, Petey?"

"I don't know who was taking care of who. Momma sat next to Kaitlin all night; she was a basket case. You know Pops. He went into your garage and straightened and cleaned for two hours. I thought he was going to give your Model A a wax job."

The eggs were good; the bread fresh. It was good to see Petey. I was coming to grips with yesterday. I did what was needed, and life goes on.

Petey made fun of my new tie, laughing and telling me that ties with purple in them are for sissies.

I was ready to return volley when I heard the sirens. At first they were far off. Then they got closer, and then there were a lot of them, getting louder and louder. Suddenly ten police cars drove up the street past the bakery. I heard the squealing of tires; the last car in the line stopped at the front door and Vinnie Castellano got out.

"I've been looking all over for you, Sean," he said. "Let's go. They just found Randall Morehouse's body."

We got in the police car and flew off. Vinnie filled me in.

"This whole business is taking on a life of its own, Sean. The FBI is coming in on it. They are claiming organized crime is involved and they are joining us. They are not taking over as of yet; they are helping out. The Chief and Chief Inspector are on the way to the Coast Guard Station below the Golden Gate Bridge. His body was souped out there. A prowler car found a 1928 Ford Model A on the Golden Gate Bridge. I ordered them to leave it there. We want to have a look first before they tow."

He flipped his notebook closed.

"Vinnie, was there a note in the car?" I said.

"The beat cops gave it a quick look. They didn't see anything. The top was down when they got there, I told them to put the top up and roll up the windows. I don't want anything flying out in the wind up there."

"Any sign of Wheeler and company?" I inquired.

"Not a whiff, it's like they were a fart in the wind. We also went by the Morehouse place. No yellow Caddie LaSalle."

I thought for a second and absorbed what I just heard.

"Call the Sacramento PD and have them raid Little Joey Patrone's bar and flophouse. They will know who you are talking about. He is in cahoots with Wheeler; they may be on the lam there."

"The Chief ordered a raid of the Morehouse's office and home. He got a friendly judge to sign a search warrant. It pays to play poker with a couple of judges." Vinnie smiled.

"Knowing Gallatin, he probably loses a lot to those judges, on purpose."

We pulled into through the gate of the Coast Guard station. It looked like a police parking lot. There was a mob of fifteen guys in a circle and there was an argument. We inched in and took a look. William Broadcreek was in the middle with Chief of Police Gallatin, going at it. Apparently the air of cooperation was over and the Feds were trying to take over. They were pointing fingers at each other and hollering. Ashwythe and Dunderbeck were there, looking worried. Then Broadcreek and Gallatin bumped chests, and it was off to the races. All the cops pulled back Gallatin, and all the FBI guys and me pulled back Broadcreek.

The problem was solved by a Coast Guard chief petty officer who walked into the middle of the pile.

"Thanks for stopping by, boys, but I need all of you to get in your cars and leave this Coast Guard property. When we complete our investigation is a few weeks, we'll let you know." He jammed a stubby cigar into his mush and started walking away.

Gallatin exploded. "What the hell are you talking about? This is our jurisdiction."

"Sorry, buddy, this is U.S. Coast Guard property, a U.S. government facility. The body was found on our property. It's a Coast Guard case now."

Broadcreek was all smiles.

"You got that, Gallatin? It's a federal case now. The FBI will take it from here, right, Chief?"

"Sorry, pal. I just got off the phone with my admiral. He doesn't want the Federal Bureau of Ignoramuses anywhere near this case. We will wait for Coast Guard investigations people to come and handle this mess. All right, men. Everybody has to leave the facility right now."

The Chief and Broadcreek were stymied. Their eyes were darting back and forth, looking around for somebody to do something. This could not happen on their watch.

I called out to the CPO. "Chief, I'm Lieutenant O'Farrell, U.S. Naval Reserve. I'm a private investigator on this case. This case is pretty huge for everyone involved. If these guys get shut out, there could be huge repercussions for them. This man did not commit suicide, Chief. This was a murder. We have to get access to the body before the trail goes cold. I promise the infighting will stop right here and everyone will behave on your base."

The Chief milked the moment.

"All right, Lieutenant. We'll play it your way. You all play nice together. Go ahead, he's over there on the shore."

The mob ran over to the shore. I stayed. "Thanks Chief. These guys are all wound up tight over this. There is a lot of posturing going on here."

"Posturing, shit. You hang out in a ward room, for crying out loud. You know all about posturing. This is standard stuff around here. Just another poor bastard joining the Halfway to Hell Club."

"The what?" I asked.

THE HALFWAY TO HELL CLUB

"When they were building this bridge, they put up nets everywhere just in case one of those steel workers fell off. If he did, he was caught by the nets. Those guys were lucky to be alive. A bunch of the survivors created a club called the Halfway to Hell Club. The only way you could join was falling into the nets. If you missed the nets, you went all the way down to the water. From that height, it's like landing on a concrete sidewalk. That's going all the way to hell."

"What a way to die," I said.

The Chief looked at the bridge. "The impact breaks your legs, breaks your ribs, and pushes the jagged bones into your heart. You bleed to death internally. If you survive the fall, the current is so strong it will drown you and drag you to the ocean. It's more like the All the Way to Hell Club, if you ask me." The Chief chomped on his unlit cigar, then continued.

"This bridge opened in '37 and the dumb bastards that jump off to end it all have been in line since then. It averages one or two a week. I finally convinced the District Commander to rotate sailors every three months, because it's too much for them to handle. That's a lot of death. You think your boy out there was murdered, do you?" He lit his cigar with a wood match he struck on the heel of his boot.

"Sure as hell, Chief. Sure as hell," I said.

CHAPTER THIRTY-SIX

The old Coast Guard stations have a brick path that leads from the boathouse to a ramp that steadily grades into the water. The old rowing rescue boats had carts with wheels. Some stations actually had a set of rails, as if for a train, for boats to be launched and retrieved. Two of the Coast Guard station sailors were taking a flat cart down to the water to retrieve the body of Randall Morehouse. I am sure that when these kids enlisted, they had no idea they might pull this kind of duty.

Randall Morehouse was face down in the water. The police photographer was taking loads of pictures as the Coast Guard chief shooed away some seagulls.

"Feathered rats!" he said.

A first-class petty officer rolled Morehouse over. His face was ghost white. More pictures were taken. What struck me was that Morehouse was wearing the same suit that he had on at Bay Meadows. They carefully placed the body on the flat cart and began to push the cart up the hill to the boathouse. No one said a word. Without being asked, five uniformed cops helped the men. It was a slow sad processional to the boathouse. Gallatin and Broadcreek were apparently done fighting for jurisdiction.

The Chief opened the tall wooden doors to the boathouse and the cart moved indoors. The sailors and uniformed cops went outside, their work done. Without anything being said, Vinnie and I nodded to Ashwythe and Dunderbeck. They nodded in the affirmative, and all four of us began searching the body.

We came up with a wallet, with one hundred dollars in fives and tens. There was no ID in the wallet; he had no driver's license. There was a picture of him and Connie. I held the photo in my hand and a bolt of lightning seared through my body. She was wearing a full-length white fur coat. They looked happy together. There was a handkerchief, eyeglass case, a package of gum, and a set of car keys. I looked over the car keys very carefully. When everyone was through, I went through the all the pockets a second time. Specifically, I went through the right hip pocket of his suit coat, looking for something that I saw Morehouse put there. The betting slip from the final race was gone. Why would he throw it away? It was worth two dollars. More than that, it was a winning slip. And he didn't win often.

I asked Vinnie to help me roll the body over. I started looking over Morehouse's skull. I parted his hair, and there it was: a large bump on the back of his head. He had been hit from behind. I was sure the autopsy would show he had a massive blow to the skull and concussion prior to death. Broadcreek and Gallatin looked at the skull as well. Vinnie started first.

"O'Farrell may be right. It looks like murder. He was cracked on the noggin, all right."

"Could he have hit his head on the way down?" Broadcreek asked.

Vinnie shook his head.

"Don't think so, the rails are set in. If he hit his head on the rail, he couldn't fall out far enough away; he would have landed on the catwalk. Somebody threw the poor bastard to his death. He was probably unconscious, since there is no sign of a struggle."

Everyone considered the options when the wagon from the coroner arrived. The Chief of the Coast Guard station directed them to the boathouse. They asked the Gallatin if we were done. He nodded to let them know that it was okay to take him away. The Coast Guard chief nodded as well.

I told Vinnie that I wanted to see the Model A on the bridge before it was towed. Three cars went to the Golden Gate Bridge. Vinnie and I were in one, the FBI guys in another, and Gallatin and his boys in yet another. Three prowler cars directed traffic away from the car.

We all stopped and got out. The others were out of the car and looking into the Model A when we walked up. Madison Cooper, a newshawk from the Chronicle, was there. He was a real self-important little shit who turned everything into a conspiracy. To him, every comment was a lie and every thought was fair game for public consumption. William Randolph Hearst must have been proud of this little muckraker, who was a critic of everyone and everything except himself. Not only is he obnoxious, he's about five foot one and pushy, in his blue suit and a gray fedora with a PRESS card in the hatband. I never liked this gee; I always thought he was cruel and sort of creepy.

As we were walking up, Vinnie whispered to me.

"How long we been friends?"

"Vinnie, you know that. Since grade school at St. Ann's."

"For all that is holy, Sean, please walk up to that guy and punch him as hard as you can in the gut. If I do it, I'll lose my job."

"What are friends for?" The Chief and Broadcreek were telling the little creep to shove off. He was whining about freedom of the press and public's right to know everything.

"Well look who it isn't, Inspector Vinnie Castellano, another lowlife cop with his hand out for another in a series of payoffs." Cooper smiled a smile that said, Go ahead I dare you to hit me.

I walked up and hit him in the gut as hard as I could; I held nothing back. The truculent, vitriolic little turd went to his knees. I am not a cruel person by nature, and I didn't know why Vinnie had me do it, but I figured it out real fast. But I had to admit, I enjoyed doing it.

He was stammering and squeaking, the little simp.

"I'll have your badge for this, your coldhearted bastard." He winced.

"No such luck, Maddie boy. I'm not a cop or an FBI guy. I'm private. They have no control over me."

Broadcreek and Gallatin looked a little shocked. Cooper climbed to his feet in total outrage. That's when Vinnie spoke up. He grabbed

Cooper by the lapel and pulled him up on his toes.

"You listen to me, you sawed-off little shit. You came into my eight-year-old daughter's hospital room, woke her up and asked her how it felt to come so close to dying. Do you even have a conscience?"

"The public has the right to know all pertinent news of the day. We at the Chronicle…" Cooper said defiantly.

I hit him a second time, a little harder than the last. I told him to fade before I threw him off the bridge, because that would be in the public interest. Cooper apparently decided that public's right to know wasn't all that important at this particular time and place, because he staggered to his car and got in the passenger side. He looked pretty green to me. He waved to the driver to take off. A uniform cop closed the car door for him, and couldn't help himself.

"Hope you piss blood later, you little asshole," he said.

The car breezed away. The Chief called the cop over.

"Just what the hell was that comment for? It was unprofessional. We have to maintain a positive relationships with the legitimate press. What is your name, son?"

"Boone, sir." The kid was a little stunned.

"Your lesson for today, son, is that you now can identify members of the legitimate press. That whining little turd is anything but. Don't say anything like that again to the press, even him."

"Yes sir." The kid quickly responded.

"Boone, when we shut this operation down have the Ford towed to headquarters" He shook the kid's hands. "Nice going, son. You said what I couldn't say to the little bastard." The Chief winked. "But now, you and your partner get this car towed out of here and get this traffic moving as quick as possible."

Broadcreek gave me a slap on the back. "You're a regular palooka, O'Farrell. Thanks for doing that. Every man here wanted to do it in the worst way."

We looked over the Model A, which was clean as a whistle. Then it hit me: There was no key on the slot on the dashboard. I pointed it out to Vinnie. He pulled out the envelope of items taken from Morehouse's body. I poured the items out on the seat and lifted up Morehouse's key ring.

"See, Vinnie, this is the key for his wife's Cadillac LaSalle, and that key is a Ford key just like mine." I took my keys out and compared. "Look, my Model A key is jagged on one side only. My '38 Ford is jagged on both sides. If Morehouse drove his car to the bridge and jumped, there would be a key in the dashboard or a key on his ring. There aren't in either location. Whoever drove the Ford Model A kept the key, out of habit. Morehouse didn't drive this car."

Vinnie nodded. "So he knocked the guy on the noodle, drove him to the Golden Gate, tossed him over the side, and a second car picked him up?"

"Think about it, Vinnie. You knock a guy on the head, he comes to, then what? You fight the guy in a moving car? I don't think so. I'd knock him out and throw him in the trunk." I said.

Vinnie looked the Model A over.

"But, Sean, this car doesn't have a trunk. It's got a rumble seat."

"Yeah, I know," I said, "but a Cadillac LaSalle has got a trunk big enough for two guys."

CHAPTER THIRTY-SEVEN

Saturday morning, Vinnie called. There was no sign of Connie Morehouse, no sign of Wheeler, no sign of any of the henchmen. All quiet on the western front. Kaitlin was working today and would get off at four. I would pick her up and run her home to get ready for the Knights of Columbus dance at the Fairmont. Since I was the treasurer of our KOC council, I was not in charge of the tickets and cash box for this event. That was Ralph Cleary's responsibility. Ralph was a milkman with Brennan's Dairy, and because of his early hours, it's hard for him to chair a lot of events. I can't really make him fish-fry chairman when he gets up at two a.m. to go to work. Ralph does as much as he can.

I drove over to the Cleary home on Greene Street. Ralph would still be at work, but I thought I could drop off the cash box and money. I parked and knocked on the front door. The curtains were drawn, but I could see movement in the living room. It took a few minutes, but Stella, Ralph's wife, answered the door. She had the chain on the door, and would only show me a portion of her face. She had been crying.

I explained why I was there, and held up the cash box. "Are you excited about going?" I asked.

She looked horrified by the question. She said she didn't know if she was going; she was under the weather. She asked me to leave the box on the doormat and closed the door softly.

I went back out to the Ford and sat for a minute. Then I got back out and walked up the driveway. Stella was standing at the kitchen sink. Her left eye was black and her lip was split. She was sobbing uncontrollably. It made me sick to look at it.

I returned in the Ford and drove as fast as I could to Vinnie Castellano's house. Vinnie was taking trash out to the can when I honked. He came over to the car.

"What's up, slick? You ready for tonight?" he said.

"I need you to come with me. We need to straighten somebody out," I said with determination.

Vinnie didn't smile, laugh or ask questions. He went into the house and came back out with his service revolver, jacket and coat. He hopped in and away we went.

"What did you tell Gina?" I asked.

"I told her you needed help and that I would be back in a while. It's the truth. Who is it, Sean?"

"Ralph Cleary. He beat the shit out of Stella. She's got a black eye and split lip. She's a mess, Vinnie."

"I'm not surprised to hear that. They have been having money troubles. I got word that a prowler has been to their house a couple of times. I kept him out of the hoosegow once, Sean. He swore to me he would buck up and do the right thing."

We arrived at Brennan's Dairy. All the drivers had returned from their runs; all twenty milk trucks were backed up and parked at the loading docks. They were all sitting around and enjoying a cup of coffee, sitting on milk crates. Ralph Cleary was in the middle of them.

Vinnie walked right up and delivered four strong punches to the gut. Ralph flew back against a file of milk crates, dazed.

"Jesus, Vinnie, what was that for?" he screamed.

The other milkmen got up and moved toward Vinnie.

"Hold it right there, boys." I flashed my .45 and gestured for them to move back.

"This is a fair fight; it's a cop against a wife beater." I said.

The others looked hard at Ralph as Vinnie helped him up.

"This is it, Ralph. This is your last chance. You go see Father Mickey, go see a bartender, come see me or Sean or any of the other brother

Knights. We can help you; we got all kinds of business guys and bankers in the Knights. We can help you and Stella. All you have to do is ask."

Vinnie got close to Ralph's face.

"You ever hit her again, and you'll answer for it. Do I make myself clear?" He voice was cold and low.

Ralph nodded, and Vinnie and I left the loading dock. Ralph fell to his knees and was bawling away. The other milkmen turned their backs and walked away in disgust.

We drove away. I asked Vinnie, "You need to go to confession?"

"What the hell for? I didn't do anything that I need to confess for. Poor Stella, she doesn't deserve that."

"How's Mimi and Gina?" I asked.

"Mimi is already milking it. Gina told her she goes back to school Monday, period." Vinnie chuckled.

His mood became serious again.

"This Morehouse case is strange, Sean. We have to find these people. It's a bad deal."

"The wife will surface, and so will Wheeler. Once you get them in a room, it's just a matter of time. Next Monday, I'm going to do some snooping around. I'll figure out what the angle is."

I pulled into Ralph Cleary's driveway. Vinnie and I got out and knocked on the door. Stella answered the door. She had put on makeup and had calmed down.

"Hi, Stella." I said. "I came by to pick up the cash box. I saw Ralph this morning and he isn't feeling too well, some kind of stomach thing." Vinnie said.

Stella smiled. "Oh, Ralph's got a tummy ache? That's too bad. Don't worry, Sean. He's going tonight and he will be manning the ticket table. There is no reason for anybody else to pick up his slack." She spoke with a smile.

Vinnie jumped in. "Are you going, Stella?"

"I wouldn't miss it, boys. Isn't that funny how a stomachache comes out of the blue like that?"

"Well, hopefully this bug that attacked his gut won't happen again," I said. "But if it does come back it could get a whole lot worse. Ralph needs to be careful; your stomach can only take so much abuse, if you know what I mean?"

Stella was smiling ear to ear. "Thanks for stopping by, boys. I really appreciate it."

As we got in the car, you could hear Stella laughing hysterically in the house. I pulled the Ford out into the street and headed for Vinnie's house.

We were driving along, not saying very much. After a while, Vinnie had some questions he had been holding back.

"How serious is this getting with Kaitlin?"

"We have been going out for five or six weeks. I feel sick when I am not with her or if I don't talk to her on the phone. Is that serious enough?"

"Sean, I'm your buddy. When Barbara and Susan died, you hit the bottom of a pit I thought you might never come out of. I don't know what it's like to lose both a wife and a child, but you can only carry that load around with you for so long. Kaitlin is making you the old Sean. It's great to see you be your old self. Is there a problem?"

"You know how much I loved Barbara," I said. "She was the world to me. I'm having a tough time because I think I love Kaitlin more. I feel guilty about how I feel."

"You got nothing to feel guilty about, buddy. Barbara would want you to be happy. What are you going to do about it?" he asked.

"Well, pal, it's almost time for a hardware store run."

"No shit, you shopping in the jewelry store? Oh, I could sell tickets to that event with the brother Knights." Vinnie laughed.

"Sean O'Farrell, private investigator, reserve naval officer, jewelry connoisseur." Vinnie starting doing a really bad French accent. "How many baguettes does this crappy piece of glass, have my good man? Is a case included in the price, monsieur? Does this candy dispenser for a penny offer better engagement rings?" He was enjoying himself.

"You're a lucky man, Vinnie," I said. "I have both hands on the wheel and I can't get to my gun at this moment."

We had a good laugh on that one.

I pulled up to Vinnie's house. Mimi was playing with a friend on the front porch. She is a cutie: blonde hair, blue eyes, innocent and pure. Vinnie and I were sitting in the car, and I know we were both thinking about how close we came to losing her and Gina. I didn't say a word, and neither did Vinnie. We just looked at each other, and we both knew what the other was thinking. Vinnie got out and picked up Mimi and gave her a big hug. Gina came out and waved. Vinnie was a very lucky man.

I called out. "Hey Gina, put this bum in a tux and put a bag over his ugly face. I'll see you both at the dance."

Mimi asked to be put down. She ran to the car and knocked on the door. I turned the motor off, opened the door and bent down to her.

Mimi gave me a big hug. "I'm not afraid to go to the dentist anymore, Uncle Sean."

Everything was going to be all right, thank God.

CHAPTER THIRTY-EIGHT

I thought I would get away quick from Vinnie's house. But Gina conned me into helping Vinnie move some living-room furniture. A little room rearranging is good for the soul. Vinnie always kids me that Gina gets rid of her stress by rearranging the furniture in the house. After yesterday, I would move furniture for her for days, if need be. I got out of there without a back injury, which seems to happen every time I help friends move furniture.

I drove over to the library without a care in the world. The radio was playing a little Glenn Miller. I walked over to the information desk and there was my girl. I stepped up to the counter.

"Drat." I said.

"Well, that's a fine how-do-you-do, mister." She was all smiles.

"I laid my library books on the dining-room table and I forgot to bring them back again. You gals here are going to fine me to death."

"We'll get it out of you anyway we can."

Mabel came out of the back room with a stack of books. She put the books on a work table, and came over for a slice of me.

"Well, well, look who it isn't. Katie, when are you going to wise up and drop this creep for a real man?"

Kaitlin blushed. "Easy, Mabel, I love this guy."

Just as she was loading up to fire more rounds, Marty Durrant came up behind me.

"Hey, Sean, how are you doing, kid?"

"I'm good, Marty. What brings you here?" I said.

"I'm getting some books and plans to make a couple new ship models.

Have you seen the lobby, buddy?"

"Now that I think about it, I haven't been back since all the action. What does it look like?" I asked.

Marty was chuckling. "The cheap landlord of ours is going crazy. All the walls in the lobby have been repainted, all the plaster work fixed and touched up. He even had all the woodwork that was damaged around my stand fixed too. He doesn't even want anybody to know anything happened there on Friday. You won't believe what he's doing now?"

"I give up, what?" I shrugged.

"There are guys on scaffolding changing the name of the building. It's gone from the Russell Building to the Bond Building."

"Who's Bond?" I said.

"Nobody knows, he just made it up. He don't want anyone walking by saying there is the Russell Building where those two schmucks got killed. Now it's the Bond Building."

Mabel joined the conversation. "Hey, you two bums got any business here at the checkout desk?"

"Yeah I got business at the checkout desk." Marty said. "I'm checking out a book and I'm checking you out, doll. What's a good-looking gal like you working on a Saturday for?"

Mabel adjusted her hair and smiled.

"Well, aren't you the smooth talker."

"Mabel, this is Marty Durrant, a retired cop and former Navy man."

It was interesting to see Mabel let her guard down a little.

"It's nice to meet you, Marty."

Marty went to work. "I come in here all the time, how come I missed a looker like you?" They went over to the side and continued their conversation.

Kaitlin got her sweater and purse. We quietly walked out. Kaitlin was giggling. "Can you believe that? How do you think those two would be together?"

"Those are two of the meanest, ornery, antisocial humans on this planet," I said. "They are perfect together. Let's fade before they start fighting."

I drove Kaitlin home, gave her a quick kiss, and told her I would see here at the Fairmont. I went home, showered, shaved, and tuxed up for the evening. In the mirror, I argued with myself: Could I carry a single .45? How hard would it be to dance with one? Would I be safe without one? Finally, I decided to go roscoe-free. I had a backup rod in the Ford. I decided to use the valet parking so I would be outside for only a minute or two.

The dance started at seven, and I left the house at six. At the Fairmont, I tossed the keys to the valet and went to the main ballroom. Outside the doors, the Knights of Columbus had a table set up with a white tablecloth. On duty, in a tuxedo, was Ralph Cleary. I just said hello, not wanting to make things awkward. Ralph gave a forced smile and hello.

This particular charity event was to benefit Catholic schools. Part of it was for building maintenance and upkeep, but the lion's shares were for scholarships for needy families. The diocese has lots of schools, a lot of maintenance, and a whole lot of children that want a good education. That is where the Knights of Columbus come in. There are the ticket sales to this event, a silent auction, and a significant amount of arm-twisting of the big rich for donations. This year we got all the big guns in local society to come, plus we talked the Archbishop John Mitty to be the after-dinner speaker. We sold out of tickets this year.

I went into the ballroom and made sure my table was up front. All of the O'Doherty's would be there with me. I made sure we had a little celebrity power at our table: Lefty O'Doul, Dominic DiMaggio, San Francisco Mayor Angelo Rossi (a fellow Catholic), and Ansel Adams, the photographer would be there. The Archbishop would be at our table also. I arranged the cards and had the Archbishop placed next to Shamus.

I went over to the bar, gave the bartender a couple of bucks, and placed a special order.

People started to arrive at six thirty; by six fifty, the room was jammed. By seven, everyone was there.

I ran into the head before the Kaitlin and her family got there. I was standing at a urinal when the spots to the right and left were filled simultaneously. I felt crowded.

"We have to stop meeting like this." I said to Righty and Lefty. "I take it the Wang's are here. How about Jimmy?"

"He's floating around here with a date, boss," Lefty said.

"Don't the Wang's ever give you guys a night off?"

Righty smiled. "Only for baseball games, boss."

I washed up and got back to the arrivals. When Shamus and Catherine O'Doherty arrived, I gave him a hard time.

"Did your driver get lost?" I asked.

"You attack a man before he has a chance to fortify himself? Shame on you, boy."

I pulled a chair for Catherine and offered to get her at drink. "A glass of white wine would be wonderful, Sean." she said.

I looked at Shamus. "I know what you drink. Where is Kaitlin?"

"She's coming, lad. She needed a few more minutes." He smiled and shrugged knowingly.

The Archbishop came in and I made a few introductions. When I got everyone settled, I went over the bar and ordered one white wine, one Glenlivet and one special whiskey. I had gone to the liquor store this afternoon and purchased the cheapest rotgut whiskey they had. The bartender gave me my order with a wink.

I went back to the table and handed everyone their drink. It was only a matter of time. Shamus was talking with the Archbishop; they were sharing a joke and laughing. Then he took a drink. His eyes bugged out, he turned red and made an awful face.

"What kind of drain cleaner do they serve here?"

I was laughing so hard I could hardly control myself. Shamus looked over at me and knew he had been had.

"Very funny, Sean."

I took a drink of my Glenlivet and almost passed out. It was like paint thinner. My mouth was burning, and some of it went up my nose. It was Shamus's turn to laugh.

"You were too cheap, Sean. You only paid the barkeeper two bucks. I paid him five."

I started laughing and couldn't stop. I had to hand it to him. He got me, and good.

Shamus took a drink, and now it was his turn to have his mouth burn; while he was rolling around laughing, I had switched drinks with him.

Catherine shook her head in disgust and held up her empty wine glass.

"Good evening, Katie. You are just in time. It's like watching two chimps at the zoo during feeding time. Sean, go get me another glass of wine and a drink for Katie. The way this evening is going so far, she'll need it."

Kaitlin stood next to me at the table. She was more stunning than ever, in an emerald-green ball gown with her red hair was down. She had on a diamond and emerald cascading necklace with matching earrings. She took my breath away.

I gave her my chair, and went to get her and Catherine a drink. The dinner and after-dinner speech came and went. I wasn't paying much attention to anyone or anything except Kaitlin. Everyone at the table was enchanting. It was the perfect evening.

I talked with the Broadcreek's and the Wang's. They were all there but avoiding each other. Vinnie and Gina Castellano stopped by to say hello, and I introduced Gina to Kaitlin.

When the twenty-piece orchestra went to work, I asked Kaitlin to dance and away we went. We started with a waltz, Kaitlin was extremely graceful, and definitely the best dancer I ever danced with. We did the foxtrot, the two-step, the tango, and she showed me how to dance the quick step. I was a little rusty, but did well, and we were having a ball.

Shamus came over and danced with Kaitlin. I offered Catherine a dance, but she declined and asked me to sit next to her.

"She's in love with you, Sean. Please be careful."

"Don't worry, I won't break her heart," I said.

"Shamus and I know that you are a good man. We worry about your business, though. It could get you killed, and that would destroy Katie. I'm her mother. It's my job to worry. Please be careful."

Shamus came over and grabbed Catherine's hand for a dance. Kaitlin sat and had a drink of water.

"My mom is making her move, isn't she? Maybe you should get another job, young man, one less dangerous?" She gave raised her eyebrows and smiled.

"Boy, you don't miss much, do you?"

"Hang in there, my love. You have the inside track now. They like you more than a lot."

CHAPTER THIRTY-NINE

Shamus and Catherine left at ten thirty. Kaitlin and I danced until midnight. When it was time to go, I asked her to wait a couple of minutes. I went down to the Ford and opened the trunk. I took off my tuxedo jacket and put on my single shoulder holster. The .45's safety was on. I made sure a round was in the chamber. I wasn't expecting any trouble, but I wanted to be safe.

It was a beautiful summer evening. We walked hand in hand all the way to her home. Suddenly she squeezed my hand, hard. "What is the matter? You keep looking around. Is something wrong?" she said.

"One of my cases went sideways. I'm just being extra vigilant."

"Well, I'm sure my mother put the careful bug in your ear. You be as careful as you need to be, but don't overdo it. That's when you might make a mistake, and I can't have that."

I understood exactly what she met. When we got to her door we kissed for a long time. I ran my hand up her back and held her tight.

After we kissed, she said, "I love a man with a shoulder holster. Is that what you were doing at the end of the dance? You didn't have that thing on when we were dancing. You slick boy, you."

I kissed her again, and we said goodnight.

I was walking back to the Ford when I heard a voice from behind me. It was Shamus sitting on the windowsill of the office, about fifteen feet away. He had two glasses in his hand.

"Take my word, lad, this is Glenlivet 30."

We touched glasses. "Nice job tonight, Sean. The Archbishop was a very happy man with the numbers. It was a record haul for the schools."

"That's what it is all about," I said.

"Just to be clear, young man: we are even tonight, but this is the early rounds. I will say, it looks like I am going to have to bring my best game. You are an experienced and talented ballbuster. I'm impressed."

"Careful, Shamus. The way Catherine was looking at us tonight, I'm not too sure I want to get on her bad side."

"Katie was happier than I have ever seen her. That's all that counts for me. You get a good night's sleep, lad."

I gave Shamus my empty glass and walked across the street. As I was getting in the car, I saw a shadow come around a bush. I drew the .45 and called out.

"Come out in the light, or I'll blast you."

He did as he was told. It was Jimmy Chin. "Hey, Sean. I'm parked next to you. Take it easy."

I put the rod away. "Sorry, Jimmy, it's been a rough couple of days. I'm jumpy."

"Don't worry, pal. Hey, give me a call next week and I'll fill you in on the two kids, and we'll settle your bill. Okay?"

"I'll give you a call, Jimmy."

At home, the phone rang as soon as I turned on the light. It was Vinnie Castellano.

"Sean, its Vinnie. Sorry to break up your night. Connie Morehouse came back to work at the hospital. We are going to pick her up for questioning. I'd like you to come along."

"Okay, swing by and pick me up. I'll get out of the monkey suit."

Vinnie's car was there in ten minutes, barely stopping. I got in and we flew away, making it to the hospital in nine minutes. Four prowl cars were there.

"A little heavy to pick up one broad, isn't it?" I said.

"I didn't call for black-and-whites, Sean. Something else must be up."

The emergency room was buzzing. They were working on two people: a sergeant with a knife wound in the shoulder and a woman on a gurney, beaten so badly that she was unrecognizable.

The sergeant was sitting in a chair, surrounded by cops, doctors and nurses. The nurse was trying to get the cops to move back, but they were staying by the sergeant. Vinnie stepped in.

"All right, boys. Give these medical people room to do their jobs."

The cops went into the waiting room. The husky sergeant gestured me and Vinnie over.

"You the inspector that caught the call?"

"No I am here for another case. I'm Vinnie Castellano. This is Sean O'Farrell, a private eye working on the same case. Your name is Mulligan, isn't it?"

"Yeah. I think my buddy Marty Durrant knows you, O'Farrell."

"Marty is a good man."

"Yeah, he was a great cop. I got to tell you, Inspector, this whole thing went to kitty litter in a heartbeat. I was out on patrol with a rookie. We answered a domestic, neighbor called it in. We got there, and the husband was calm as a cucumber. Told us everything was fine, no problems. We asked to look around and he said okay, that his wife wasn't even there. So the rookie is looking around the room. This gee is wearing a tuxedo, for crying out loud. The rook looks behind the couch and there is the old lady, beaten half to death and not moving. She's right over there; she may be dead for all I know. Next thing you know, the bastard has a kitchen knife. He catches me off guard, knocks me down, and before I know it he's on top of me and stabbing me in the shoulder. He has the knife in both hands and is about to finish me off when the rookie comes through and put three rounds in the guy. He's dead before he hits the rug in the living room. The kid got me upright and helped stop the bleeding. I'm lucky to be here. That D'Amato kid's a hero."

I looked over at woman on the gurney. Tommy D'Amato was there, holding her hand. Vinnie and I went over. The doctor was checking her stomach and middle, and looked very concerned. He took the nurse aside and talked to her.

"Get the operating room ready, and call Dr. Morehouse. She just finished an emergency heart surgery. Tell her we have a woman that has severe internal bleeding from a beating. She'll need to operate immediately."

The woman was trying to get Vinnie's attention. She was whispering, gurgling, and making noises when she tried to talk. Vinnie put his ear to her mouth. He turned white as a sheet. He stood up and looked carefully at the woman, and then he glanced at me. He talked to her quietly.

"It's going to be all right, Stella I don't know about Ralph. I'll see what I can find out."

The nurse raised the side rails and started rolling Stella Cleary towards the double doors to the surgery wing.

Another nurse appeared with another gurney and asked for help with the sergeant. We got him on the gurney and the young doctor reappeared.

"We are going to prep you for surgery, Sarge. You have a very deep cut in the shoulder, and there are a lot of veins and arteries in there that got nicked. We need to get you in surgery so Dr. Morehouse can stabilize the wound and ensure you don't start bleeding again. I can't give you anything for the pain since you are going into surgery. I need you to tough it out for me."

The Sarge was woozy. "Hey, kid, tell me about this Dr. Morehouse. Is he any good?"

"Dr. Morehouse is a she, and she is the best surgeon in this town. She has saved four cops from gunshot wounds in the last three years. She is a magician. If I were going under the knife, I'd want her, hands down, more than any other surgeon. She saved a little boy's leg this morning, she saved a rabbi from a massive heart attack, and now she's in with the woman you brought in. She'll take good care of you too, Sarge. She's the greatest."

He patted the Sarge on his good shoulder and moved to another emergency case that came in.

We went to Tommy D'Amato and sat on each side of him. Tommy was pretty pale.

Vinnie put a hand on his leg. "I know you feel low, kid. You pulled your service revolver and took a life tonight. I know it eats at you."

He turned and looked hard at Tommy. "You remember this more than anything: You saved a woman's life. You saved your partner's life. You did what you had to do. You were a cop tonight. I'll ride in a prowl car with you anytime, anywhere, officer, and so will all the guys waiting in this room. I'm going over to the Sarge's house and get his wife. You come along with me. Give me a minute first; I need to talk to Mr. O'Farrell."

The kid nodded and we went to the corner of the waiting room. All the cops there came over and slapped him on the back.

"Did we do enough for Stella, or did we let her down?"

"We did all we could, Vinnie. Some men can't be helped or saved. Ralph was one of them."

Vinnie was thinking hard. "Do you think this Morehouse dame was in on her husband's murder?"

"Yes, I do."

"Well, so do I. I can feel it in my bones, Sean, this broad may not have done it, but she knew the score. For that, she is going in for questioning. I'm going to squeeze her until she pops, so help me God."

He put his hand on my shoulder. "But not tonight. Tonight Dr. Constance Morehouse is going to save two more lives. Come tomorrow, though, her ass is in a room and she's mine."

CHAPTER FORTY

Vinnie and the kid went to go pick up the Sarge's wife at home. It suddenly occurred to me that I didn't have a ride, and there was no reason for me to hang around.

I was getting ready to shove off and was standing just outside the side door of the emergency room having a butt when that young doctor came out for what looked like the same purpose. He was no older then twenty-five or six, fresh out of medical school. He had a baby face, and he didn't look old enough to shave yet. But it has been a long day for everyone and he looked tired and weary. I held up my pack of Luckies and offered him one. He smiled ear to ear as I struck a match and fired the kid up.

"You look tired doc, long day? I said.

He shook his head in the affirmative. "I swear it's like we were giving away free medical care today.

"How so?"

"We have had two bar fights, two car crashes, an accident down on the piers with a crane, an old Model T that thought it could outrun a cable car at an intersection, and now the cop, and the lady victim. I have been up over thirty hours straight."

"That was pretty nice things you said about Doctor Morehouse, is she that good?" I said fishing around.

The young doctor was not playing along, his yap was shut tight, he was a smart kid. He stuffed out his butt and started going back in without a word.

"Look doctor I'm a detective, I'm not some janitor hanging around the water cooler looking for two cent gossip. I need to know about this Doctor Morehouse."

The kid turned around and was thinking things over. He wasn't saying yes and he wasn't saying no. He just stood there, I didn't push him. Finally he piped up. "Got another smoke pal?"

I fixed the kid right up. He inhaled down to the bottom of his lungs and he seemed to relax a little. He was looking down, ran his fingers through his hair and nodded to himself that he had made up his mind. He gave a hard long stare.

"Okay he said." First the kid looked around and over both shoulders making sure no one was listening in. He leaned in and lowered his voice. "I wasn't kidding, if I was that cop I would want Doctor Morehouse working on me, PERIOD!"

He looked over both shoulders again gripped in either fear or paranoia, probably both. "She may be the most talented surgeon on the planet, but that twist is one stone cold bitch." He dragged on his smoke.

"Really?" I said.

"Look most doctors are uptight and hard to please. Surgeons are known for being almost maniacal, but she is heartless."

I asked him what he meant by that.

"Okay you know how guys talk about broads and getting laid every chance they get?

"Sure" I said. "What gee doesn't?

"Morehouse is creepy. There was this intern named Jacobs, he worked here in the ER, good doctor. He was single and Morehouse didn't know he was alive. The guy got married and next thing you know old Connie is after the guy, morning, noon, and night. After a couple of months of softening this idiot up, she got a few drinks in him and the next thing you know he's nailing her in her office. One screw and she was done with him."

"You are right doc that is pretty cold."

"That's nothing, Jacob's wife got an anonymous letter in the mail clueing her in. Next thing you know Jacobs wife leaves him. He swears that it was Morehouse that sent the letter."

"I gave the doc a knowing nod.

"Okay you hear one story, its rumor. You hear a second and you start to listen. There was a Negro orderly called Darnell. I was going up the stairs to the second floor when I saw Darnell screwing Morehouse from behind in the stairwell, she has her skirt up around her waist, and she was holding on to the handrail for dear life as he was giving it to her, and good. I just froze there, they couldn't see me, but I just wanted to crawl away and hide. I didn't what to make any noise so I stayed hidden under the stairwell. When they were done she told him "Fuck break is over back to work." I heard the second floor stairwell door open and slam and went back the way I came." The young doctor looked white.

"Anything happen after that?" I asked.

"The very next day, Doctor Morehouse went to the hospital administrator and she told him that she saw Darnell steal some money out of a patient's room. He fired him on the spot.

"Jesus, that's cold." I said. "Let me be the devil's advocate here. Was Darnell stealing from patients? I said.

"Not a chance, but this is the super twisted part of this whole damn thing."

"What is?"

The kids swallowed hard. "I have been here for one year. Ever since I have been here, little piddily stuff goes missing from patients rooms. Compacts, lipsticks, lighters, little stuff. I don't give it a second thought, then one day this eighty year old woman is checking out and she is tearing her room apart. She claims she brought her late husband's pipe lighter. She didn't smoke, she just wanted it near her." He looked at me. "You ever seen one."

"I think so, is it the kind you pull apart and there is a round hole that fits over the pipe"

"Exactly" the kid smiled. "The lady described it to me. Gold, with brown leather on both sides, and two green emeralds that join together when it is closed.

"Two months later I'm in Morehouse's office getting my ass chewed and she lights a smoke with guess what? The kid held up his flat palm for me to guess.

"Don't tell me a gold pipe lighter with brown leather and emeralds." I said.

"The doctor smiled.

I lite another smoke for myself and then it hit me, when did I lose my lighter? Shit it was at Connie Morehouse's place.

I caught a cable car down to the wharf to get something to eat. It was two in the morning and only Molly's Diner would be open this late. I was all keyed up and needed something to eat. I jumped off the cable car by the docks, a block from Molly's.

A cold breeze came off the water, giving me a damp chill. I turned up the collar of my wool overcoat. It was a little foggy and it started to drizzle. I lit a butt and was tossing the match when I heard the noise. At first I thought it was a cat crying. Then I heard laughter, several men in a group. I made my way to the docks, closer to the sound. A blood-curdling scream pierced the night, followed by more laughter.

I unbuttoned my overcoat and suit coat, and quietly drew a .45 with my left hand. I let it hang down at my side. What I saw in the middle of the pier under a shabby lamp made me sick.

Madison Cooper was hanging on a massive fish hook that was suspended from a wire secured between two iron bars. A fish scale was under his feet. The hook was in his overcoat and suit coat, right behind his collar. It might have been in his shoulder, I couldn't tell for sure. His nose was bleeding and he had a cut over his right eye. His hat was crushed on the dock and his shoes were three feet above the pier. He was swinging back and forth, his face frozen in terror.

The five men around him were some pretty tough-looking

longshoremen. They were all dressed in black trousers, black turtleneck sweaters and black watch caps. A couple of them had on pea coats. The tallest one had some kind of wooden bat and was hitting Cooper in the side like the reporter was a Mexican piñata.

"Come on, Crusher. Hit the nosy little turd again," a bald fat one said.

The tall one stuck the bat under Cooper's chin.

"All right, shorty, I'll ask you again: What are doing down here poking into union business here on our docks?" He brought the bat down and hit Cooper in his side.

Cooper was pleading. "Please don't hit me anymore. I'll leave and never come back."

The bald man opened his pea coat and pulled out a long serrated knife from a sheath. "Don't worry, shorty. We know you won't ever be back again." He smiled a wolfish grin. The others laughed as he raised the knife between Cooper's legs.

"Evening, boys," I said.

They all turned and faced me. The tall one did the talking.

"This is a private dock. Shove off," he said.

I held the .45 behind my leg so they couldn't see it.

"That gee looks like he weighs a buck fifty. Do you think all five of your mutts can handle him by yourselves?" I said.

The tall one wiped his mouth with the back of his hand.

"This newsie was poking around in a place he ought not to be poking around. Take a walk, pal. This is none of your business." He spit on the dock and gave me a menacing look.

I was looking at their leader when I noticed every pair of eyes shifting to my right. I could feel someone creeping up behind me. I brought out the .45 and pointed it at the crowd.

"If the guy behind me doesn't move to my front, one of you rummies is going to walk with a limp for the rest of their life."

I pulled the second .45 and aimed it at the leader.

"I guess we'll all start calling you Hopalong."

The leader threw up his hands. "Jesus, Wally, come out from behind there before the gee shoots."

A gaunt black kid came out of the darkness and joined his buddies, doing his very best to look tough. He had a long knife in his hands. I told him to drop it. He didn't. I squeezed off a round. It went into the wooden pier post between the black kid and the leader. Splinters flew through the air. All six longshoremen dropped to the dock and covered their heads.

"Jesus, mister, you don't have to shoot. We'll leave the newsie alone," the kid said.

I put one .45 away. "Get on your feet and start walking, all of you. Anybody turns around and I'll drop you where you stand."

They scrambled to their feet, and backed away down the pier and into the fog.

The leader had a little starch left in him. "What's your name, pal?" he said.

"O'Farrell," I said.

The leader pointed at me. "Next time you come down here and mess in our union business, we'll boil your mick ass like a potato." He gave himself a satisfied smile.

I fired another round into wooden sign directly over his head. The sign said LONGSHOREMEN ONLY. The pieces fell on his head and shoulders.

"Thanks for the tip, pal." I said.

They drifted away. I waited about a minute to make sure they were really gone before taking a small barrel and placing it next to Cooper. I jumped on top and put my arms around his waist.

"Cooper, are you hurt? Anything broken?"

Cooper was doing his best to keep it together, but he was in shock and scared to death. "I'm okay. Please get me down."

I lifted as high as I could and took his weight off the hook. "Cooper, can you reach behind your head and get the hook out?"

It took him a few tries to get it out, but he eventually worked the hook free. I was busy looking over my shoulder, making sure the welcome wagon didn't come back. I lowered Cooper to the ground. His legs didn't hold him up. He slid to the dock with his legs splayed out. He tried to reshape his stomped fedora, but it was pretty much a lost cause. Slowly he started to stand. At first he leaned on me, then the post. After a couple of minutes, I offered him a butt. His hands were too shaky to light his lighter, so I took it from him and lit his smoke. He took a deep drag and held it. He exhaled and seemed to settle down.

His hand was still shaking as he lifted the butt to his lips.

"I thought I was dead for sure, O'Farrell. Thanks. I owe you my life."

"What the hell were doing down here anyway?" I said.

"I was chasing a rumor that the longshoreman's union was going to strike the docks tomorrow. I was poking around, like the guy said."

I handed him what was left of his fedora. "Come on, Cooper, I'll buy you a coffee."

We walked the block over to Molly's Diner. Cooper looked up at the neon sign and gave me a funny look. "O'Farrell, this is a cop diner. I'm not exactly welcome here."

I gave him an impatient look. "Come on, Cooper. They don't bite."

We strolled in and the place was almost empty. Breakfast, lunch, or dinner, it was the same menu, twenty-four-seven. It was a greasy spoon, but it was clean, and there really was a Molly. Her old man was a cop who was killed in the line twenty years ago. Cops from all over town came to Molly's. They came before shift, after shift, after church, after poker. Cops never forget the fallen.

Cooper and I grabbed a couple of stools. Tommy O'Mara, a brother Knight, came to the register to pay his tab. He was in uniform, either coming or going on duty.

"Hey, Sean, how you doing, lad?" he said.

I gave him a short wave. "Hi, Tommy, how's tricks?"

"Doing well, Sean. If I were you"—he gave Cooper a hard look—

"I'd find better company than this piece of shit." He didn't wait for a response. He said goodnight to Molly, took his hat off the rack, and found the front door.

Cooper was a little dejected; it had not been a good night for him. "I told you, O'Farrell, I wasn't welcome here."

"First off, call me Sean. Second, I'm sorry Tommy was hard on you, but you earned your reputation. It's up to you to change it."

He gave a little chuckle. "Easier said than done."

"What do your friends call you?"

He shuffled a little. "I don't have many friends, but my old buddies used to call me Coop."

"Well, Coop, my old man was not very tall," I said. "He was sensitive about it; he was so worried about it that he took every comment and slight to heart. He could be a mean little bastard. When I got into high school, he changed. He made a decision to not let it bother him ever again. And I'll be damned, I never heard another person every mention it again. I never saw my old man come unglued like he did when I was little."

Cooper was listening, taking it all in. I lit a fresh smoke as the counter man refilled our coffees.

"Look, I read your paper every day, front to back. I read every article you write. You are a great writer. But you go negative about everything. You can see in your articles that you are pissing people off. Even when you write a great story you end up in the used-car section buried in the back. You got to give a little to get a little in this world. If you wrote about the good that cops do occasionally, you won't be treated the way O'Mara just did."

I tossed fifty cents on the counter. "Coop, I've never seen an article by you on the front page. If you go up there, you get your picture and byline plastered there for everyone to see. You deserve a lot better than hanging on a hook down at the docks."

I told him I had to get home. He said he was going to stay for a while, that would walk home from here. He thanked me again. I turned up my collar as the wind tried to take my fedora. As I walked by the front window, Cooper was looking into the mirror behind the counter. The wheels were turning. If there was hope for Madison Cooper, only time would tell.

CHAPTER FORTY-ONE

The next morning, I was pouring cream in my coffee when Vinnie knocked on the door.

"Want some eggs, Vinnie?"

"Absolutely. I only got four hours of sleep, but it's better than no hours of sleep."

I poured Vinnie a cup of coffee and started another pot brewing. "Everything okay at home, pal?"

"Yeah, I'd rather take the family to church, but duty calls. Connie Morehouse has been in surgery all night. She will be done with the Sarge around ten. I have a little gift from Judge Reinholt."

Vinnie held up a search warrant.

"While the good doctor is slicing and dicing, I have four inspectors rummaging through her house. Do you want to come along and help search that yellow boat of hers?"

"You never take me anywhere anymore," I said.

"I'll take that as a yes. When she is done, I'm dragging her down to the station for the questioning. I figure I'll get her while she is tired. Maybe I'll get lucky and she won't have a scumbag lawyer on a leash who comes running when we get her in a room."

"Eat your toast. You're evil, Inspector, and stop saying harsh words about my fellow brethren of the bar."

"You know, I keep forgetting that you too are a scumbag pettifogger. And by the way, pal, she's your client. I don't see you running in on a white horse and saving her."

"She's not my client anymore. I am just an interested bystander. We'll see if she needs saving first, all right?"

Vinnie took his car and I drove the Ford to the hospital. We parked in the DOCTORS ONLY parking area and started looking over Connie's Cadillac LaSalle. It felt great to get dirty looks from doctors coming to work. Yes, I am parked in your space. Drop dead.

Vinnie looked in the jockey box; I looked under all the seats. We ran out hands between the front seat and the center console. Nothing. I checked the ashtray; there were Camels with red lipstick and English Ovals without the lipstick. Randall Morehouse was a Lucky smoker like me. I found it kind of strange that he didn't have a deck of butts on him when he died.

We opened the trunk. I lifted the rubber mat and lo and behold, we found a blue piece of paper. I had Vinnie put it in an evidence bag for future use. Just as we closed up the car and moved our rigs to the front of the hospital, out came two uniforms with Connie Morehouse in tow.

The procession of cars headed to police headquarters. I met the group in an interrogation room. Dr. Constance Morehouse was looking pretty carefree about the whole thing. This was Vinnie's show, but I knew I couldn't keep my mush shut.

I offered Connie a Lucky. She accepted and I lit it for her.

"Sorry, I know it's not your usual brand, English Ovals. Oh, sorry about that. You smoke Camels, Wheeler smokes the Ovals."

She gave me a dirty look, but she kept her mouth closed.

Vinnie came in and got right after her. "Doctor Morehouse, what is your connection to Anthony Giovanni?"

"Who?" she responded coolly.

I cut in. "That's Jonathan Wheeler's real name."

"Oh. He is my late husband's business partner."

A couple of uniforms came in, and a couple more inspectors joined the party. The extra cops made the room feel smaller and Connie more nervous. That was the idea.

Vinnie was really good at this. He liked to keep suspects off balance by changing the questions around, and speeding up and slowing down the interview.

"When did you find out your husband was dead?"

"Yesterday when I got to the hospital," she said softly.

"Wow, four surgeries in one day. Your old man wasn't even stiff yet and you were going about your business."

That got a rise out of her. "I guess that's what separates doctors from the rest of us: that cool-under-pressure demeanor."

He looked through the file he had in his hands.

"When did you last see your husband, Doctor?"

"He left the house last Monday and I haven't seen him since."

"Are you absolutely sure about that, Doctor?"

"Of course I am."

He looked at me. "Hey, Sean, where were you last Wednesday afternoon?"

"I spent the late morning and entire afternoon at Bay Meadows following Mr. Morehouse and Mr. Giovanni."

Vinnie was playing it up.

"So the last time you saw your husband was Monday, and you didn't see him any time after that, is that correct Doctor?"

She was starting to steam. "How many different ways do you want me to say it, pal? No."

"Well, I don't understand something, Doctor. How did this get in the trunk of your car?" Vinnie slid the piece of paper we found in her car trunk.

"What is that? I've never seen it before. What is it?"

Vinnie smiled and pointed to me. "It's your turn, pal."

"That, Doctor Morehouse, is a betting slip from the last race on Wednesday at Bay Meadows Racetrack. Your husband placed a one-dollar bet on the final race, two-to-one odds, and won. The line was so long to collect that he put it in his hip pocket of his suit. How did a Wednesday betting slip end up in the trunk of your car when you hadn't seen him since Monday?"

She was holding together, but showing signs of cracking.

"You hired me to find out what your husband was up to. It was gambling, not another woman. You wanted to know who held his debts. You used me to find out if there was anybody other than Wheeler. So you and that lowlife Giovanni cooked up a great deal. He kept him gambling and drinking, all the while you and he are splitting the sheets. I really felt sorry for your husband; he deserved a better deal than you for a wife."

"Screw you, O'Farrell." She spit the words out with relish.

I was all fired up and kept up the assault.

"I'll tell you exactly what happened to your husband. He was falling apart and you were tired of him. You had a new boyfriend, one with special skills. He got your husband alone, clubbed him, and threw him in the trunk of your car. Your husband came to and hid the betting ticket under the mat for a clue. My guess is Giovanni drove your old man's Model A. It didn't have a trunk, so he drove his car and you drove your husband to the Golden Gate Bridge. Giovanni clubbed him again. You kept watch for headlights, and when the coast was clear, he threw Randall Morehouse to his death. You make me want to puke, lady. You are one sick twist. I'll bet you got wet hearing your husband scream all the way to his death."

She came out of the chair and flailed her hands at my face. I pushed her back into her seat, hard.

"My, my, Miss Kitty has claws. You screwed up in a couple of areas, angel. First, Giovanni took the key for the Model A with him. Your husband had a set of keys on him, but it didn't have the Model A key. Where did it go? Your husband was a chimney. He was always smoking. No butts on his person. Once again, Giovanni was nervous and took your husband's smokes because he needed one. A man needs a smoke right after a quick murder. Giovanni is a crook, but that doesn't mean he is smart enough for you. Right after you fired me, I broke into the offices of Morehouse and Wheeler. I found this little interesting piece of paper."

I threw a legal document on the table. "It's a copy of the partnership agreement between Morehouse and Wheeler. A fifty-fifty partnership, how cozy, Morehouse does all the work, gambles and drinks, while Wheeler covers his backside. He was expecting a big cut. Giovanni knows how to murder little kids; he should have paid attention to learning how to read. In the event of Randall Morehouse's death, it all goes to his widow, Doctor Constance Morehouse, and Giovanni and the Chicago boys get squat.

"What a convenient time for his death. The final payment for his services in designing the Oakland Bay Bridge is coming now that the project is complete. Six hundred thousand dollars and it's all yours, baby; you don't have to share it with your boy toy."

Connie looked trapped now. I kept pouring it on.

"Everything was going great for you, until you fired me and I kept poking around. Wheeler got scared and brought in a chopper squad from Chicago to get rid of a loose end, and then you stood across the street and fingered me for the shooters. By the way, Connie, this is Inspector Vincent Castellano. It was his wife and daughter in the lobby when the shooting started. His little eight-year-old got hit in the leg. I am sure he would like to hit you, but he can't. He would lose his job."

I hauled off and backhanded her. "But, I can do anything I want. I'm a private guy. I have a rule about never hitting a woman. But I am breaking all the rules today."

I backhanded her again. She was steaming, but she kept her mouth shut.

Vinnie took over. "We can't stick you for the murder, but we got you for accessory to murder. Once we get your boyfriend in custody, we'll get the whole picture."

The door opened and a couple of police matrons came into the room. "On your feet. Doctor Constance Morehouse. You are under arrest for accessory to murder."

The matrons cuffed her hands behind her back. Connie was keeping it together, but I was sick of her smug look.

"Hey, Vinnie, do me a favor, will you. When you leave the room, turn out the lights. I want to save as much juice as we can, so there is plenty when they give blondie here the electric solution. Connie, still want me to rub your back and other parts for you?"

She went completely insane. It took both of those matrons to haul her ass out of the room. She was screaming all the way.

"O'Farrell, you asshole, I'll kill you for this. I'll take care of you, you'll pay for this, you coldhearted bastard. Do you hear me, O'Farrell?"

The door was still open, and we could hear her being dragged down the hall, kicking and screaming.

Vinnie was impressed. "Nice going, Sean. The matrons are going to love you for this. She is going to be a handful until we get her in front of the judge. Couldn't you keep your pie hole shut just this one time?"

I smiled and ignored Vinnie. "Think she'll make bail?"

"Doctor, loads of cash, good looking, helps cops with bullets in them. She'll get a mouthpiece that knows the score. She'll arrive in court looking like a lost puppy. The judge will cry and she'll walk on bail. But that will be tomorrow morning. For the time being she gets to sit in jail and meet all the nice hookers we grab up tonight."

"Couldn't have happened to a nicer gal. Hey, Vinnie, do me a favor, will you?"

"Sure, what's that?"

I took an envelope out of my suit coat jacket. "I need you opinion. Should I deliver her final bill down in Central Booking or should I just drop it in the mail?"

Vinnie was laughing.

"You really are a coldhearted bastard, aren't you?"

I lit a butt and threw the match in the ashtray. "Yes, I am."

CHAPTER FORTY-TWO

It was just like Vinnie called it. Connie Morehouse made bail the next morning. I sent my bill in the mail, and to my surprise a check for the entire amount arrived two weeks later.

One Sunday after mass, Danny O'Day came up to me and filled me in on Connie's case. It wasn't a federal case, but he had talked to Mark Maple, the deputy district attorney who was assigned the case. He was sitting tight until they found Giovanni or Wheeler or whatever the hell his name was. I had to admit, the case against her was largely circumstantial. Wheeler could have used her car without her knowledge. She could have been a victim of this scumball just like her husband. It was strange; I had moments when I was convinced she was involved, and others when I just wasn't quite sure. Time would tell.

Kaitlin and I had the best time on Labor Day weekend. We went to a Seals game on Saturday, then dancing in the evening. On Sunday, I went to an early Mass with her family at their church, St. Brigid. We had started to go back and forth between my church, St. Peter and Paul, and St. Brigid. I was starting to like St. Brigid's, just being a parishioner instead of running around and taking care of everything.

We went for breakfast with her folks at the Top of the Mark; it was wonderful, the food and service was excellent. They could have served chipped beef on toast and I would have been happy, because I was with Kaitlin.

The afternoon was beautiful, sunny and breezy. Kaitlin and I had been planning an outing for some time, and I put the top down on the Ford Model A. We drove across the Oakland Bay Bridge and went to

THE HALFWAY TO HELL CLUB

Oaks Stadium for the last game of the regular season game between the Oaks and the Seals. The Seals lost, 11-9, but it was a great game.

We drove across the bridge as the sun began to set. It was breathtaking. When we got back on our side of the bay, we drove to a little joint on Fisherman's Wharf. We sat outside at a table and had clam chowder and fresh sourdough. The sun produced all of the colors you would expect: yellow, orange, red, blue and purple. We sat holding hands for over an hour. We chatted, but mostly we enjoyed the view and each other's company.

When it got dark, I put the top up and we drove over to Kaitlin's. It was six forty-five, and the Jack Benny Show would be coming on in a few minutes. It was my job to make popcorn. As the kernels were popping away, Kaitlin got a couple of glasses with ice and two bottles of Coke from the refrigerator. A moment later, I put the popcorn in a big bowl and we sat on the couch just in time for Jack Benny.

But it was not meant to be.

I heard the siren from a distance; I could hear it coming up the hill. When the car turned into the driveway, it left no doubt that the police were here. Crap!

I opened the door and walked to the driveway. Vinnie Castellano was leaning against the car door with one foot on the running board.

"Come on, Vinnie. It's Sunday."

"Get your hat, pal. Chin Wang was just murdered in his club."

I knew when not to barber. I got my hat and kissed Kaitlin, then got my .45 out of the trunk and put it on. I slipped my coat on. By this time, Shamus and Catherine were in the driveway. They said nothing, but there was concern in their eyes.

I started to get in the prowl car when I changed my mind and walked over to Shamus. He was standing to the side; Kaitlin and her mother were talking separately.

"Shamus, I can't live like this anymore. I need to change things for myself, and more importantly for Kaitlin."

I didn't wait for an answer or a response; it was more of a statement to Shamus and myself.

The prowler peeled out and headed for Chinatown.

"What do you know, Vinnie?"

"Not a whole lot. All I know is Wang was sitting at his desk. He took a couple or more in the pump. The Chief assigned me this case because of my connection to you. He thinks you are a straight shooter, Sean; he thinks you might be able to help us out here since you worked a case for Wang. His people might be more cooperative with you involved."

We pulled up the Chinese American Club and it was like the circus had come to town. Six prowl cars, photographers everywhere, loads of reporters. But, surprisingly, not Madison Cooper. Maybe he had found a better story to write.

We walked through the club. Right outside Wang's office, the real show was underway. Chief Inspector O'Malley was already there and was verbally sparring with William Broadcreek. Ashwythe and Dunderbeck were standing behind them, looking out of place. Guess what they were arguing about?

Broadcreek was in rare form. "This is an organized crime figure. We are currently investigating his organization. We are in charge of this investigation, period."

Gallatin jumped right in undeterred. "There is no evidence of anything right now. It's simply a homicide. It's our case, period."

These two just can't play nice in the sandbox. I told Vinnie to pull his guys back and I would talk to the FBI guys.

I grabbed Broadcreek's arm and jerked him back to a corner. Ashwythe and Dunderbeck followed.

"Look Mr. Broadcreek, you can't get anywhere near this case. Not right now, anyway."

"Like hell. I have full authority over this case, and if—"

I cut him off. "Think this over. You claim jurisdiction and every newshound in the area, including that little shit Cooper, will dig until they are in China. Imagine the headline: SENIOR DEPUTY ATTORNEY GENERAL SUSPECT IN CRIME BOSS DEATH."

"I had nothing to do with this and you know it."

"Of course I know that. I don't know you real well, but I know you well enough that you would never do anything like this. But your only daughter is dating Wang's only son. You have had a long antagonistic relationship with Wang, throw in the personal element, and you are served up fresh with hash browns by the press. The truth doesn't mean anything to William Randolph Hearst; all he wants to do is sell newspapers. You don't want to be the next Fatty Arbuckle, do you?"

"Jesus" was all he could say. The wheels were working in his head.

"Vincent Castellano is a top-drawer inspector. You let the locals take the lead. Bill and Dave here will join in and be kept fully in the loop; they will be part of the investigation. But as far as the press is concerned, you guys are providing technical assistance and expertise. You are extending a handshake of cooperation and all that crap to the press. It keeps your name out of it. When the press dies down in a week, you can step in, and no one's hair gets mussed. You duke it out with the locals, it will make you look petty. And if the press makes the connection with your daughter, it will look like you have something to hide.

"You wanted the investigation so you could control it, because you were involved. GET IT? Plus, you will slow everything in the investigation down."

When emotion isn't ruling him, Broadcreek is a smart guy.

"Okay, Sean, work it out with the locals. We'll play along."

Chief Gallatin was less than cooperative.

"Like hell I will let them play on this one. Broadcreek can go screw."

"That's not the smart play, Chief. If Broadcreek pushes and gets a federal judge to sign a writ, you will be standing out in front of this building with your dick in your hand. Then you will have to explain to all those newsies out there how you had the rug pulled out from under you in your own town by the FBI."

Chief Inspector O'Malley nodded. "It's the smart political move, Chuck."

I kept going. "Vinnie here will head things up; Broadcreek's guys will join in and help. You take the lion's share of the credit. You and Broadcreek can walk out together and kiss each other's ass in front of the press. You both put a positive face on both organizations and you look good doing it. Meanwhile, we get going and investigate and keep a lid on this thing."

Now Gallatin was nodding.

"You are a smart one, O'Farrell. Vinnie, why isn't this guy one of my inspectors?"

I have to hand it to the Chief and Bill Broadcreek. They went out front and had a brilliant press conference. The Chief was smooth and thanked the FBI for their valuable assistance. Broadcreek told the press that this very well could be a federal case in the future, but the SFPD was handling the case so well that their role would be advisory. Broadcreek praised Inspector Vincent Castellano for his professionalism. Chief Gallatin praised Special Agents Ashwythe and Dunderbeck for their expertise and assistance. Both men shook hands and the flash bulbs popped.

And I missed Jack Benny, popcorn, and Kaitlin's company for this? I would have puked, but I had to get to work helping Vinnie.

CHAPTER FORTY-THREE

Now that all the glad-handing was over it was time to get to work. Vinnie opened the office doors and we got our first look inside.

Righty and Lefty were sitting in the two client chairs. Their eyes were red. The instant I had a look, I knew Chin and Loc were not involved. I had grown to respect these two men. They weren't simple muscle. They protected the Wang's, and they were taking this murder hard and personally.

Vinnie and I looked at the body. Wang had taken two in the pump at close range. The shooter had been in front of the desk, point blank; there were powder burns on the white shirt. I pulled his chair back a little and found that Wang had been shot in the groin once or twice. It was a mess. There were two .32 automatic shell casings in front of the desk and two under Wang's chair.

I looked at Righty and Lefty. I knew I would get straight answers. "Where were you guys when this happened?"

Chin spoke up. "We took Mrs. Wang to luncheon at the University Club, it was some charity thing."

Loc added: "Mr. Wang told us to take her and stay with her. He had a phone call he was expecting and a meeting in his office at five."

"Where is Mrs. Wang and Jimmy?"

"She's all broke up, boss," Chin said. "Jimmy took her upstairs to the bar to get her away from all this. He asked us to stay here until you guys arrived, then bring you upstairs to see her."

Loc was struggling to hold it together. "She's the toughest woman I have ever met. But she's broken, boss. I've never seen her like this."

"Where did you go after the luncheon?"

"We took her home and waited for Mr. Wang to call. We listened to the ball game on the radio. After it was over, Mrs. Wang asked us to head back to the office and wait for Mr. Wang. We were getting ready to leave when Jimmy called. He found Mr. Wang. We brought her right here, boss."

"I trust you guys, but I have to check your story. Run down the top of the ninth of the game."

Loc started. "The Professor laid down a bunt and made it to first. Harley Boss fanned looking for the first out. Orville Jerkins popped up for the second out."

Chin picked up from there. "Casper Carlson, that bum, had four foul tips. Then he stood there like a statue for a called strike three. Moron."

"Yeah I know, guys. Kaitlin and I were at the game."

The crime-lab guys showed up and started gathering evidence. Vinnie, Ashwythe, Dunderbeck and I took the elevator to the top floor.

Dunderbeck asked: "You know those two guys, Sean. Are they on the level?"

"Those two are capable of just about anything. But betraying the Wang's is not one of them. They would die before they would do that."

"Whoever pulled the trigger shot Wang in the privates," Vinnie said. "That seems like the kind of thing a wife would do to a cheating husband."

"The Wang's are like a couple of vicious sharks. They kill out of necessity, not pleasure. There is always a plan, always a motive. If Mr. Wang was cheating on Mrs. Wang, I guarantee, we'd never find his body. She is too cunning and too smart to do this one. But it sure was set up to make it look like she did."

Mrs. Wang was sitting in the corner looking out the window. She was perfectly calm. Jimmy Chan was sitting on a barstool drinking a beer, looking pretty shook up.

"Hey, Jimmy. Where were you when this happened?"

"Mr. Wang sent me to the telephone exchange to receive a call."

"Who from?"

"That's the strange part. He wouldn't tell me who it was that would be calling, only which phone bank to wait by. The call never came."

"Chin and Loc told me Wang had a meeting. Who with?"

"Sean, I have been working for Wang for years. I know everything about him, his family, his schedule, everything. I had no clue he had a meeting today. He told me he was waiting for that phone call, that's it."

"How's Mrs. Wang?"

"She's brokenhearted, Sean. But stand by. I know her. In a couple of hours her rage is going to take over. Whoever did this will regret the day that they were born."

I patted Jimmy on the shoulder and we all went over to Mrs. Wang. She was calm-looking, but numb.

"I'm so sorry, Mrs. Wang." She nodded but remained quiet.

"I hope you know that I have your best interests at heart, but I am going to be brutally honest with you. I am not trying to hurt or offend you. But I have to be hard and fast."

She nodded.

"Mr. Wang was shot in the groin. This is usually the act of an angry wife of a cheating husband. Did Mr. Wang ever cheat on you?"

Jimmy cringed like an explosion was about to come. It didn't.

"No, never. He has been faithful every day of our marriage."

"Mrs. Wang someone has gone to great deal of trouble to make it look like you did it. I need you to allow the police to search your home and this building right now."

She considered the idea. "I have nothing to hide; you have my permission to search wherever you feel is necessary. It is with the proviso that it be information-gathering for this crime, this may not be a fishing expedition for the FBI to gather evidence against my late husband's business interests."

The FBI guys nodded. I told Jimmy to stay with Mrs. Wang. We went down in the elevator.

Dunderbeck asked: "Do you expect to find anything at the house, Sean?"

"This whole thing stinks on ice. My guess is we will find the murder weapon, and in a pretty incriminating location."

The Wang's lived on the same street as Connie Morehouse: Pacific Avenue in the Pacific Heights. We pulled into the circular driveway and rang the bell. The housekeeper answered the door and stood aside.

At the bottom of the stairs, Vinnie made a good point. "Mrs. Wang is cooperating. I'm with Sean; this thing seems too easy. Let's start in the bedroom and be gentle. We may need more of her cooperation and assistance. We are not rolling a whorehouse or some two-bit dope dealer."

We marched up the stairs and found the master bedroom. My house could fit in this room. Bill went to the bathroom; Vinnie the nightstands. Dave took the closets, and I got stuck with the lingerie chest. I felt strange rummaging through a woman's undie drawer. But there it was, in the second drawer from the top.

I called out. "Bingo, boys."

Vinnie came over and moved the silk items to the side with a pen. He lifted it out by the trigger guard. It was a nickel-plated Walther PP automatic. The perfect ladies' weapon: small compact, white grips, goes with any outfit.

Vinnie gave it a sniff. "Guess what? It's been fired recently." He put the pistol on the dresser and the pen in the muzzle. He picked up a hairbrush and used the handle to press the eject button. The magazine slipped out. It was missing four rounds. Once again, very convenient.

Bill was the first to say something. "I don't know, boys. If Mrs. Wang pumped two in Mr. Wang's pump and then shot off big Jim and the twins, I don't think she'd park the roscoe in her unmentionables drawer."

Vinnie agreed. "If she had anything to do with this, she would have had a mouthpiece at her side and she never would have talked to us, or let us search the house."

Dave added: "I have been chasing the Wang's for two years. There are a lot of smart people in on this investigation in Chinatown. I have to be honest: We don't have shit. The Wang's have outmaneuvered us every step of the way. I don't get it. In my personal opinion, I think Mrs. Wang is smarter than Mr. Wang was. She just isn't this stupid."

I asked Dave and Bill: "Is there an enemy in Chinatown that would benefit from both of the Wang's going down?"

Bill gave it some thought and scratched his head. "There are probably forty or fifty players that are already planning their moves to take over Chinatown. But to be honest, all the major players were killed off by Wang. It's all small fry, Sean."

We all stood around and mulled it over. I had a thought, but I didn't like it.

"Let me make a phone call," I said. "I need to do some digging around in the morning. Let's call it a night. We are going to let the principals stew in their own juices till morning. I think we need to smoke out a rat." I didn't like those words coming out of my mouth.

Vinnie looked confused. "You got a hunch, Sean?"

"I am sorry to say, yes."

CHAPTER FORTY-FOUR

Vinnie dropped me off at Kaitlin's at two a.m. I quietly got into the Model A and drove home. It was raining cats and dogs. It was the one bad thing about this car: it leaked when it rained. Plus, it was a warm rain, and the windows fogged up and made it hard to see. I was all bundled up in my trench coat just trying to stay dry.

I pulled in the driveway; the Ford was in the garage. I was trying to decide if I wanted to change places to get the Model A back in the garage. The easy answer was: Go in the house and worry about it in the morning when the rain stopped. But then I saw standing water on the floorboards. Decision made.

I backed up the Model A all the way to the end of the driveway, opened the garage door, and pulled the Ford out. Next move was to pull the Model A into the street.

I had just gotten out of the Model A when it came out of nowhere. I bent over to get in the car, and whatever hit my shoulder was deflected by the roof of the car. I fell to the ground. Whoever it was, was dressed in all black, complete with a black ski mask. I was on the ground, about to be clobbered, and I was wondering where a gee gets a ski mask in San Francisco. It's funny what runs through your mind when you are in danger.

He pulled the stick over his head but he accidentally hit the trim on the garage. I rolled over and the stick hit the driveway. It was a baseball bat. I had on the double shoulder holster, but my coat was closed and I couldn't get to either one. He brought the bat to his right to wind up, but he missed and hit the mirror on the Ford. I sat up and leaned against the car door, and he swung again and hit the door hard.

I rolled and reached into my sock and pulled out a knife. As the guy pulled the bat over his head, I drove the knife into his thigh and pulled down. The scream was bloodcurdling. With the bat still in his hands his limped down the driveway with the knife in his leg.

It took me a minute to stand up. I was a little shaky. Uncle Gino and Cousin Petey came running up the street. My shoulder was killing me, but I don't think he broke anything.

Uncle Gino was beside himself.

"Sean, are you okay? What happened?"

"Another unsatisfied customer, I suppose."

Petey helped me re-park the cars. My poor Ford, my baby, was all dented up. It broke my heart, but that car helped save me.

We went in and got the bottle out. I asked Uncle Gino not to tell Aunt Celia; she would be worried to death. I polished off an extra whiskey and called Vinnie at home.

"Vinnie, its Sean. Somebody just tried to take me out at home." I described what happened.

"You are a popular guy, Sean. Any ideas?"

"Hot news flash, buddy. I know who did it. I know who killed Wang, and why. I'm going to call Mrs. Wang. I want you and me to meet her at the club in the morning. We are going to close the book on this whole business once and for all."

"Your call, pal," he said.

I asked Vinnie to pick me up, since I didn't know how strong my shoulder would be in the morning. I called Mrs. Wang, who was awake. I asked her to have Righty, Lefty, and Jimmy in her office at eight. She agreed. I asked to speak to Loc or Chin.

Chin came on the line. "What's up, boss."

I explained what had happened and what I wanted done. There was no hesitation.

"Just as you say, boss." The phone clicked off.

Uncle Gino and Cousin Petey left and I got ready for bed. I put a

.45 under the covers with me. But I knew the attacker was not coming back tonight.

At seven thirty, Vinnie knocked on the door.

"Holy shit, look at your flivver," Vinnie cried.

"It's enough to make a grown man cry."

We drove to Chinatown in silence till we were almost there. "You're okay? The shoulder's going to be fine?" he said.

"Nothing more whiskey won't take care of."

We walked in. Jimmy was in the lobby. "Mrs. Wang can't go in the office," he said. "She asked if we could meet upstairs."

We went up. Mrs. Wang was seated in the corner again. Lou was directly behind her shoulder. Jimmy sat next to her and Vinnie sat on Mrs. Wang's left. I sat next to Jimmy.

"Mrs. Wang, I think we have figured out who killed your husband," I said. "I think we have a pretty good guess."

Mrs. Wang usually had a good poker face, but not this time. "That is completely unacceptable. I hope you have more than a guess, Mr. O'Farrell."

As she said this, Chin walked in the door with a baseball bat in his hands. He threw it to me; I caught it with one hand.

Jimmy was sitting on a bar stool and doing his best to look disinterested.

"Wow, Chin. I haven't seen one of these since college." I turned to Mrs. Wang. You don't see these much anymore, Mrs. Wang. This is a Louisville Slugger baseball bat. It's made out of kiln-dried northern ash."

I pointed to the label in the middle. "Do you see those letters right there?"

She looked and nodded.

"Those three letters, COL, indicate that this is a college model. Hey, Chin, what do these numbers of the end of the bat mean?"

I looked at Chin, who smiled and played along. "The 30 that is engraved on the knob tells you it is a thirty-inch bat, boss."

"Then what are these numbers that are painted on the knob?" asked Mrs. Wang. "It looks faded."

"It is the number twenty-two. We used to paint our uniform number on our bat so when it was in the rack, you could tell your bat from everyone else's."

I continued with Mrs. Wang.

"You see this number. 125? A lot of people think that is a model number. It really means that this is the best-quality lumber that they have. This is without a question, their best bat."

Mrs. Wang looked confused, but didn't say anything.

I looked the bat over.

"Hey, Chin, what are these marks on the barrel?"

"Looks like maroon paint to me, boss."

"Actually, Chin, it's midnight burgundy, the same paint that is on my 1938 Ford Coupe."

Mrs. Wang was paying close attention.

Jimmy was starting to look around the room nervously.

"Where did you get this baseball bat, Chin?"

"I got it from Jimmy Chan's apartment, along with this stuff."

He threw me a bag. In it was bloody gauze and my pocket knife. I threw it on the table.

"How did the bathroom look, Chin?"

"Just like you guessed, boss. A slaughterhouse. Blood was everywhere."

I looked at the knob of the bat.

"Number twenty-two." I shook my head. "That was your number in college, Jimmy. You never could swing a bat for shit, buddy."

I took the knob of the bat and drove it into Jimmy's thigh. I got to hear that bloodcurdling scream again.

Chin grabbed my pocket knife. Loc grabbed Jimmy and lifted him out of the chair. Chin used the knife to tear away Jimmy's pant leg. He was bandaged like a mummy, but the wound was starting to bleed again. Jimmy was crying in pain.

Mrs. Wang was on her feet, her eyes as large as saucers.

"Why Jimmy, why?" she demanded.

He didn't say a word. I answered for him.

"Because Jimmy wanted to be part of management. Your husband counted on Jimmy, but he wasn't family. He was never going to take over the family business. Jimmy asked and was told no. So he murdered your husband and set you up for the fall.

"If you managed to get out of the fix, Jimmy would be there to help you manage the operation. Good old reliable, helpful Jimmy. It was perfect. Jimmy knew right when to hit. He made sure you, Mrs. Wang, were busy, and that Chin and Loc would not be around. He probably told your husband that someone was coming for a meeting, and when everything was quiet Jimmy killed him and made it look like you did it, Mrs. Wang. Old Jimmy even made a special trip to your house to plant the murder weapon in your lingerie drawer. When you didn't get hauled in by the police last night, Jimmy panicked. He thought I would figure it out, so he came after me to close the loop. Strike three, Jimmy, you're out."

Mrs. Wang was stunned. She sat back down; Loc brought her a glass of water.

The phone rang at the bar, and the bartender called to Vinnie. "Inspector Castellano, there are four men from the police department downstairs here to arrest your suspect."

As soon as the doors closed behind Vinnie, the fun began. Loc clubbed Jimmy on the head and he fell to the floor. I started to get up, but Chin put me in a bear hug and Loc held my shoulders down. I wasn't going anywhere, but I put up a fight.

"You can't murder him in cold blood, Mrs. Wang. Don't lower yourself to Jimmy's level. You are better than that."

Six little Chinese guys in those silk pajamas, round red Chinese caps, white socks, and black slippers emerged and moved with unbelievable speed. They tied Jimmy up and hauled him out through the kitchen in all of ten seconds.

Righty and Lefty were still holding on me. Loc whispered in my ear.

"We are sorry, boss. You weren't going to stop this. Not now, not ever." They released their grips.

I looked at Mrs. Wang. "His murder will solve nothing."

Mrs. Wang was cool as gin and tonic.

"I give you my word. Jimmy Chan will not be harmed; he will not be injured, or maimed in any way. He will also not be murdered. You have my solemn word on this fact. What Jimmy Chan will receive is justice."

Vinnie came back up in the elevator, hopping mad.

"What the hell, Sean? There was no one down there. Where the hell did Chan go?"

"He escaped, Vinnie."

"Escaped, my ass. You were sitting here. You had these two gorillas to stop him. Don't bullshit, Sean. Where did he go?"

I shrugged and looked at Mrs. Wang.

"Silence is a friend that will never betray you," I said.

She smiled broadly. "Very, very good, Mr. O'Farrell. You quote Confucius. I am very impressed."

Vinnie walked over to the bar and called headquarters.

"This is Inspector Castellano; I want to put out an all-points bulletin for a Jimmy Chan, description to follow."

I called out, "HEY, VINNIE."

He stopped talking and looked at me.

"He's gone, Vinnie, and we'll never find him again. This is justice, Chinatown style."

Vinnie hung up the phone. Mrs. Wang gracefully exited the room. Vinnie and I were all alone. It was eight thirty in the morning. "Bartender, two Bloody Mary's, please," I said.

Vinnie just sat in a stool next to me. We didn't say anything. I started to drink my Bloody Mary.

"How good of a buddy was Jimmy Chan to you, Sean?"
"Jimmy who?"

CHAPTER FORTY-FIVE

It was an interesting meeting. Vinnie and I were in the large conference room in Broadcreek's office. The Chief of Police and Chief Inspector were there. Ashwythe and Dunderbeck were there as well. And there Vinnie and I were, on the skillet, getting a nice toasting. We told the story about three times each. Nobody liked it.

Broadcreek was upset, but not so much.

"You expect me to believe this crap? What happened to all this air of cooperation, Chief? I'm not all that upset with you, but it looks like O'Farrell and Castellano here went cowboy on us and decided to do this little act solo."

I'd had enough. "Look, pal, this thing took on a life of its own. How long have you been working this Chinatown caper?"

His voice lowered and he said sheepishly, "About two years."

"Two years of the big goose egg. Let's wrap this up so we are all clear here. Jimmy Chan murdered Mr. Wang. He got caught by his own people and they cleaned that mess up, period, end of story. There is nothing more to tell, and that's just how the people in Chinatown want it."

After about five minutes of everyone in the room staying quiet, Chief Gallatin, Chief Inspector O'Malley, Vinnie, Bill and Bob got up and left quietly. It was just me and Bill Broadcreek.

"I'm just a private dick. I don't know much more than the average Joe. But I am going to make a couple of observations for you. You can throw them in the garbage can as soon as I leave. Mr. Wang is dead; his widow is running the show. His right arm, Jimmy Chan, is long gone. You keep trying to bring down the Wang organization and all that you'll get is a bloodbath. It will be all-out war in Chinatown, like the Barbary Coast days when Wang set up shop. All the petty crooks, trying to take over Chinatown, killing each other and innocent civilians along the way.

"I know you are supposed to get rid of organized crime in San Francisco, but you are missing the bus, pal. Wang and company are small potatoes now. Their organization is firmly in control of Chinatown. It's about a twelve-block area. It's everywhere else that's up for grabs. The boys from Chicago got their hooks into the architect who designed the Oakland Bay Bridge. He designed all three of the new bridges in the Delta up to Sacramento. That's contracts, construction, payroll and graft. And the mafia wants a big piece. They missed their opportunity on the Golden Gate Bridge; they won't make the same mistake again. Prohibition is over; the mob wants new revenue streams. Their organization just doesn't have broad-shouldered street thugs anymore. Organized crime is guys who went to Harvard, Yale and the Wharton School of Business. It's a new organized crime."

I think I was getting through. Broadcreek wasn't arguing.

"I know it was you that nailed Al Capone. Eliot Ness got all the press, but he couldn't do anything in a courtroom. That was your doing. It must be nice to know that every night when you go home on that ferry that old Al is scrubbing toilets, just another number?"

Bill Broadcreek seemed to think for a moment, then spoke.

"That son of a bitch murdered many good federal and local agents over the years. Many of them were my friends. I got a call from the warden on Alcatraz a couple of weeks ago. It seems old Al nearly got his throat cut for cutting into line at the barber shop. Just another number, just another convict. He's a nobody now."

I got up to leave.

"I'm sorry for all of this. I hope everything works out for your family, Mr. Broadcreek."

I extended my hand and he shook it.

"You ever get tired of the private life, son, give me a call. You'd make an outstanding FBI agent."

I breezed. The rest of the day was mine. I went home and slept.

Around one p.m., I got up and drove the Ford over to a body shop. It broke my heart, the condition she was in. The estimate was over one hundred and fifty bucks. Ouch!

I spent the rest of the day at the office looking at bills and returning phone calls. Some woman wanted her cheating husband followed. I told I was busy for the next three to four weeks. I gave her the Pinkertons' number. Like I need another Connie Morehouse type for a client. I took the cable car home at seven and read in bed till nine, and then it was lights out.

In the morning I took a cable car to meet Vinnie for breakfast at Molly's Diner. I worked on a cup of Joe and watched the place crawl with cops coming off duty. Molly was behind the counter, holding court and giving hell to all the rookie cops.

Madison Cooper came in grabbed the stool next to me.

"I'm not staying long, Sean. I'm sorry for being a jerk in Chinatown. I have to learn to keep my mouth shut and pick my spots." He was looking at himself in the mirror.

Cooper nodded to Molly and went to a stool at the end of the counter. A couple of the cops started giving him crap. Molly jumped right in with both feet.

"You flatfoots button it up. Cooper's all right. Don't you mugs read?" She slapped a Chronicle down on the counter in front of the two cops. They started to read.

Vinnie came in took the stool next to me.

"What's shaking', Sean?"

"I'm not sure, but let's find out." I said." I gestured to Molly. She brought a cup and filled Vinnie's and re-filled mine.

"Hey, Molly, what's in the paper the patrol guys are reading? Cooper have a story about the Chinatown murder last night?"

She had a surprised look on her face. "No nothing like that at all. Did you two see the paper this morning?"

We both shook our heads. Molly went over the cash register and got another paper. She slapped it down in front of us with the banner and headline in large letters: MURDER IN CHINATOWN.

We started reading when Molly grabbed it off the counter.

"You two mugs are reading the wrong article." She flipped the paper over to the bottom half. The headline read, HERO COP SAVES PARTNER IN DOMESTIC SHOOTOUT. It had Madison Cooper's byline. I guess he had found a better story, after all.

It was a great article. It painted Tommy D'Amato as a real hero, saving the life of his partner and an unconscious woman. Cool under pressure, he fired his service revolver an instant before the suspect could plunge a knife into the chest of Sergeant Patrick Mulligan. The article went to talk about the dangerous and thankless job that policemen do for the citizens of our fair city. There were a couple pictures from the crime scene and one of D'Amato helping lift the gurney into the ambulance. It was a real nice piece of work, the best I had ever seen from Cooper.

"Gees, is this the same Cooper?" Vinnie asked.

I smiled. "He doesn't look so small all of a sudden, does he?"

Every cop in the place shook Cooper's hand and thanked him for the article. Vinnie laughed. "Who knows, Sean, there may be hope for this gee."

"I think you are correct, Inspector," I said.

Vinnie and I ate bacon and eggs, and downed more coffee. We talked about how much a wedding set was going to set me back at the jewelry store.

When the hubbub died down, Cooper came over. "Hey, Sean, I forget to tell you something, if you have a minute." He sounded sheepish.

"Sure, Coop," I said.

He was nervous, he looked at Vinnie.

"Inspector, I'm sorry for going into your daughter's hospital room.

It was a lowlife thing to do. I should have known better." The kid swallowed hard.

Vinnie put down his knife and fork.

"You are right. It was a lowlife thing to do. I'll be honest; I didn't think much of you, but it took starch to walk in here and apologize in person. Nine out of ten guys don't have that kind of guts." Vinnie extended his hand and shook with Cooper.

"Maybe I was wrong about you. By the way, it's Vinnie, and that was a great article. Nice work."

He worked up a little more nerve. "Listen, the real reason I came over here was to give you both a tip. I know that you are both working that Morehouse killing. I did some digging and I found out something that might be of interest to you."

"Anything would be a help, Coop," I said glad that he had changed the subject.

"I was doing some background info on Morehouse and his wife. It was all pretty normal. Then I found out something funny. I found an article in the society pages ten or fifteen years ago announcing the engagement of Morehouse. It listed his soon to be wife's name as 'Constance Nagle.'"

Vinnie shook his head. "So what?"

Cooper lowered his voice. "Her medical degree is from Johns Hopkins University in Baltimore. She graduated as 'Constance Miller.' I called the Baltimore Sun paper and asked about Constance Miller or Nagle. Turns out Doctor Connie was married to another doctor named Miller; Nagle is her maiden name. Her first husband was shot three times with a small-caliber handgun, a supposed street mugging. The Baltimore Sun guy told me that the cops questioned old Connie for five days, till they were blue. They liked her a lot for it, but they had no evidence. The detective in charge, some gee named Kowalski, told me he was convinced that the good-looking doctor iced her hubby, but he just couldn't prove it. After five days of questioning the DA told him to kick her loose, and she moved away. He told me something really creepy, guys." Cooper broke out an evil toothy smile.

"Okay, we give up, come on Coop, give," I said.

"He said the twist enjoyed it, that she was real sick, and he said she would do it again if she got the chance. He said he was absolutely sure she would kill again. That she got off on it, she liked it."

A chill went down my spine.

CHAPTER FORTY-SIX

We took the cable car down to Union Square, then walked down Ellis to Samuel's Jewelers.

"I was beginning to think you had changed your mind there, cowboy." Vinnie said.

"Fat chance of that," I said.

Vinnie and I looked over the rocks for four hours. It would have been be easier to swim to Alcatraz and back then spend all morning looking at jewelry. I picked a very nice set. Vinnie kept telling me I was too cheap and should get a bigger diamond. I asked him who died and left him a bucket of money.

"Hey, pal, she's a Knob Hill girl. You better hurt when this is over."

He was right. I bought big and it would hurt. I set up an account and payment schedule. My wallet needed to go to the emergency room for a transfusion.

Vinnie and I walked across the street to John's Grill. We went to the bar, and on the way I made reservations for dinner at six on Saturday. Believe it or not, I ordered only a Coke at the bar.

Vinnie had some lingering thoughts.

"I'm sorry, Sean. I kind of came off like you were part of the operation that allowed Jimmy to get away."

"Don't apologize, Vinnie." I told him what had transpired.

"Crap, what did you figure they will do with him?"

"I don't know, but my guess is it won't be pretty or fun for Jimmy."

Vinnie took a pull on his beer. "Are you okay, Sean?"

"Yeah I'm okay. You know, I am pretty good at being a detective?"

"Sean, you would be the ace in the Inspector bureau. And I'm not saying that because I am your friend. It's true."

"I'm going to ask Kaitlin to marry me on Saturday night. I think it is time for me to practice the law again," I said.

"Where are thinking about hanging a shingle? District attorney's office, U.S. Attorney's office, public defender, what?"

"I don't know. All I know is Kaitlin is afraid of me getting hurt or killed. She has never come and asked me to give it up. But I know she wants it and I know I have to. Last night we were ready to listen to Jack Benny when the sirens came up the street, and Kaitlin turned white with fear. I can't live my life in fear of scaring her to death at every corner. I think it's time to find a big heavy box and store all of my .45s."

"Can you give it up, pal?" Vinnie asked.

"For her, I could give up anything."

"Well, since you are in a giving mood, maybe you want to give your best friend that Ford of yours in the shop."

"Sorry, I'm dizzy for that redhead, but I plan on keeping the Ford."

Vinnie turned serious. "You worried at all about the Morehouse broad?"

"She's going to hide under a rock until things cool off. I should be okay. It's only a matter of time before they bring in her boy-toy Giovanni. When that happens, old Connie has a whole new set of problems."

"Are you going to keep packing for a while?"

"I'm going to ask Kaitlin to marry me on a cable car on Saturday night, and you think when I go to hug her she wants to feel a double rig of .45s?"

Vinnie's face turned grim. Sean, I need to come clean with you about something."

"Go ahead Vinnie."

He was looking deep into his beer. You remember four years ago when I got transferred from the Chinatown station?"

"Sure, Mimi was still crawling around."

"I was transferred out because Madison Cooper ran a story that a bunch of cops were on take from the Wang's. I lost being promoted to Inspector for two more years. I never took a dime, but I got punished like I did. I never forgave Cooper for it. That's why I treat the gee so crappy. A lot of cops had to take retirement because of that mess."

He lowered his voice. "I had you punch Cooper on that bridge not for seeing Mimi in her hospital room, but for almost ruining my career. My God, I used my kid for an excuse to get even with that newise."

I looked at Vinnie. "None of us are perfect, Cooper included. It's time to move on.

We drank up and he gave me a lift home. Grandpa Mario was waiting on the porch.

"Hey, Sean, both of my kids are going to be out in the morning. I need you and one other guy to go fishing with me."

"You are on, Grandpa. I know just the guy."

I called Shamus at his office. "What does your schedule look like at four in the morning?"

"It doesn't look like anything, boyo. I'll be sleeping."

"I need a man who isn't afraid of a little outdoor work. You'll love it, take my word."

"All right, lad, I'll see you at four a.m. What time will I get back? We should be done at noon."

I called Kaitlin and told her what I was up to. She agreed to meet me at noon.

In the morning I picked up Shamus at his front door at four and handed him a cup of coffee. A few minutes later we pulled up to Fisherman's Wharf. There was a dive right on the end of the pier called Bobby's. I went in with Shamus and asked the bartender if Boston Bobby had my order.

Bobby came out with a large cleaver in his hand. He looked pretty mad. "Look, O'Farrell. I've told you before we don't serve your kind in here."

Bobby was big, strong-looking with a ruddy complexion. The kind of guy who finishes any trouble that he starts.

"And what do you mean by my kind, pal?" I said.

Shamus looked pretty nervous.

"Officers, you are all a bunch of high-strung sissy boys. How are you, Lieutenant?" Bobby was suddenly all smiles. He threw the cleaver on the bar and gave me a big hug.

"You know what, Lieutenant? You are okay for an officer."

I introduced Shamus.

"Shamus this is Petty Officer First Class Robert O'Mara, United States Navy, Retired. He hails from Boston, hence the Boston Bobby."

Shamus was ecstatic. "Well, it's always a pleasure to meet a fellow Boston man."

"Where from?" Bobby asked.

"I'm a Southie Boy."

"I'll be damned. So am I."

Grandpa Mario broke up the party. "Let's go, boys. We will be burning daylight soon."

Bobby had three Tiffin carriers full of breakfast and a big thermos of coffee. We got on board, threw off the lines, and made for the Golden Gate Bridge. The Sun Dancer was humming right along. We got to our fishing ground and Grandpa Mario had us let go the nets. We were going after sardines today. As soon as the nets were set, the sun came up and we set up for breakfast. There was a little folding table in the pilothouse, and we sat on some stools and ate.

Shamus opened his Tiffin and exclaimed. "Red flannel hash and eggs! Jesus, Mary and Joseph."

"Remember, Shamus," I said, "that's Boston Bobby. He would know how."

"Well, now I have a place to eat breakfast now."

"I would not show up there in a suit. It's a fisherman's place."

The rest of the morning was spent tugging and pulling on lines, to bring the nets on board. The Sun Dancer has an arm with a block and tackle to bring up the nets, but it is still hard work. Shamus was having the time of his life. We all got excited when we saw the net was bursting. Even Grandpa Mario was pretty happy, and he has been doing this all his life.

We headed for home as soon as the nets were on board. We arrived at the terminal and offloaded by eleven thirty. At noon sharp, Grandpa Mario was backing the Sun Dancer into her berth at Fisherman's Terminal. It was like a science with Grandpa Mario; he hates being late for anything.

Standing on the pier was Kaitlin and her mother, and to my surprise Righty and Lefty were there as well. What was no surprise was that Kaitlin and the boys were arguing about where Dominic DiMaggio would end up in the big leagues. Also no surprise: Kaitlin appeared to be dominating the conversation and winning the argument.

"There is no way the professor is going to those stinking Yankees. Joe has the ego for six men, and there is no chance he would allow his little brother to show him up. He'll sign with the Red Sox, mark my words," Kaitlin said.

Chin and Loc weren't giving up so easily.

"As long as Boston stays in that little dinky stadium, Fenway, they will never compete with New York," Chin said. "And Yankee Stadium seats more than double the capacity of Fenway. It's simply a matter of revenue. The Red Sox need to move to a new stadium. Besides, the White Sox, Cubs and Red Legs are in the hunt."

Chin was pretty convincing, but eventually the combatants decided the debate was a draw. I gave Kaitlin a kiss on the cheek.

"You are a lucky man, boss. Good looks, smarts, and she knows baseball." Loc spoke, but Chin's head bobbed in agreement.

Shamus suggested we all go to lunch. Chin and Loc said they had an appointment, but needed to speak to me privately.

We walked to the end of the pier. Chin did the talking for the pair, as usual. He handed me an envelope.

"Mrs. Wang wanted me to give that to you. It is the agreed-upon amount of two hundred and fifty per day for the month plus three days that you have been working on this case."

"I can't take this. It's too much," I said.

"Boss, please take it. To Mrs. Wang, that is pocket change. What was important is that you caught her husband's killer, and fast. That meant the world to her. I have been with the Wang's for a lot a years, both me and Loc. I've never been told to say this to anyone, ever. Mrs. Wang wants you to know that she owes you one."

"I don't know what to say."

"Don't say anything, boss. Also, this is from me and Loc: We don't say anything to anybody about what goes on. I promised you that Jimmy wouldn't be hurt. You are a good man, and you were straight with both of us. We owe you one, and here it is. This is between us. Jimmy Chan was sold for four hundred dollars to organization in Hong Kong. Mrs. Wang threw him in as a sweetener to a deal. One hour after he left the club, he had a ten-foot length of chain attached to his ankle. The chain was welded to the deck of the freighter. He will live his life washing dishes on that freighter. He can make it to a head, the dishwashing room, and a bed in the supply room. The chain won't reach to a hatchway or porthole for him to look out of. He may be alive, but he ain't living a real life anymore. He has an existence. It is the price he will pay for his betrayal. If there is a hell, he is all the way there now. Stupid bastard."

"Greed consumed Jimmy. It was his downfall," I said.

"You want to know the funny part, boss? The way that Jimmy handled this deal with their son Kuai, Mr. Wang was thinking about retiring and putting Jimmy in charge. He wanted to ride off into the sunset with Mrs. Wang and play with grandbabies." He shook his head in disgust.

I laughed. "The best-laid plans of mice and men."

"You take care of yourself. And Kaitlin? She's a keeper, boss."

I shook hands with both men. They piled into the Duesenberg and flew off into traffic. Kaitlin and her parents were waiting, and Kaitlin asked what it was they delivered.

"It was a check from their employer," I said. "And something far more valuable than that to me: their respect."

CHAPTER FORTY-SEVEN

Thursday evening was spent in an important meeting. Vinnie Castellano, Dave Dunderbeck, and Bill Ashwythe and I attended a law-enforcement symposium at my house: beer and poker night. It was a load of fun. I owed it to the FBI guys; this had been a tough case for everyone. Dave cleaned us all out. I felt like a little kid in short pants the way he worked the cards. I thought I was a pretty savvy poker player from years of cards in the Navy. No such luck.

Friday morning, it was back to business. I was rummaging through my desk trying to find more envelopes. I looked up and Vinnie was there.

"Follow me, Sean."

Vinnie told me I wouldn't need my hat and coat. We took the elevator to the third floor in silence. I had a feeling.

We walked into the offices of Morehouse and Wheeler. Crime-lab guys and photographers were everywhere.

We went to Wheeler's office. There, sitting in his leather office chair, was Anthony Giovanni. He had been strangled with piano wire.

Vinnie and I didn't say anything. What was there to say? We went to the other offices and found the other three thugs, murdered in the same fashion.

Vinnie shook his head. "I'm not surprised, Sean. Wheeler got sent here to get the mob into those bridge projects, and he didn't get it done. I guess this is his termination notice from the front office."

"Damn. That means right, wrong or indifferent, the DA is going to drop the charges against Connie Morehouse. She walks, but not before collecting the life insurance and the money for the completion of the

Oakland Bay Bridge. Plus she gets to keep a two-dollar betting slip. Hell of a note."

I had enough and went back to my office.

I was going to ask Kaitlin to marry me on Saturday. But her mother called me in the late afternoon to tell me that Kaitlin came home sick with the flu. Apparently she was very sick. I called John's Grill and rescheduled our dinner for a week out.

The next week I worked a quick case. Some parents wanted their teenage daughter found. Turns out she had lammed off with her best friend. She told the parents of the friend that her parents were out of town.

Shamus called and asked me to breakfast at the Palace Hotel on Friday morning. One must see the Irish Pope when summoned.

Thursday afternoon, I went to go pick up the Ford. I thought about calling them last week and have the entire car painted, but that was a lot of money. I was saving for a honeymoon. When I got there, the car looked fantastic. To my surprise the entire car was painted, and it was paid for. Bert the owner told me two big Chinese guys came in and paid for it. They also said the paint job wasn't even and told him to paint all of it. When I got behind the wheel, I found a note from Chin and Loc. It said there was a small gift in the back seat. I turned around. It was Jimmy's baseball bat. The note was signed Righty and Lefty, not Chin and Loc.

Kaitlin was finally over the flu and back to work on Thursday. She said she was better and was looking forward to Saturday night.

On Friday morning I took the cable car to the office and walked to the Palace Hotel. Unlike the best hotels in San Francisco, the Palace is different in its location, in the heart of the financial district. This hotel is all about business, money and power. The big rich in the area meet here. It is a beautiful hotel, but it has a reputation for being snobby, as I would soon find out.

I'd never been to the hotel so I went to the front desk to find directions to the Atrium Room, where they serve breakfast. The desk attendant had been working there too long, as apparently he thought himself to be aristocracy. If his nose were any higher in the air he would fall over backward. I stepped to the desk and he first looked me over to see if I was worthy of his service.

He said, condescendingly, "May I help you, sir?"

"Yes, where is the Atrium Room?"

Again he looked me over. Apparently my suit wasn't expensive enough. "And you wish to find the Atrium Room for what purpose, sir?"

I was getting irritated.

"I am meeting someone for breakfast."

He looked down that long nose of his again.

"Perhaps you might be more comfortable at the lunch counter across the street, sir."

"No, thank you. I am meeting somewhere at seven in the Atrium Room. Which way is the Atrium Room, please?"

The phone rang and this dope picked up.

"Good morning, the Palace Hotel Front Desk, this is Bartholomew, how may I assist you? We serve breakfast in the Atrium Room until nine. Yes, madam, you are most welcome."

Good old Bartholomew looked up from the desk.

"Oh, you are still here."

I was almost done with this clown. "The Atrium Room?"

"Yes, sir, right down this hallway, and the last set of double doors on your left. Enjoy your breakfast, sir."

I said thank you and was walking away when I him say, under his breath, "asshole." I went back to the desk.

"What did you call me?"

He was all smiles and smugness. "I'm sorry, sir. I didn't call you anything at all."

I turned to walk away and swung around and hit him square in the schnozzle. He started to bleed instantly. As he stuffed his snot locker with tissue, he sounded like a whimpering baby.

"What did you do that for?" he cried.

"I'm an asshole," I said.

The hotel manager came out from a door behind the desk.

"Oh, my goodness, Bartholomew. You are bleeding all over the register." He grabbed more tissues to clean the mess.

I waved to the manager. "Those nosebleeds, it must be the dry air."

I found the atrium room and Shamus. We ordered the breakfast special. The waiter apparently had gone to the same finishing school. He seemed like a good guy, though; just a little too dry and stiff for me. The table next to us had a pair of Texans. The waiter asked them to remove their hats. They complied, and asked for a spittoon.

"I'm sorry, sir. This isn't a saloon or a bowling alley."

Shamus and I chuckled, then Shamus got to the point.

"What are your intentions, young man?"

"Boy, you don't fool around, do you?" I said. "With your permission, I am going to ask Kaitlin to marry me on Saturday. I was going to come over and see you and Catherine after work and ask your permission. You are a little ahead of my schedule."

"I had a sense that you were up to something special. I only have one question, Sean. And I'll be honest: It's a little hard to ask."

"Shamus, when I ask Kaitlin, I plan on handing her two things: an engagement ring and my private investigator's license. If I am going to get married, it's time for me to practice law. It's a lot safer."

"It will make Catherine and Kaitlin very happy, my boy. But I have an offer for you. I know you can practice the law anywhere. Standard Oil of California is expanding my office. We are adding over two hundred people. We are exploring for oil in Alaska, the Yukon Territory, the Middle East, and offshore. I have been authorized to hire an in-house counsel and an in-house investigator. I called New York and cleared it with them. I want you to handle the legal and any investigative work that needs doing. You can hire a couple of lawyers and a couple of investigators to work for you. You will work directly for me and will also be responsible for security of the offices.

"Sean, this job will be safe. You can practice the law, and you get out in the field when you want. Of course, the money is very good. I want you to know I wouldn't do this if I didn't want you for the job. I don't find jobs for future son-in-law's. This is the right time, the right place, and you, my boy, are the right man for the job.

"With all that said, yes, marry my daughter. You have both Catherine's and my blessing. As far as the job goes, think it over. If it's not for you, I will understand."

We finished breakfast and Shamus talked about what a great time he had on the fishing boat. "It feels good to work hard and produce something. My arms are killing me, boyo."

We shook hands and off went Shamus to work.

I stopped by the front desk and waved to the manager, who was all smiles. Bartholomew was standing behind him. His nose looked like he had a cork up each nostril. He smiled and waved. He wouldn't ever be rude to a customer again.

I walked back to the office. When I got parked the phone rang. It was Danny O'Day from the U.S. Attorney's office.

"Hey, Sean, it's Danny. Two things. Fred Patton has agreed to be the fish-fry chairman for a year."

"Good news. Now we will have Father Mickey off our backs. I'm tired of carrying that guy around."

"The other is not unexpected news. I just got word that the local DA is dropping any and all charges against Constance Morehouse."

"Danny, you still have the third Chicago shooter who can testify."

"No chance of that, Sean. He was found an hour ago in his cell. You'll never guess how he died?"

"Wait, don't tell me. Piano wire?"

"Give the man a cigar."

THE HALFWAY TO HELL CLUB

"Shit" was all I could say.

CHAPTER FORTY EIGHT

I had just hung up the phone when my thoughts began to run wild. Something that Vinnie said was stuck in my craw.

I walked down to Marty's stand. I exited the elevator and sat on the empty stool. Without asking Marty poured a cup of coffee and slid it across the counter to me. I said nothing.

Marty smiled broadly. "Cat got your tongue gumshoe?"

I shuffled the cup back and forth in my hands and didn't look up.

"Sean, something is eating you, spill it." Marty demanded.

"Vinnie Castellano told me he was transferred out of Chinatown a few years ago because of an article about cop corruption. Madison Cooper wrote the piece. Vinnie thinks his promotion was held up a couple of years because of it. You were in Chinatown back then Marty, what was the story?"

Marty suddenly looked away in pain. He closed his eyes and held his head down over the counter. He opened them slowly and looked at me long and very hard. His forehead was wet, he was shaking.

"All right Sean, I will tell you. One rule, you say nothing to Vinnie, not a word, not ever. Okay?"

I nodded approval.

Marty drew a cup of coffee for himself, took a swig, and dropped hard on the stool behind the counter. He looked defeated and relieved at the same time.

"You got to understand about Chinatown, the rules don't apply there. You walk a beat and get to know people, they get in trouble with powerful people, like the Wang's, and they ask you to look the other way, and you do, just this once."

Marty's eyes were red and moist. "The next thing you know restaurant owners are picking up your check for a favor. Some cops did favors and they had an envelope handed to them. Me I never took money, but I knew a lot of cops who did, friends, buddies, gees who had my back."

Tears were running down his cheeks. "That article ran and the shit hit the fan. Every cop in Chinatown was under the microscope. I got hauled in and questioned. They wanted me to name names, give people up. The word was the mayor and chief wanted ten cops to go down for this. They gave me an option to name somebody or take a fall. They gave me twenty-four hours to make up my mind.

I was scared out of mind, being a cop was all that I was ever any good at. Marty brushed away the tears and took a big slug of coffee. He was re-gaining his composure.

Later that night I was on patrol when say some street thug smacking some broad around. I ran down the alley, and the gee pulled a roscoe. He fired three times, I fired once and he took it right in the face and down he went. I had two fellow cops behind me. COPS, GOD DAMN IT." Marty was shaking in uncontrollable rage.

"I got shot twice, one in the arm, and one in the left leg. It was the leg that was damn near destroyed.

Marty refilled his cup. "I woke up in the hospital and the chief and mayor were there. They told me they had lined up nine cops that were eligible for pension that would fall on their sword and do the right thing. They told me they wanted me to be the tenth, but that plan went out the window when I got injured in the line."

Marty mindlessly wound his pocket watch. "They left it up to me, I could take the rap and get a full disability retirement, or they drop the blame on Vinnie Castellano."

"I would have decked the bastard, but I couldn't move. I told him Vinnie was clean and didn't deserve any blame at all. The Chief shrugged and said, ten had to go down, and go down hard. Vinnie had a baby for Christ's sake. He was a good cop, and he was CLEAN.

Marty shook his head. "I confessed in a written statement, and they agreed to move Vinnie out and get him promoted in twenty-four months. They kept their part of the bargain. The mayor got his ten scalps, and I opened my shop here.

Marty tossed the contents of his cup in the sink. "Bottom line is, I wasn't a dirty cop, but I wasn't exactly clean either.

I got up from the stool. "Marty, honor and mercy mean a lot in this world. You gave up your place on the force for Vinnie. You can always be proud of that."

I took it on the heel and toe, and headed for the elevator.

Marty called out. "Sean, please don't ever tell Vinnie, I'm too ashamed for him to know. He warned me and the others about taking favors, we ignored him. Guess what? He paid for it."

As the elevators closed I could hear Marty in the distance sobbing.

We all commit sins, it is human to error. Living with it is the hardest part.

CHAPTER FORTY-NINE

My Saturday started with bread making with Petey. I was finished by ten and got home in time to clean .45s until one. I was listening to the radio and working along when the phone rang. It was Vinnie Castellano.

"Hey, buddy. Tonight's the night?"

"Correct you are, my friend."

"You got the ring, and you got your license?"

"What, are you pushing me into retirement?"

"Easy, cowboy. It was your idea to go soft and return to the bar. Wait, is that the drinking bar or the practice-of-law bar? I forget."

"Go talk to Mimi. You are better off talking to someone with the same mental capacity."

Vinnie chuckled. "Easy, pal. You better develop a little charm before dinner. I don't think Kaitlin will appreciate the marriage proposal at gunpoint: Marry me or I'll fill you full of lead, lady."

"Don't worry, Daddy. I'm leaving the roscoe's at home. This will be a gun-free marriage proposal. The whole idea, Vinnie, is for Kaitlin to say yes and not no."

"You keep telling me how smart she is. I don't know what she sees in you."

"I'm hanging up now. I need to do something constructive like drive over to your house and shoot you."

Vinnie was laughing hard. "You have fun tonight and give Kaitlin our best. Don't screw this up, O'Farrell."

"Thanks, Vinnie. I'll see you at Mass in the morning."

I spent the rest of the afternoon giving the car a bath, then running over to the Standard station to fill up. I ironed a shirt for tonight. Then Aunt Cilia called from her house: the kitchen sink was backed up and Uncle Gino was at the restaurant. After my plumber duties were taken care of, Aunt Cilia told me how much they enjoyed meeting Kaitlin's parents.

"I understand you might be asking a question tonight?"

"Yes, tonight I will be asking Kaitlin for her hand in marriage. I do have one question for you."

She looked confused. "Sure, what?"

"You wanted to ask me that question all day. How much stuff did you have to jam down the drain to get it to plug?"

Aunt Cilia howled. She gave me a big hug. "We are all proud of you. Now go get Kaitlin and ask that question."

Back home, I shaved, showered, dressed, and went off in the Ford in search of a future bride.

I knocked on Kaitlin's door and Shamus answered the door. He and Catherine were there. Gee, I wonder if they know what is going on? Kaitlin came out and she was as radiant as the first time I met her. She simply took my breath away.

We got into the Ford and we went. I couldn't help myself. "So the folks were just out for a walk and stopped by, did they?"

Kaitlin was smiling and shaking her head side to side.

"A wee bit of a smartass indeed."

"I told your father that I might be asking a very important question tonight."

She was all ears. "I'm listening."

"Well, it's a little early, but, do you think the Yankees will make it to the World Series?"

Kaitlin reached over and whacked my shoulder.

"Ouch, this is going to hurt for weeks."

"Tough it out, big boy." She giggled that wonderful giggle of hers.

We arrived at John's Grill and had a wonderful time. The food was world class. I had a steak, baked potato and asparagus. Kaitlin had pork chops with baked potato and apples.

She commented that her appetite had finally returned. She was a little weak on Thursday and Friday at work, but was her old self today, she said.

I had cheesecake and espresso, and Kaitlin had chocolate mousse and coffee. When our dessert arrived she started picking at my cheesecake.

"Hey, that's my cheesecake."

"Well, I wanted to try both."

It was fun skating around the issue. But it was about time to fish or cut bait.

"Kaitlin, do you want to have children?"

"Yes, very much. Do you know anyone willing to be the father?"

"And you call me a wee bit of a smartass."

We talked for over an hour over coffee. It was just about time for the big question. I make sure I had the ring in my pocket. I paid the bill and took her across the street to the window at Samuel's Jewelers. I asked her to look in the window and see if there was anything that caught her fancy. I asked the jewelry store to put a copy of my ring dead center in the window and give it the best light. Kaitlin went right for that one.

"That one in the middle is beautiful."

"You have excellent taste, my dear." I reached in my pocket for the ring. Then I lost my balance and fell forward into Kaitlin's arms. At first I thought maybe I was sick. Then I heard the second shot. One had ripped into my left shoulder; the second went tearing through my right shoulder. Kaitlin was screaming and trying to hold me up. I slid to the ground, and Kaitlin was under me. She was screaming uncontrollably.

I turned my head and heard the voice.

"I told you, O'Farrell, that I would kill you."

It was Connie Morehouse. She was wearing a white full-length fur coat. She had a nickel-plated automatic in her hand.

All I could say was, "Please don't."

Connie laughed. "I'm going to shoot you dead, but first I think I'll give you a little company for your trip to hell. Let's just take out your bitch girlfriend." She started to lower the gun.

A gunshot sounded.

In an instant my life flashed before my eyes. I have spent all my life trying to be a good man, doing the right thing, being honest. I spent my life in service to others, through works of charity and church. I was not a perfect man, I was anything but. I was imperfect, flawed, mistake-prone and weak. Every time I tell a lie, I go to confession and ask to be forgiven. I would have to go to confession on Sunday for telling a lie. I lied to my best friend Vinnie Castellano. Sometimes when you lie, it can be for a good reason. This was not one of these cases. I was weak; I was unable to say no to myself. I just simply could not control my internal struggle with myself to be ready for anything. I lied to my best friend. Could he forgive me? Would God forgive me? I just had to bring my guns, because you can't be too careful.

Connie Morehouse was standing three feet away from me with a bewildered look on her face. She looked like someone had bumped into her. She was walking around in a tight circle with the gun down to her side. She looked at her feet. She was questioning herself: Did I bump into something? Did I trip on something? Suddenly she stopped looking and transferred the gun to her left hand. She took her right hand and reached into her coat. It came back out covered in blood. She was outraged.

"You son of a bitch. I'll see you all the way in hell, O'Farrell." She raised the pistol to fire.

"My policy has always been, ladies first," I said.

I fired both .45s, one round at a time. Connie Morehouse danced in place like a marionette puppet. As each round exploded into her body, her arms flailed and her body contorted until she landed against the jewelry store window. The last four rounds blew out the window. Glass was everywhere. She slid down the wall to the sidewalk in a seated position, her white fur covered in blood. Her coat opened to reveal white lingerie. Her eyes were wide open. She was all done; she was taking the big dirt nap.

I was flat on the sidewalk. I couldn't move. I heard sirens in the distance.

I called out for Kaitlin. There was no answer.

Tommy D'Amato came running up the street. He got to me and told me to hang on.

"Tommy, check on Kaitlin, check on Kaitlin."

"Sean, you are losing a lot of blood. I need to sit you up."

Tommy lifted me and leaned me against the street clock in the front of the jewelry store. It hurt a lot; my shoulders were throbbing like I have never felt before. Kaitlin was face up on the ground next to me. Her face was covered with blood. She wasn't moving.

I lifted my hand. It was covered in blood. I felt cold and damp. I couldn't move my legs. I was cold.

"It was such a shame to shoot holes in that beautiful fur coat," I babbled. "Crap, this was a brand-new suit, I only wore it twice. They never explained what it was like getting shot in law school. They talked about never upsetting your clients to the point where they want to shoot you. Hey, Tommy, is there still an engagement ring in my suit pocket? I want to ask Kaitlin to marry me."

Kaitlin was not moving at all.

"Tommy, what's wrong with Kaitlin? Help Kaitlin will you. TOMMY, ANSWER ME, GOD DAMN IT!"

I remember waking up with a lot of bright lights over my head. There were six faces close, all of them talking loudly. One gee was screaming for another unit of blood. "We are losing this guy," he said. That guy was me, based on the way I was feeling. Then I heard something that made me go cold.

"God damn it! Where the hell is Doctor Morehouse? She may the only doctor that can save this poor bastard."

I was laughing to myself. Is life full or irony or what? Everything went black.

CHAPTER FIFTY

I woke up in a strange place. I tried to sit up, but I discovered that I didn't have the energy or the ability. I could move everything, just not very well.

I was trying to clear my eyes, but things were blurry. I didn't see anyone but I heard a female voice yell.

"Doctor, he is coming to."

A guy in a white lab coat leaned over, six inches from my face. "Mr. O'Farrell, I'm Dr. Livingston. Do you know where you are?"

I tried to move my arms. It was slow going.

"Not really," I said.

"Mr. O'Farrell, do you know what day it is?"

"It's sunny out, it must be Sunday."

I don't remember what he was saying, but I think I dozed off to sleep. When I woke up Vinnie Castellano was there.

"Sean, how are you doing buddy?"

"Hell if I know, Vinnie. You tell me. What's the story, what happened?

"Connie Morehouse came after you with a .32 caliber Smith and Wesson auto. She got off two rounds; she hit each shoulder. She managed to hit an artery and you lost a lot of blood. The doctor says you are very lucky to be alive. You lost a shitload of blood, pal."

I heard chuckling behind Vinnie. There was no mistaking Swede Amundson's laugh.

"Hey, O'Farrell you just cost me three bucks in the office pool. I bet you were going to bleed out or turn into a potted plant." He laughed generously.

Vinnie exploded. "Get out of here Swede, NOW."

"Hey O'Farrell stay weak and die already will ya." I heard the door slam somewhere behind me, and that blood curdling laugh fading down the hall.

"Why did the doctor ask me what day it was?"

"Sean, you have been in a coma for ten days. After five days they weren't sure that you would pull out of it, and if you did there was concern about brain damage. Not that your brain could be damaged any more than it is."

I looked around. "Funny. Where's Kaitlin? Is she okay?"

Vinnie was slow to respond, and that scared me. "Sean, Kaitlin wasn't hit, but she was covered with your blood and she went into severe shock. Her breathing was very shallow. She was in the hospital for three days. They were worried for a while that she may have deprived her brain of oxygen. Don't worry, she's fine, but she is very fragile. Frankly, Sean, she's a train wreck."

"When can I see her?"

"Sean, she had a real trauma. She was psychologically wounded. She saw you blow Connie Morehouse away. The whole area was a bloodbath. She overloaded, Sean. She hasn't left her house since the shooting. I talked to Shamus. He told me that Kaitlin doesn't want to see you."

All I could manage was to sit up in bed. Vinnie bear-hugged me back down on the bed.

I was dizzy, but I quickly got back on the important subject at hand. "You mean she won't see me until I get out of here? I can understand that I…"

Vinnie cut me off.

"Sean, Kaitlin doesn't want to see you ever again."

The words were slow to sink in.

"Sean, she might change her mind someday, buddy, but that is down the road, way down the road. Shamus thinks it would be best if you kept away from her."

"Isn't that nice of him? You can call them and tell them I came out of my coma."

Vinnie changed the subject. "We have been looking for Jimmy Chan. No can find."

"There's the news of the century, what a surprise."

"The doctor wants me to get you up and start walking. He wants to throw you out of here as soon as possible. Do you feel like giving a walk a try?"

"Let's get moving, pal. I got places to go, people to see."

"Oh, you have plans already."

"Yeah, I have a couple of library books that are overdue. There is a redheaded librarian is going to send me to hell for being so late."

It was time to get the hell out of bed. I stood up and looked out the window. I wobbled like a drunk to the window. I opened the drawer of the table next to my bed. My butts were in there. My private-eye license was in there as well. It had a bullet hole and it was covered.in blood. I lit my smoke and threw the match into the ashtray. It was four in the afternoon and the fog was rolling in from the bay.

I never felt so alone in all my life. It's like I had joined the Halfway to Hell Club.

Too bad there was a net.

MARK J. McCRACKEN

Sean O'Farrell will return in:

THE ALL THE WAY TO HELL CLUB

THE HALFWAY TO HELL CLUB

About the Author

Mark McCracken ia an award winning author, travel writer, chef, and a retired U.S. Coast Guardsmen with 25 years of service. He followed his service as a high school English and Social Studies teacher as well as coaching sports. Mark is currently a Financial Management Analyst fo the U.S. Navy. Mark is a memeber of the Mystery Writers of America.

CPSIA information can be obtained
at www.ICGtesting.com
Printed in the USA
FSHW021334220119
55177FS